P9-DEA-488

the LOVE LETTERS of ABELARD and LILY

the LOVE LETTERS of ABELARD and LILY

LAURA CREEDLE

Houghton Mifflin Harcourt

Boston New York

www.hmhco.com

The text was set in Adobe Casion Pro.

Library of Congress Cataloging-in-Publication Data
Names: Creedle, Laura, author.
Title: The love letters of Abelard and Lily / by Laura Creedle.
Description: Boston ; New York : Houghton Mifflin Harcourt, [2017] |
Summary: Lily, who has attention-deficit hyperactivity disorder, and Abelard, who has Asperger's, meet in detention and discover a mutual affinity for love letters—and, despite their differences, each other.
Identifiers: LCCN 2016037229 | ISBN 9780544932050 (hardcover)
Subjects: | CYAC: Love—Fiction. | Letters—Fiction. | Attention-deficit hyperactivity disorder—Fiction. | Asperger's syndrome—Fiction. |
Single-parent families—Fiction.
Classification: LCC PZ7.1.C737 Lov 2017 | DDC [Fic]—dc23
LC record available at https://lccn.loc.gov/2016037229

Manufactured in the United States of America
DOC 10 9 8 7 6 5 4 3 2 1
4500684860

For Isabel

the LOVE LETTERS of ABELARD and LILY

CHAPTER 1

The day Abelard and I broke the wall, we had a four-hour English test. Seriously. Every tenth grade student in the State of Texas had to take a four-hour English test, which is too long to sit still even if you are a normal person. And I'm not a normal person.

After the test, I told my feet to take me to geography. If I didn't tell myself where to go, if I let my mind drift, I'd find myself in the quiet calm of the art wing, where the fluorescent lights flickered an appealingly low cycle of semipermanent gloom. Or I'd stand in the empty girls' room just to be alone. Sometimes I think I'm not attention deficient but attention abundant. Too much everything.

When I got to geography, Coach Neuwirth handed out a boring article about the importance of corn as a primary crop in the early Americas. Then he left the room. He did this a lot. Ever since basketball season had ended, Coach Neuwirth seemed like someone who was counting the minutes until the school year was over. To be fair, he wasn't the only one running out the clock.

Thirty seconds after Coach Neuwirth left, the low murmur of voices turned into a conversational deluge. I sat in the back of the room because that's where the two left-handed desks were — in the row reserved for stoner boys who do not like to make eye contact with teachers. Two seats in front sat Rogelio, turned sideways in his chair, talking fast and casting glances in my direction.

"Cosababa, pelicular camisa," Rogelio said, and the boys around him all laughed.

Okay, this is probably not what Rogelio said. I'm not a great listener. Also, my Spanish is terrible.

"Camisa," he repeated.

At the word *camisa,* Emma K. turned to look at me, and whispered something to the blond girl next to her. I instantly wondered if I'd been talking to myself, which is a thing I do. It attracts attention.

Then it sank in. *Camisa.* Spanish for "shirt."

Maybe there was something wrong with my shirt. Maybe the snap-button cowboy shirt I got at a thrift store was not charming and ironic as I'd imagined, but seriously ugly. Emma K. had whispered about my shirt. Even Rogelio and his friends, who often wore snap-button cowboy shirts, had laughed at my shirt. Or maybe not, because my Spanish isn't good, and anyway, Rogelio could have been talking about someone else. Not Emma K., though. She looked straight at me.

What if I'd popped open a button at bra level and I'd

been walking around all day with my bra exposed, and was I even wearing a nice bra, a sexy black bra? Or was it just one of those tragic old bras with a ribbon or a rose that might have been cute once but, over repeated washings, had turned slightly gray and balled up like a dirty piece of dryer lint stuck to the center of my chest?

I clutched the front of my shirt, and Emma K. and the blond girl giggled. My shirt was properly buttoned, but I couldn't sit in my chair for another minute. School was a molasses eternity, a nightmare ravel of bubble sheets and unkind whispers unfurled in slow motion. I had to leave, even though I'd promised my mother that I would under no circumstances skip school again.

I stood. My feet made a decision in favor of the door, but a squeaking metallic noise stopped me.

I turned.

Directly behind me was an accordion-folded, putty-colored vinyl wall, along with a gunmetal gray box with a handle sticking out of one end. The squeaking noise came from the metal box. The handle moved.

When our school was built in the sixties, someone decided that walls impede the free flow of educational ideas, because some of the third-floor rooms are all double-long, cut in half by retractable vinyl walls. Apparently, the architect of this plan had never been to a high school cafeteria to experience the noise associated with the unimpeded flow of ideas. The wall doesn't get opened much.

Last time anyone opened the wall was during Geography Fair. One of the custodians came with a strange circular key he inserted into a lock on the side of the box. He'd pushed the handle down and the wall had wheezed open, stuttering and complaining.

Now the handle jiggled up and down as if a bored ghost was trying to menace our class, but no one else was paying attention. I wondered if the custodian was trying to open the wall from the other side. It didn't make sense.

I left my desk and walked to the box. I leaned over and grabbed it, surprised by the cool feel of solid metal. And suddenly, I felt much better. The world of noise and chaos faded away from me. The touch of real things can do this.

The movement stopped. I shook the bar up and down. It didn't range very far before hitting the edge of what felt like teeth in a gear.

I pushed down hard on the handle. After a momentary lull, it sprang up in my hands, knocking with surprising force against my palms. I put both hands on the bar, planted the soles of my Converse sneakers, and pulled against it with all my might.

There was a loud pop, followed by the whipping sound of a wire cable unraveling. The bar went slack in my hands. The opposite end of the vinyl wall slid back three feet.

Everyone stopped talking. Students near the door craned their heads to see into the other classroom. Dakota Marquardt (male) said, "Shiiit!" and half the class giggled.

A rush of talking ensued, some of it in English, some in Spanish.

I dropped the handle and slid back into my chair, too late. Everyone had seen me.

Coach Neuwirth ran back into the room and tried to pull the accordion curtain closed. When he let go of the edge, it slid away, leaving a two-foot gap.

He turned and faced the room. "What the hell happened here?"

It's never good when a teacher like Coach Neuwirth swears.

I waited for someone to tell on me. Pretty much inevitable.

Dakota Smith (female) stood and straightened her skirt. She pulled her long brown hair over her shoulder and leaned forward as though reaching across a podium for an invisible microphone.

"After you left, the handle on the wall began to move," she began. "Lily put her hands on the handle and pushed down and the cable broke and — "

"Thank you, Dakota." Coach Neuwirth strode to his desk. "Lily Michaels-Ryan, please accompany me to my desk."

I followed him to the front of the class, keenly aware that every set of eyes in the room was fixed on me. Coach Neuwirth filled out a form for me to take to the office, not the usual pink half-page referral form, but an ominous shade of yellow with pages of carbons. As I stared at the razor stubble on top of his pale head, I realized I'd messed up pretty badly. So badly, I probably wouldn't be allowed to see my father in the summer.

"It wasn't just me," I said. "There was someone on the other side pushing down. I didn't mean to break the door, it's just . . ."

Coach Neuwirth ignored me.

"You'll note, Miss Michaels-Ryan, that I have filled out a *Skrellnetch* form for you. Your mother will have to sign the *kerblig* and return it to the main office before you can *be burn to clabs . . .*"

This would be a good time to mention that I'd stopped taking my ADHD meds about a month earlier because they made me puke randomly and caused my head to ring like an empty bell at night. Side effects.

". . . Your parents will have to sign the *kerblig* before you can *be burn to clabs*. Do you understand me?"

He waited, holding the *Skrellnetch* form that I needed to take to the office. Clearly, he had no plans to hand me the all-important *Skrellnetch* form until I answered him. I contemplated my choices. If I said yes, he would hold me responsible for remembering every clause in his statement, and I would be made to suffer later because I had no idea what he had just said. My heart pounded with a weird mixture of fear and exhilaration.

However, if I said no, Coach Neuwirth would consider

it a sign of insubordination and general smart-assery. It didn't look good for me.

"So . . . what copy does my mom sign again?"

Peals of laughter erupted from behind me. Someone muttered, "Ass-hat," and the laughter increased.

"Get the hell out of my classroom," Coach Neuwirth said. He threw the *Skrellnetch* paper across his desk at me.

I began my trek to the office, hoping I wouldn't run into anyone while I held the stupid *Skrellnetch* form. After the noise and glare of the classroom, the quiet calm of the hall, with every other row of fluorescent lights off to save on electricity, was a relief. Six steps of cool dark, six steps of bright white burn. Down the stairs. The first floor had a band of colored tiles at shoulder height: white, mustard yellow, white, blue. I held my right hand out and touched only the blue tiles as I passed through the hall, feeling my jittery state of anxiety mute into a dull, sad place in the center of my chest.

Down at the office, kindly Mrs. Treviño eyed my yellow *Skrellnetch* form with visible regret.

"Lily, what happened?" she said, as though I'd twisted an ankle in gym, or had some other not-my-fault kind of accident.

"I broke the sliding wall between Coach Neuwirth's and Ms. Cardeña's rooms."

Mrs. Treviño sighed deeply.

I looked away as my lips started to quiver. A gray cloud of shame descended on me with remorseless speed. I'd like to be the good, thoughtful person Mrs. Treviño had mistaken me for. A person who doesn't break stuff.

"Well, you're not the only one," she said. "Come on back."

She escorted me to the inner chamber. There, by the vice principal's office, were two ugly orange chairs. On one chair sat Abelard Mitchell. I took one look at him and knew he'd been on the other side of the wall pulling up on the handle while I pushed down.

Mrs. Treviño gestured to the empty chair and left us alone in the waiting area.

I'd known Abelard since kindergarten. Since my last name was Michaels-Ryan and his was Mitchell, we stood next to each other at every elementary school function. Abelard was tall and slim but broad-shouldered, with a mop of sable brown hair and dark blue eyes. He was gorgeous, but he had some sort of processing delay, mild autism or Asperger's syndrome or something. He didn't interact like everyone else.

But sure. Neither did I. When I was seven, I accidentally smacked Abelard with my metal lunchbox because I couldn't stop swinging my arms. I cut his cheek, but he didn't cry, and no one noticed until later, so now he had this little scar, which was weirdly sexy. Abelard never said anything. He had to have noticed that I was standing there in front of him swinging my Hello Kitty lunchbox with happy, maniacal abandon.

I liked to believe that he could have cashed me in to the teacher and he didn't.

I dropped into the chair next to him, feeling suddenly nervous to be sitting on a chair that was actually bolted to his chair—as though even the furniture was there to be punished.

"Hey," I said, a little too loudly. "So you were on the other side of the wall? Who knew it would break like that? You'd think a handle roughly the same age as the *Titanic* would be sturdier. Although I guess that's a bad comparison."

He said nothing. He was probably thinking about computer games, or quantum physics, or the novels of Hermann Hesse. From all available information, which I'll admit was limited, Abelard was pretty brilliant.

"You were on the other side of the wall." Abelard glanced at me and looked away.

"Yes." I felt a strange thrill of complicity. "Usually, I'm here by myself. Why did you . . ."

I stopped before I asked him the stupidest of questions: Why did you break that? My least favorite question in the history of questions.

"The mechanism was squeaking. One of the gears is rusted. They need to oil it."

I nodded. I didn't know what to say, or if there was

anything to say. I thought of Abelard, under the same anxious impulse to touch everything in the world of the here and now that we could feel with our hands. But unlike me, he was thinking about the hidden gears in the box, years of neglect and humidity, gears rusting away unused. He wanted to fix things, not destroy them. A more evolved monster, Abelard.

He leaned over and peered at me from under his shaggy fringe of hair. I caught a hint of his warm scent. Nice.

"Lily Michaels-Ryan," he said. "You were in my English class last year. You hit me with a lunchbox in first grade."

"Yeah, sorry about that," I said. "I hope it didn't hurt too much. On the plus side, I really do like the scar. It makes you look like a pirate, a little disreputable, you know?"

Abelard brought his hand to his cheek and traced the edges of the scar as though checking to see if it was still there. Suddenly, I wanted to run my hand along his cheekbone to feel for that slightly raised skin, proof of my earlier bad act.

The sight of his hand on his cheek made me conscious of where my hand was on the arm of the chair, touching the sleeve of his shirt. A phone rang in the office around the corner. Mrs. Treviño's voice came from the outer office, but it felt like she was on the other side of the world. We were alone.

"Abelard, why didn't you tell anyone that I hit you with my lunchbox?" I said. "I never got in trouble for that."

Abelard frowned in slow motion. He seemed slightly offended, like I'd accused his seven-year-old self of being a tattletale and a snitch. I'd been right. He had protected me, one freak to another. I felt a swell of something more than gratitude, more than surprise.

Abelard's lips parted slightly, like he had something to say that he didn't want anyone else to hear. I wanted to know what he was thinking. Suddenly, what Abelard had to say seemed like the most important thing in the world.

I turned my head and put my arm down on the chair to lean in so he could whisper in my ear. My arm slipped on the ancient vinyl, and I accidentally moved too close to Abelard, which is a thing that I do. I'm not good with personal space.

Abelard didn't say anything. I felt his warm breath on the side of my face, a thousand little hairs on my cheek moving in the soft breeze, and I thought of his cheek and how I'd wanted to run my finger along the edge of his scar. And still it seemed like Abelard had something to say, but it wasn't coming, and maybe he was too anxious to speak. I didn't know what to say either. My brain was not forming thoughts in English.

I lifted my face and he looked away. But his lips were there, centimeters from mine.

I kissed him. The kiss was over before I really knew what I was doing, just a momentary soft press of my lips against his. A stray impulse that didn't make sense, my wires crossed by the randomness of the day.

What was I thinking?

"Well, it was nice of you not to tell on me, even though you were only seven." I went on talking as though I hadn't just kissed him. I do this a lot. When you live at the mercy of your impulses like I do, you pretty much have to.

"Maybe you should have told someone? You probably needed stitches. Not that I don't like the scar—it's a great scar."

Abelard brought his index finger to his lips and frowned. He had one of those serious, symmetrical faces that a slight frown only improves.

"Lily," he said slowly, "I—"

I braced myself for a quick, awkward rejection, but before Abelard could finish his sentence, Vice Principal Krenwelge rounded the corner. I didn't know whether to be disappointed or relieved.

CHAPTER 2

My mother came to get me at school. She arrived looking frazzled, a small coffee stain over the left breast pocket of her shirt, lipstick reapplied but the rest of her makeup faded, leaving her skin blotchy, nose reddened by the sun. I expected her to be mad, but this was far worse. She looked defeated. Friday, the end of a long week, and now this.

Mom had a brief conference with Vice Principal Krenwelge, and then we drove home in silence. I was tired, beyond tired, needing the comfort of a darkened room.

"Are you mad at me?" I finally said.

We were stopped on Lamar at the light in front of Waterloo Records, where Dad's band had a CD release when I was five. I remembered Mom in a tight camisole and brightly colored skirt, holding a sleepy baby Iris on her shoulder. Her hair dyed magenta red. Happy clothes. Sexy, even. Afterward, we walked to Amy's for ice cream. Life in the before time.

"No, Lily, I'm not mad. You're just lucky Abelard's mom volunteered to pay the damages."

This made me sit up.

"Why? Abelard and I broke the wall together. It was as much my fault as his."

"Not according to your vice principal. Mrs. Mitchell seemed to think that it was Abelard's idea to break the wall, and you were just following along."

Mom rolled her eyes to let me know what she thought of this explanation. Me in close proximity to a broken thing: cause and effect. Mom knew who was at fault.

Why would Mrs. Mitchell think that Abelard was at fault? There could be only one reason. Abelard must have taken the blame for me. It didn't feel right. Abelard wasn't the breaky type. If I hadn't pushed down on the stupid handle, Abelard might have found a janitor to oil the gears.

"Abelard said the wall was already broken. Abelard said the gears hadn't been oiled in an eternity."

"Well, the next time Abelard decides to 'fix' something, don't volunteer to help, okay?"

"Volunteer to help," I mumbled.

I liked the idea that I'd jumped up because I'd intuited that the situation needed my special breaking expertise. But what if breaking and fixing were really the same activity, reversed?

Did Abelard really "fix" things, or did he just break things, like me? I wanted to ask him about his experience fixing things and breaking things. I thought about the time I'd pulled up too hard on the back seat handle of the car door while pushing against the door with my hip, and the handle broke. And then for some reason, I flipped the child lock switch thinking it might fix the door, only it didn't. It locked the door, permanently. I'd tried to fix it, I really had.

". . . and Mrs. *Screngle* says *tuber work*." Mom glanced over at me. "Lily, are you listening?"

"No," I admitted. No point in lying.

"Did you eat today?"

I had to think about it. The day seemed like an eternity, as though the time before I broke the wall and the time after served as a clear demarcation of events, like the birth of Jesus or the arrival of the dinosaur-ending meteor off the coast of the Yucatan. And now my mind was filled with thoughts of Abelard. Why had he covered for me?

"I don't remember," I said.

"Is your lunch still in your backpack?" Mom asked.

I dug through the backpack at my feet. Sure enough, my lunch was untouched in the outer pocket.

"I would have eaten, but they told us to eat during the test, and I was still working, and I just sort of forgot about it, and then we had to go straight to sixth period, so I didn't have time."

"Are you hungry now?"

I nodded.

We drove through P. Terry's for veggie burgers, and we split a chocolate shake on the way home, like I was being rewarded for screwing up. I was happy enough, but

I couldn't let things go. I kept thinking about my dad in Portland.

At the start of the school year, Mom had promised that I could visit Dad if I kept my grades up and didn't skip class. I'd been trying, but things hadn't been going too well. My grades are all over the place, and I try not to skip, but sometimes I can't help it.

"So, Mom, about the summer . . . I mean, could I still see Dad?"

Secretly, I planned to go visit Dad and just stay on. Dad taught English at a homeschool cooperative connected to the farm where he worked, kids getting life credit for milking goats and picking organic beets. Heaven. I'd miss Mom and Iris, but clearly I belonged in a "less-structured learning environment."

"I know you want to see your dad." Mom paused. It wasn't quite a pregnant pause, just an awkward millisecond or two. "But it's not that simple. We'd have to talk to him, and he may not be in a position to have houseguests . . . and of course, your grades . . . and no more skipping . . ."

I stopped listening. A qualified yes is almost a full yes. I'd have to improve my grades and attend all my classes, blah, blah, blah. I could do that.

"You know, Lily, seeing your dad again isn't going to solve all your problems."

I nodded to let her know I'd heard her and stared out

the window. She was wrong. My father had solved my biggest problem. There was no reason to think he couldn't solve my smaller ones.

My father taught me how to read.

When I was in second grade, the school reading specialist decided I was dyslexic. She told my mom to read to me every single night, but Mom worked nights. So Dad read to me.

In the beginning, he read me books about cat warriors while he drank craft beer. When Dad got tired of reading books about cats, he picked up *Nancy Drew* and the *Three Investigators* from a used book store. These books amused him with their gee-whiz 'thirties and 'forties references: chaste country club dances, German housekeepers devotedly making strudel, and clubhouses with secret tunnels made out of packing crates and junk. Nancy Drew ushered in cheaper beer: Tecate in cans. I laughed at Dad's earnest voice for Ned Nickerson, Nancy's straight-arrow boyfriend, and I fell asleep worrying how Nancy was going to get out of that cave by the ocean before high tide.

"Choral reading," my mother said, echoing the reading specialist's advice. "Dad reads a passage, Lily reads a passage."

My father sat by my bed with the book held between us as I painfully sounded out each little word. I learned to read the same way Hercules learned to hold a full-grown bull in his arms, by having to brute-force sound my way through every syllable until the words got longer and heavier. At first, I read individual words, then sentences, and eventually paragraphs.

Together we read all of Harry Potter; *The Lightning Thief*; *The Lion, the Witch and the Wardrobe*; *Inkheart*; and Diane Duane. When the words began to swim on the page, Dad read to me from his own personal library of medieval classics. By this time, I was sharing a bedroom with my sister, Iris, and she listened with rapt attention.

Dad read *Le Morte d'Arthur* and *Physica* by Hildegard von Bingen, *Sir Gawain and the Green Knight*, and *The Letters of Abelard and Heloise.*

At about the time we started on Tolkien, with a nightly supplement of *The Prose Edda* and the *Nibelungenlied*, my father had discovered vodka. Cheap, easy to hide, and packed more of a punch than beer.

I never questioned the hours I spent sequestered away in my bedroom with Dad, reading while he drank. It was fun, and it was too good to last.

The end came when I was in fifth grade. My mom caught me alone in my room with her copy of *Jane Eyre*.

"Are you reading?" she asked, hands on her hips. Her dark green eyes glittered with some internal fire I recognized as hopefulness. She had a sort of feral alertness that alarmed me.

"What? . . . No," I replied, thrown off my guard. I quickly regained my composure. "This book is weird. I can't understand this language. What's it about?"

"It's a love story about a girl with a strong moral compass. It's an older book, so the language can seem a little stilted, but it's really good." She smoothed the hair away from my forehead and attempted a wan smile. She looked sad. "You should have your father read it to you."

"I will."

I felt bad about lying to her, but mostly I felt relieved. Crisis averted! My father read me *Jane Eyre*, or he reread me *Jane Eyre,* because I'd already finished it by then. I didn't care. Mom was happy; Dad was pleasantly drunk. Life was golden.

At the end of fifth grade, the school tested me again. I'd never seen my mother so thrilled. She came home waving her copy of my test results over her head.

"Your phonemic scores are still relatively low," she said. "But your comprehension is off the charts. You've made amazing progress, Lily."

I didn't immediately get the magnitude of what I'd done, but I think my father did. He greeted the news that I was in the 98th+ percentile in reading comprehension with a queasy smile. I'll never forget the look he gave me. It was as though his usefulness on the planet had suddenly ended. Maybe he knew divorce was not far off.

"I've heard about this book *Wuthering Heights,*" I said,

hoping I wasn't overplaying the wide-eyed thing. "I don't think I can read it by myself, though. It's for older people, right? But we could read it together."

"Sure thing, Lil," Dad said, his eyes distant.

We all smiled at one another. The happiest part of my life ended there in the fifth grade.

CHAPTER 3

Monday morning my mother woke me while it was still dark. She stood by my bed with a cup of tea and a piece of toast.

"Eat the toast," Mom said. She hovered over me, already dressed for work in a white linen shirt and a fifties beaded cardigan that may have once been an ironic statement for her but that she now considers an heirloom.

"It's the middle of the night." I rolled over to face Iris's twin bed next to mine. "Look. Iris is still asleep."

My sister was an inanimate lump of covers. Iris usually springs out of bed like Snow White, ready to polish silver and sing with birds, but it was so early she wasn't even stirring.

"I have to go to work early today," Mom said. "You need to take your medication."

"I can't take it on empty stomach."

"Hence the toast." Mom thrust the plate at me.

Reluctantly, I bit into the toast. At this hour of the morning, food seemed like a human rights violation. I chewed twice and swallowed with difficulty before slumping back on the bed.

"Now your medication."

I took the pill and swallowed without hesitation. She handed me the lukewarm and very weak tea with milk to wash it down.

"You don't trust me anymore," I said.

"It just doesn't seem like you've been taking your medication lately, Lily. Maybe you've forgotten. I thought I would help you remember."

Every morning for the past month, Mom had left a cup of tea, a piece of toast, and a pill on a plate for me by my bedside. And every morning I'd taken that pill and stashed it in an old pickle jar under my bed. I didn't like the drug. It sucked the creamy goodness out of life.

Antidepressants tend to do that. I should know. This wasn't the first one I'd been on.

Bells and whistles went off in my head. On Saturday, the day after Abelard and I broke the wall, Mom offered to take me and Iris to a movie. She didn't go with us, and at the time, it seemed kind of weird. She must have gone home and searched the room for missing pills.

I probably should have flushed the medicine in the toilet so downstream fish and migratory waterfowl could experience an unexpected rush of jittery calm and the sudden ability to meet deadlines and organize paperwork. Yes, I could have shared my drug bounty with the ecosystem, but a strange frugality had stopped me. The stuff was expensive.

Once Mom left, I looked under the bed. Sure enough, the pickle jar was gone.

I'm sure Mom was relieved to find my hidden stash, because I'd saved her a couple hundred bucks. One thing was for certain: She would never mention the pickle jar, and neither would I.

School. I met Rosalind at our usual spot under the live oaks in the courtyard for lunch.

Rosalind is my oldest friend all the way back to kindergarten. She's tiny and plays small children in local theatrical productions. With her long dark hair in braids and her giant brown eyes, she can pass for twelve. Maybe ten on a really big stage.

Rosalind was eating out of a bento box filled with brown rice, raw carrots, and seaweed salad. Rosalind's parents are restricted-calorie-intake people who have formulated a plan to live for all of eternity. Like the children of vegan, macrobiotic, gluten-shunning parents everywhere, Rosalind's favorite food is pizza—though she likes classy pizza: feta cheese, black olives. Her dream is to move to New York and eat nothing but pizza. Also—acting.

"Lily, how was your trip to the vice principal's office?" Rosalind asked.

"Gripping and poignant. I laughed, I cried—"

"Was your mom mad?"

"Weirdly, no. I have a week in detention, but that's it. She even said I can still see my dad this summer."

"Really?" Rosalind raised a skeptical eyebrow. "Your mom said you could go to Portland?"

"If I keep my grades up and don't skip class."

Truth be told, Rosalind didn't entirely approve of my plan to visit my dad and then refuse to return. She didn't think I was cut out to be an organic beet farmer. Also, she would miss me.

I glanced across the courtyard. Abelard sat at his usual spot on the low wall under the crepe myrtle. Alone. The sight of him through the milling crowd sent a jolt of electricity up my spine. I realized I'd been scanning the halls all day, hoping to catch a glimpse of him.

I settled on the bench next to Rosalind, carefully avoiding a patch of grackle poo, and opened the lunch that Iris had packed for me. A tomato sandwich, apple, Oreos. I nibbled on an Oreo and set the rest aside.

"You're not eating?" Rosalind said. "Why, if I had a sandwich on actual bread—bread made from real demon wheat, mind you—"

"Here, have it. It's yours. Taste the evil."

I handed Rosalind my sandwich, but she just shrugged. I suspect she actually likes brown rice.

"So you aren't eating. What's up?"

"I'm back on my drug-based diet. My stomach will

refuse all food until five thirty, at which point I will eat my entire day's calories in two hours, mostly in potato chips. Straight out of the bag. If we even have potato chips. Might be stale crackers."

"Healthy," Rosalind said. "I thought you weren't going to take the drugs anymore."

"After my little trip to the vice principal's office, my mother decided she would watch me take my meds, like some hospital matron in one of those old movies your parents love."

"*The Snake Pit,* Olivia de Havilland," Rosalind said.

"Whatever."

Rosalind frowned.

"The drugs aren't good for you, Lily. They change you."

"It's not like I have a choice."

"Um, you know how my mother is always talking about . . . balance between . . . gluten and sugar can . . . talk to your mother . . . only if you . . . off the medication . . . take you to a dark place."

I shrugged, uninterested in the topic of my medication and diet. Abelard was eating cookies or crackers, reading something on his phone, dark hair falling over his eyes. I couldn't stop thinking about him. He was an attractive nuisance, a shiny object.

"What do you think of Abelard?" I asked.

Rosalind followed my gaze. "I don't know. He's kind of in his own little bubble. Why do you ask?"

"He was on the other side of the wall when I—when we broke it." Breaking the wall was beginning to feel like a shared secret, a source of pride. Abelard and I destroyed something—together.

"Okay," Rosalind said slowly. Dubious. I know that look.

"He took the blame. For both of us. He didn't have to do that."

"And you think that was about you?"

"Maybe it was about me," I said.

I continued to stare. It was easy to stare at Abelard. He never lifted his head, never glanced in my direction. Plus—kind of beautiful. Rosalind had a point, though. Abelard was self-contained. Maybe he hadn't thought about me once since I'd kissed him in the office. And here I was thinking obsessively about him, imagining we had some sort of secret kinship just because ten years ago I hit him in the face with my lunchbox.

"I'm just saying, don't construct an elaborate fantasy about him before you find out what's really going on in his head," Rosalind said. "Abelard is not like everyone else."

"Neither am I."

Rosalind sighed.

"You know what I mean, Lily. Unlike Abelard, you can carry on a conversation—"

"Almost like a normal person," I interrupted.

"You are a normal person," she said.

I kind of loved that Rosalind thought there was nothing wrong with me that couldn't be cured by regular helpings of wheatgrass shots and a little extra understanding. This was why she was my best friend—but it bothered me to hear her say Abelard was not like everyone else. Broken.

Whether she admitted it or not, I was also not like everyone else. Why be polite—why not just say "broken"?

I am a proud Broken American. There. I've said it.

CHAPTER 4

Normally I leave school each afternoon like I'm running the bulls at Pamplona. Not that afternoon. I went to the bathroom and fought for space at the mirror with the girls who did their makeup. I brushed my hair in the corner, but then one of the mirror regulars, a raccoon-eyed blonde named Montana Jordan or Jordan Montana, took pity on me.

"Here." She waved me to a free spot in the mirror.

I touched up my base and put on some lip gloss.

"You should really *sclur* your *blash*," Montana Jordan/Jordan Montana said. Her voice echoed noisily against the bathroom tile. "*Screeb* pretty."

"Sure," I replied. *Screeb pretty.* That was me.

"*Sclur* your *blashes*," she said, holding out an eyelash curler.

"Oh." Curl my eyelashes. My brain took the visual cue and made sense of the words. "No thanks. I'm on my way to detention. Coach Neuwirth."

I stared at my reflection in the mirror—a slight bump

on the bridge of my nose, skeptical green eyes. My wavy brown hair already starting to look like my time with the brush had been an exercise in futility. I couldn't see how curly eyelashes would be much of an improvement.

"Really?" she said. "Me too."

And then she went back to curling her eyelashes.

Abelard was already in detention when I arrived. The only other people in the room were Richard Hernandez from my algebra class and Rogelio. An emo boy I didn't know wandered in after me.

I dropped my backpack on the floor and sat at the desk in front of Abelard, my heart pounding. Coach Neuwirth could show up at any moment. I turned around and faced Abelard before my heart rate settled.

"Okay," I said. Extraneous hand movement. I do this when I'm nervous. "Why did you take the blame for breaking the wall when it wasn't just your fault? Because my mom said that your mom told the vice principal that you said you were to blame."

I stopped because I'd run out of breath. Also—tortured sentence.

Abelard looked up. His eyes were a clearer, deeper shade of blue than I had remembered. He looked away.

"And when I hit you with the lunchbox in first grade, you never told anyone, but you probably should have. It wasn't like we were really friends or anything—"

"You came to my house," Abelard said in a surprisingly loud voice.

Tectonic shift of the earth's crust, a realignment of everything. Abelard and I had a prior history, a reason I'd felt a natural connection between us. I wished I remembered.

"You came to my house," Abelard repeated. "I was five. We watched *Pokémon* together. You insisted Charizard was a dragon, not a lizard."

I've had an obsession with dragons ever since Dad read me *The Poetic Edda.* There's a dragon in Norse mythology who chews on the roots of the tree of life. A bad thing, right? But my father contended that without the dragon, the tree of life would become overgrown and eventually choke itself out of existence. My personal spirit animal—the destructive dragon.

"Because—fire-breathing," I said. "I mean, hello, dragon?"

Abelard blinked.

"Char—lizard, Charizard," he said slowly. "Etymology."

Beside us Richard and Rogelio switched their conversation seamlessly from English to Spanish. Should have been a hint, but I was too excited to pay attention. A rustling noise at the front of the room and throat clearing.

"Turn around."

"Oh, you did not just play the *Pokémon* etymology card," I said, experiencing a rush of word-borne feels. More fun words than I'd had in a long time. "Dragons are everything! It's a dragon who nibbles on the roots of the tree of life, because otherwise—"

"Miss Michaels-Ryan! Turn around!" a voice boomed. "Stop pestering Mr. Mitchell."

Pestering. I was pestering. A word invented by teachers to mean "bothering" but sounding infinitely worse, like something you'd get arrested for doing in a movie theater.

I swiveled, and Coach Neuwirth locked eyes on me. I felt my stomach flop, but at that moment Rogelio muttered something hilarious in Spanish. Rogelio is a natural-born confrontation clown, one of those guys who always have to get the last word in. It didn't help Coach Neuwirth's mood that the last word was in Spanish.

"We're going to break up your little party," Coach Neuwirth said. "Mr. Mondragon, please move next to Mr. Kreuz, Miss Michaels-Ryan, next to Mr. Hernandez."

I moved back a row next to Richard Hernandez. Abelard turned sideways in his chair and stared out the window. The room went quiet, unearthly quiet. Montana Jordan/Jordan Montana slid soundlessly into the room and took a seat across from the emo boy. Coach Neuwirth glared at her from his desk.

"Nidhogg," Abelard said in a voice that cut through the thick stillness. "Yggdrasil."

Nidhogg—the dragon. Yggdrasil—the tree of life. I didn't remember the names from Norse mythology, but

Abelard did. Abelard, my secret cartoon-watching friend from a childhood I didn't quite remember. Abelard, who knew Norse mythology and the finer points of gear maintenance. Was there anything he didn't know?

Detention was pretty boring. Half an hour later, I'd finished my homework. I hadn't eaten my lunch, and I was hungry and tired, too burnt to read. There was nothing to do.

Richard Hernandez sat at the desk next to me, drawing. I leaned over, expecting to see badly drawn girls with gravity-defying breasts, motorcycles, guns—the standard *Grand Theft Auto* love letter to chaos and faceless sex. The stuff boys draw.

Instead, Richard was drawing Abelard. Abelard with a three-quarter profile, his right cheekbone illuminated by sunlight streaming in from the window. Richard had drawn the barest line of a mouth and was filling in the details of Abelard's chin, muscles in his jaw shaded diagonally from top left to bottom right.

The only part of the picture Richard had finished was Abelard's eyes. He'd perfectly captured the way Abelard's dark blue eyes held the light, the open, almost mystical quality of his gaze.

I glanced at Abelard and felt a strange thrill in the pit of my stomach. There was something otherworldly about him. It wasn't my imagination—Richard saw it too.

Richard finished Abelard's chin and moved to his hair.

"Wow," I murmured.

Richard wrapped his right arm around his picture to shield it from my view and looked up. He had close-set, intelligent eyes and dark hair in a Caesar cut.

"That's really good," I whispered. *Good* was an insufficient word for his drawing, like telling a rock star his music was nice. I felt a little stupid about that, but what could I do? Drugs kill thought—even the happy, helpful drugs.

"Shhh . . ." Coach Neuwirth hissed.

"Thanks," Richard mouthed silently.

Richard returned to drawing, and I continued to watch. Minutes passed while he sketched in rapid, assured movements. It was calming, watching Richard, as soothing as a lullaby. I almost forgot that I was hungry and that the skin over my skull was beginning to crawl and itch.

One of the basketball players came by to talk to Coach Neuwirth. They stepped out into the hall, and I leaned over toward Richard.

"You're left-handed—like me. Also Leonardo da Vinci," I whispered. "You shade in the same direction—top left to bottom right. Do you know they think da Vinci was dyslexic?"

I held my hands out to visualize this, making the classic *L* for loser with my left hand. Kindergarten tricks. They never get old.

"You're making that up," Richard said. "How could anybody know?"

"I'm not making it up. I saw it on *Nova.* Da Vinci wrote letters backwards and misspelled words. Classic dyslexic tendencies. I should know. I'm dyslexic, too."

"No you're not." Richard looked up, his close-set eyes in a savage frown. "You can read."

Richard said the word *read* with the naked bitterness I usually reserve for the terms *late slip* or *instruction sheet.* Dyslexia. You can pass for normal for a while, but eventually the anger gives you away. The monster will out. I decided I liked Richard.

"Yes, I'm totally normal," I replied. "That's why I've been in the same algebra class with you for two years running."

"But I see you reading all the time. You always have a book—"

"I hear talking," Coach Neuwirth boomed.

Richard startled at the sound of Coach Neuwirth's voice. His pencil slipped, and the picture of Abelard floated off the desk, slid across the floor, and landed face-up in front of Rogelio Mondragon.

Richard froze, a stricken look on his face.

Coach Neuwirth was in the hall talking, his back half turned but still in the line of sight. I eased out of my seat in a crouch and moved slowly toward the picture, hoping to snatch it before Rogelio noticed.

I was too slow. Rogelio spotted the picture and grabbed

it. He glanced at Abelard and back to the picture as his expression changed from perplexed to positively gleeful. It was as though he'd found a secret love letter, ready-made for a million stupid jokes. Someone was going to be made to suffer in both English and Spanish. Rogelio scanned the room, searching for his victim.

At the exact moment Rogelio's eyes settled on me, Coach Neuwirth strode down the aisle and ripped the picture out of Rogelio's hands.

"Whose picture is this?" Coach Neuwirth demanded.

Richard looked a little sick.

"It's mine." The words were out of my mouth before I realized what I was saying. Lies are like that sometimes.

Coach Neuwirth held the picture and examined it carefully.

"So, this is your boyfriend?" Coach Neuwirth chuckled. "Pretty good likeness of our friend Abelard here."

Hard to determine who he was trying to humiliate at this juncture, Abelard for being unlikely boyfriend material, or me for being, well, me. Sometimes I think Coach Neuwirth lets the cruelty fly randomly just to see who might get hit.

Abelard turned to look at me briefly. I couldn't tell whether he was horrified, embarrassed, or intrigued that Coach Neuwirth just told the whole world he was my boyfriend. I looked away.

Coach Neuwirth handed the picture to me.

"Put it away, Ms. Michaels-Ryan," Coach Neuwirth said.

I folded the drawing of Abelard and slipped it into my book.

In the afternoon when I returned home, the picture fell out of my book. Abelard, beautiful and distant. Richard Hernandez's own version of the *Mona Lisa,* a mystery for the ages. Abelard, no doubt named for Peter Abelard from the twelfth-century text *The Letters of Abelard and Heloise.* Strange.

I drew a thought bubble over his head and wrote the words *I am Abelard, medieval French philosopher and time traveler. I have come to the future on a quest for love and beauty, but find only the barren wasteland that is high school. My travails are for not!*

I stuck the picture on the bulletin board and collapsed on my bed, empty. I opened my book, a novel about a girl on the run with her brilliant, eccentric father. After three pages, I quit reading, because I didn't care what happened with the father's new girlfriend or the daughter's desire to go to a normal school for more than three months at a time. My head had begun that drug-fueled end-of-the-day descent, circling the empty runway of a town called Apathy.

I put my book away.

My sister came into our bedroom.

Iris is in seventh grade. Tall like me, brown eyes to my green. Same wavy brown hair, same bump on the bridge of her nose. Iris doesn't seem to have inherited my mother's large breasts like I have. She wishes that she had my breasts, but she is wrong about this.

Iris attends the Liberal Arts, Math, and Engineering Academy—LAMEA, or LAME as everyone calls it. She is the perfect student, equally adept at the long-form essay and robotics, and building musical instruments out of found objects. Found objects are a big part of the curriculum at LAME.

For someone with such a full curricular life, Iris has an overdeveloped interest in my activities. Like being me has a 1950s-motorcycle-and-leather-bomber-jacket sort of glamour for her, because she has never tasted the fruits of failure. I could tell her that living outside the lines is not all that, but she probably wouldn't listen anyway.

"What are you doing?" Iris said.

"Nothing."

"Who is that?" She leaned over the picture of Abelard, studying it with the dreamy intensity she usually reserves for K-pop stars with ice-blond dyed hair and too much mascara.

"No one," I replied. "A kid at my school. His name is Abelard."

"He's adorable," she said.

"No." I stared at the picture. "Well, yes, he is."

I thought about my impulsive kiss, and my heart flopped in protest. Continued exposure to the sight of Abelard's faraway eyes was unfair.

"It's dinnertime," Iris said. "Mom told me to tell you."

"Not hungry," I replied.

"Mom made a really good salad. We've got *Supernatural* cued up."

Supernatural. Salad. These are the things we do together, eat salads and watch *Supernatural* because all three of us, Mom, me, and Iris, think those guys are hot. Iris likes the taller baby-faced one, but Mom and I prefer the deep-voiced snarky brother. It's like a miracle, Mom says, to find such transgenerational hotness on TV.

This was our familial idea of a good time. It meant nothing to me at that moment—good TV, hot guys in a seventies ride, salad.

"No thanks," I said. "I'll just lie here and listen to the inside of my skull buzz."

Iris wandered off. I played *Candy Crush* on my phone until I saw little orange and blue striped candies exploding on the insides of my eyelids when I closed them, and still it wasn't enough. It wasn't enough pleasure, not enough light or color to fill the emptiness of my brain. It didn't feel good or fun, but it was motion of a kind. If I stopped playing, I would realize that there were no thoughts left in my head and I was truly alone. This was what happened when my ADHD medicine wore off. This was why I hated drugs.

I left the picture of Abelard in my room, thinking I would show it to Rosalind over lunch. But when I packed my stuff up for school in the morning, the picture was gone. This didn't surprise me in the least. Most pieces of paper I come into contact with disappear suddenly and without reason. It's just the way it is.

CHAPTER 5

Nothing disappears forever. The universe is a swirling mass of lost jewelry, paperwork, and people, a vortex of missing cell phones and spare keys. When I pulled my bed away from the wall looking for my lost math homework, I found a take-home history test from eighth grade and a copper ring I'd never seen before. My math homework was in Kansas or stuck behind the dryer; either way, searching for it was pointless. I wasn't going to find it before it was due that day. My math homework still existed; my favorite eye shadow wasn't lost—it was buried under a pile of towels at the bottom of the laundry hamper. My dad wasn't missing; he was on a goat farm in Portland, Oregon.

When you lose things constantly, as I do, it helps to remember that matter can never be created or destroyed. You will always find what you are looking for later, probably when it's no longer important to you.

So I expected to find Richard's portrait of Abelard—one day.

* * *

Math was my last class of the day. I'd mostly done my homework, but I didn't really understand it, so I'd left a few problems blank. It was about logarithms and natural log and inverted logarithms, which are something else. I didn't understand the way X turns from one thing into another, and it made me angry and anxious just thinking about X as an exponent, like X doesn't have enough to do just being a line position variable.

Still, I could have gotten partial credit if I hadn't lost the assignment. I had to pass algebra to see my dad, and I was just barely scraping by. I needed the grade.

I tore through my backpack, looking for the assignment. I sorted frantically through the pile of loose and crumpled paper at the bottom of my locker, getting angrier by the minute. The bell rang, and then I was in the hallway with a few other stragglers and no math assignment in sight. My giant math book was on the floor, blocking the door of the locker. I slammed the book in the locker five times in a row and then kicked the locker five times. It hurt my foot, but it didn't make me feel any better. I shoved the book and my backpack into my locker and closed the door. The locker was slightly bent at the bottom, and I had to push it hard to get it to close.

Next thing I knew, I was walking down Lamar Boulevard in the bright sunshine. It happens this way. I'm upset, I start walking to cool down, and before you know it, I've skipped school. It's never a conscious choice.

After a while, I dug in the pocket of my jeans and found a five-dollar bill. Enough for a Coke at the 7-Eleven and a bus home. I lingered over my Coke on the curb in front of the 7-Eleven and tried not to cry. I didn't have my house key, and I couldn't get in until Iris got home. If I failed math, I'd never get to Portland. Plus, I'd skipped school—again.

Out of the corner of my eye, I noticed a guy sitting in his car, staring at me. He was a bald old man in a sedan. I got up and walked to my bus stop and sat on the bench. It occurred to me that not only had I skipped math class, but I'd skipped detention as well. Coach Neuwirth would make me suffer.

Worse yet, I wouldn't get to see Abelard. I'd been thinking about him all day.

"Needer scride?"

I turned. The bald man craned his head out the window of his car. He'd followed me from the 7-Eleven.

"Crab sand walk," he said. *"Nedderly be home in sure hours."*

I blinked. I couldn't understand him.

"What? What did you say?"

I realized that I'd made a big mistake. I should have just ignored him. He got out of the car and walked toward me, smiling, his eyelids strangely droopy. It freaked me out. I'd left my phone in my locker. There was no one at the bus stop.

"*Screw* look upset. *Canner hell?*"

Just then, one of those whippet-thin guys in spandex who ride up and down Lamar on racing bicycles stopped and told the guy to fuck off. Literally he said, "Fuck off, old man. Go be a predator elsewhere"—and a bunch of other stuff I didn't catch. The old man drove away quickly. Then the bicycle hero got back on his bike just as my bus arrived.

For every horrible person in the universe, there is a truly amazingly good person waiting to undo the evil. It's all a matter of timing. A bicycle hero is only good if he arrives at the right moment. If only I had a bike hero to help me find my homework. Then maybe I could stay in school.

"Lily," Mom said, "I got an automated notice from school that you weren't in class in the afternoon. Did you leave school?"

"Um—yes."

No point in lying. You can't argue with a robocall.

Mom had come home late from work with one of those time-stamped, grocery-store baked chickens and a premade salad. Chocolate-covered ice cream bars in a sad attempt to retain nice-mom status while simultaneously crawling up my ass about attendance. Might have worked if I was still ten. She put the ice cream bars in the freezer and turned toward me.

"Did something happen to make you want to leave school?" she said in a soft voice.

"No."

She pursed her mouth in a tight line and shook her head. In the range of maternal responses to failure, I'd have taken anger over defeat any day. I couldn't stand that I made my mother look old and tired. I was the most exhausting person in the world, apparently.

"You can't keep leaving school, Lily," Mom replied, not looking at me. "Do you want another visit from CPS?"

Child Protective Services. In middle school I skipped so many classes that CPS sent a small, earnest guy in a shirt and tie to question Mom. He talked to me alone for what seemed like hours. I thought he was nice, but Mom remembers the CPS visit differently than I do. Mom remembers the CPS visit as the "Worst. Day. Ever."

"What can CPS do?" I said, beginning to get angry. "I mean, school is hell. How can CPS punish me worse than I'm already being punished? Has CPS discovered a deeper level of hell for people who skip school?"

Okay—Dante's *Inferno* in AP English last semester. Metaphorically useful. But then I remembered that my trip to Portland was contingent on staying in school. I had hopes of crawling out of the stygian marsh to dry land.

"Coach Neuwirth called me," she said, ignoring my CPS question. "He said to tell you that you just earned yourself three extra days of detention."

"Fine."

I didn't mind detention as long as Abelard was there.

Abelard didn't show up for detention the next day. I thought he might be late, but ten minutes into it, I realized he wasn't coming.

"Where is Abelard?" I blurted out.

"Well, Ms. Michaels-Ryan, your 'boyfriend' isn't in detention anymore," Coach Neuwirth replied. "Apparently Abelard's mother felt that two days of detention was punishment enough for the wanton destruction of thousands of dollars' worth of school property. I respectfully disagree."

No Abelard!

I took the late bus home. Rosalind had texted me a half-dozen times since school ended, expressing frustration that I had not yet turned on my phone. Sometimes I forget.

When I finally got back to her, she sent me a link. I opened it and found Richard's picture of Abelard on Tumblr with my stupid thought bubble clearly in view. I followed the comment trail. It started with Iris and her best friend, Exene Ybarra, conversing about an English assignment on intertextuality and the internet and cute boys and *The Letters of Abelard and Heloise,* which Exene had never heard of. Somewhere in the day, a multitude of their friends jumped on the thread, and then someone wrote, *OMG! That's Abelard Mitchell.* I felt sick.

And then people from our school appeared on the thread, and it got worse.

Iris. I was going to kill her. Why would she post this online? It was a public declaration that I was crushed out on Abelard for the whole internet to see. I checked the thread to see if anyone had figured out I was the person who wrote this. So far, no one. My heart slowed just a little. Dozens of comments, some of them funny, but a few were mean to Abelard. Heart-twistingly, middle-school-depths-of-hell, I-am-sad-to-be-a-human-being mean. Yes, I was going to kill Iris.

"You asked about Abelard," Rosalind texted. *"Did you do this?"*

Rosalind. She knows me too well.

"Yes and no." I texted back. *"My words. Iris took it and posted it."*

"WTF? Iris?"

"I will kill!" I sent back.

"Who drew the picture?"

"Richard Hernandez," I said. I was pretty sure Rosalind didn't know Richard. They didn't travel in the same circles.

"He's an amazing artist."

I wondered if Abelard had decided not to come to detention because of the picture and all the craptacular things people had posted about him. My heart sank to a new low.

* * *

Detention made me late, and Iris was already home when I arrived. I found her in the kitchen, chopping carrots for dinner. I stood in the kitchen doorway and stared at her long enough to make her really uncomfortable.

"What?"

I let her twist for a moment before I spoke. She deserved to suffer.

"I believe you have something that belongs to me," I said slowly.

Iris blushed and hurried over to her backpack on the dining room table. She opened the top and carefully pulled out a manila folder with my picture of Abelard inside. The picture looked like she'd ironed it. Really, it looked better than when I'd brought it home. So there was that.

"Sorry," she croaked, her voice failing her.

"Sorry? You posted this online! Did you even read the comments?"

"It was for an English assignment on intertextuality," she said. "I was supposed to find a feed that referenced a literary work."

"Doesn't your school have a closed network?" I asked.

"Yes, but this was supposed to be something we found outside of school."

LAME. It's an all-pastiche, postapocalyptic playground until someone gets hurt. I blame LAME for unleashing mutant geniuses on the world with limited supervision.

"So, instead of searching, you stole one. Lazy." Calling

her lazy was the sickest burn I could ever offer Iris. And it worked. She looked like she was about to cry.

"Please don't tell Mom," she begged.

For some reason, this touched my heart just a little. What could Iris possibly be worried about? She'd always been Mom's favorite. Plus, there was no way Mom could ever punish her. What could Mom do? Ban her from extracurricular activities? Send her to norm school?

Not that Iris knew that.

"You know, that's a good idea," I replied. "I should tell Mom."

I didn't tell Mom. It was enough to watch Iris squirm. I put Abelard's picture back up on the bulletin board. And I hoped that, like so many things on the internet, the site with Abelard's picture would disappear in a day. But of course, that didn't happen.

CHAPTER 6

My English teacher, Mrs. Rogers-Peña, loves books and reading more than anyone I've ever met, except perhaps my father. She lets me slide on the deadlines and details as long as I get my work in. She has chin-length dark hair and thick glasses, and tends to wear skirts that look like they were made out of 1950s kitchen curtains. She knows everything that goes on in school. Which can be a problem.

I headed to her desk after class to talk about the novel at hand, *The Stranger*. Mrs. Rogers-Peña is always trying to get people to discuss whatever novel we happen to be reading. I wanted to talk to her, but not in front of other students.

"This is depressing. I mean, I get that the point is pointlessness . . ."

"You're right, Lily," Mrs. Rogers-Peña said. "All books should be happy and pleasant."

This was why she was my favorite teacher. She never stinted on the irony.

"I'm glad you're here, because I have a question for you," she said. "Is high school really a barren wasteland?"

She turned her laptop to show Richard's picture and my words:

I am Abelard, medieval French philosopher and time traveler. I have come to the future on a quest for love and beauty, but find only the barren wasteland that is high school. My travails are for not!

Busted. My heart sped.

"What makes you think I wrote that?" I asked.

"Lily, please." Mrs. Rogers-Peña peered over the edge of her glasses. "You referenced *The Letters of Abelard and Heloise* in a paper last semester. Also, you misspelled *naught*. You might as well have signed this."

Dyslexia. No matter how much you try to hide it, the spelling always gives you away.

"It wasn't me," I said. "I mean it was me, but it wasn't me. I wrote this, but—"

"It doesn't matter who did what. I know you didn't intend for this to happen, but people have posted some pretty mean things about Abelard. You need to apologize to him."

My stomach did a flip-flop. I did not want to apologize to Abelard. No, I did not.

"But if I apologize, Abelard will know that I wrote this about him."

Endless possibilities for mortification presented themselves, like I'd scrolled his name in curlicues on my notebook. Abelard, looking for "love and beauty." So middle school! What had I done? What had Iris done?

"Yes," Mrs. Rogers-Peña said. "And that's the point. Bullying thrives on anonymity. You have to put a face on this thing. Are we clear?"

I nodded. When she said it that way, it seemed like I owed Abelard an explanation. But still.

At lunchtime I met Rosalind in the courtyard. I didn't even bother to unpack my lunch. Eating was an impossibility. My fourth day back on the medication, and my appetite was pretty much gone. Supposedly it takes a couple of weeks for the antidepressant to build up in your system, but I could already feel the drug working its dismal magic.

Abelard was in his usual spot under the crepe myrtle, looking at his phone. I wondered if he was studying his picture. I hoped not. I hoped that he'd managed to miss the whole fiasco.

Rosalind was on her phone, staring at the picture of Abelard, eating a salad wrap.

"Mrs. Rogers-Peña thinks I should apologize to Abelard because of all the stuff people said on this thread."

Rosalind scrolled down and made a face.

"Definitely apologize," she said. "It's not your fault that people are horrible, but you did start this."

"What if Abelard didn't see it?" I asked hopefully.

"Oh, he saw it," Rosalind replied. "If he didn't find it himself, somebody pointed it out to him. You know how school is." I nodded. Whatever Mrs. Rogers-Peña believed about the nature of high school, I stood by my "barren wasteland" assessment.

I lunged in Abelard's direction, stumbled, and caught myself. Behind me, Rosalind sighed at my lack of personal elegance. I walked the open space of the courtyard, arms at my sides, feeling like the entire school was watching me: the stoners returning from the parking lot, shiny blond seniors sipping low-fat caramel extra-whip lattes for lunch, the Hispanic girls eating school lunch on trays in the blazing sun. If I hadn't been on drugs, I probably wouldn't have cared, because I wouldn't have noticed all the other people. But suddenly, talking to Abelard seemed like a really bad idea. A people-will-be-joking-about-this-for-months bad, because two freaks in the same vicinity was an order of magnitude more hilarious. I stopped, but it was too late. Abelard looked up and made eye contact.

"Lily," he said.

Almost like he'd expected me.

His dark blue eyes skittered away like some incredibly rare and beautiful animal you catch a glimpse of through the forest canopy.

"Abelard," I replied.

I took a deep breath and sat down next to him. "Have you seen your picture online?"

I tried to wait for Abelard to respond. I made it maybe a second and a half before I started talking at my usual breakneck pace. Ninety miles an hour with gusts up to a hundred and fifty.

"Well, okay," I began. "So I had that picture after detention, and I took it home and wrote something about Peter Abelard, the twelfth-century French monk on it, just as a private joke. I didn't plan on showing anyone the picture, but then I lost it, and it . . . ended up online."

I paused and waited for a response from Abelard. A sign that he was mad, or indifferent to the ramblings of internet trolls because he'd evolved into a superior mind-based being. Nothing. Abelard sat perfectly still, staring into the middle ground. The grape Kool-Aid scent of mountain laurel drifted in from the vines by the teachers' parking lot.

"You've read *The Letters of Abelard and Heloise,*" he said finally.

"My father read it to me when I was little."

I thought about how weird that sounded. It's not a happy bedtime story. It's not a novel, either. It's a slim volume of letters sent back and forth between two medieval geniuses who had the misfortune of falling madly in love. Real people.

"My father read it to me in Latin," Abelard said.

"Latin?" I said. "You know Latin?"

Abelard nodded.

I wondered why he wasn't over at LAME magnet school with all the other geniuses. Abelard felt the gears of the world turning; he spoke Latin. What other talents was he hiding?

"Okay, well, I just wanted to say I'm sorry." I stood up slowly.

"So when you kissed me," he said. "Was that a joke, too?"

My mouth went dry. This wasn't how I pictured this conversation going. Not at all.

"No, it wasn't a joke. So . . . what happened there was . . . Well, I went off my medication, and I guess I've been having a little problem with impulse control."

"Impulse," he said. "You had an impulse."

He said the word *impulse* slowly, as though trying to understand the full meaning of the word. As in, "impulse: a sudden strong and unreflective urge or desire to act." Emphasis on desire. I desired to kiss him. And now he knew.

My face went hot as an awkward pause fell over us. "I'm back on my medication now, so you don't have to worry. I'm not going to do anything weird. Again. Okay, so . . . Bye."

I turned and bounded toward the doors and away, narrowly missing a full-body collision with Dakota Smith from geography.

"Lily!" Rosalind called. "You forgot your lunchbox."

Rosalind had grabbed my lunch and followed me. She's done this hundreds of times since kindergarten. The only reason I still have a purse and a backpack is because Rosalind is my best friend.

"How did it go?" she asked.

"Great! We had a nice talk about my impulse control issues and my struggles with prescription drugs. Also, he speaks Latin." I paused, strangely out of breath.

"Latin—okay," she said slowly. "So why are you hyperventilating?"

"I'll tell you inside." It felt like the whole entire world was listening in to our conversation. I pushed through the double doors and moved quickly past the cafeteria. I found an empty place in the hall and stopped.

"I didn't tell you this because it was just so awkward," I whispered. "I kissed Abelard in the vice principal's office. He wanted to know why I kissed him."

"You kissed Abelard? What made you do that?"

"I don't know. It was just one of those—"

"Lily moments," she said.

I grimaced. I don't like it when Rosalind refers to what she calls my "Lily moments," but in this case, it was pretty accurate.

"So you really do like Abelard?"

"No," I said quickly. "I mean, maybe. Okay—yes."

And there it was. I'd admitted to Rosalind that I liked Abelard—which was enough to make me admit it to myself.

CHAPTER 7

"*Let's stop pretending that sixteen* people is a viable breeding population," Iris yelled at her laptop. "Two hundred years down the line, everyone will be so inbred they'll have three thumbs on each hand and speak only in grunts."

"Could you possibly text, like a normal human being?" I asked.

"Can't." Iris gestured to the piece of posterboard on her bed. "Craft project. Need my hands free."

Iris sat cross-legged on her bed, talking to Exene Ybarra on speakerphone while one of her beloved K-pop videos played on her laptop: spastically cheerful Korean girls leaping around in a crayon selection of miniskirts and matching thigh-high stockings. I was still trying to read my novel about the girl on the run with her brilliant father. Trying and failing.

Iris and Exene were working on a project where you had to design a fallout shelter and underground survival community for sixteen people, only in this homework scenario of the damned, thirty people arrive at the shelter and fourteen people have to be left outside. Iris and Exene had the names, the ages, the IQs, the job descriptions, and the breeding potential of everyone who showed up to the shelter. Iris and Exene also had an inexplicable faith that the decision of who lived and who died could be solved with a rational, community-based process. In real life, their bomb shelter would quickly have filled with the kind of gym-muscled douchebags who were not in the least bit concerned with the continued survival of the human race and had devoted their lives to maintaining physical superiority and minimal body hair. This was what you learned in norm school.

"Well, if they can't breed, what's the point of survival?" Exene asked. "They might as well all leave the shelter right—"

"Human dignity?" Iris replied. "The chance to leave a message for an alien race—"

"Pointless. If the human race doesn't survive, it doesn't matter," Exene said.

"What do you think, Lily?" Iris said, in a naked attempt to open a line of communication between us. I'd returned Abelard's picture to the bulletin board, but I was still mad at her for posting it online.

"Kill everyone who isn't a farmer," I replied, without looking over at Iris.

Exene laughed.

"'Holiday in Cambodia,'" Exene said. "Dead Kennedys."

Exene Ybarra's parents are semifamous musicians with a late-seventies California punk fetish. I think her mom once played bass in a band with my dad. They named her after Exene Cervenka of X.

My phone on the bedside table buzzed. I ignored it.

It buzzed again.

"Are you going to get that?" Iris said.

"No." I turned the page of my book, though I couldn't remember what I'd read. My eyes skimmed over the words without gathering any meaning. Pointedly demonstrating my displeasure with Iris took more energy than I had at this hour of the day.

My cell buzzed again.

And again.

Iris snatched the phone off our bedside table.

"Hey, Exene, I'll call you back, okay?" Iris handed the phone to me. "You need to read this."

It was Rosalind.

"Check out the picture. Abelard is on!" Rosalind texted, followed by the link.

I clicked on the link. There were now about a million new posts starting with my words: *"I am Abelard, medieval French philosopher and time traveler. I have come to the future on a quest for . . ."* and replacing my comments about love and beauty with ones suggesting that Abelard had come to the future to get wasted while willing future sluts to perform various and sundry sexual acts upon his person.

Iris was giving the laptop her undivided attention, which meant she was also reading the comments.

"You shouldn't be reading that," I said.

"*You* are," Iris shot back.

"I'm older," I said. "Plus, you learn things in norm school that they don't teach over at LAME."

Iris was uncharacteristically silent.

"Creepy," I texted. *"All the trolls."*

"*Scroll down,*" Rosalind replied. *"Look for 'Real Abelard.' That's got to be him, right?"*

Three-quarters of the way down, I found the comment: "*I am Abelard, medieval French philosopher and time traveler. I have come to the future on a quest . . . to find a woman of surpassing beauty and purpose among you! She alone would know to email me at the initial of my Christian name, followed by Abelard, initial of my surname, all lowercase @gmail.com for further instructions — Orator of Paraclete.*"

I leaned back against the headboard and closed my eyes as a wave of golden happiness overtook me, like a drug strong enough to counteract the late-day letdown of my ADHD meds. Abelard understood my sense of humor. Not only had he understood, but he'd called me a "woman of surpassing beauty and purpose."

Abelard.

"Well?" Rosalind texted.

And just as quickly, doubt filtered in. This many internet-borne feels could only be the result of a cruel joke.

Anyone could have Googled Abelard and come up with Peter Abelard's history and his nickname, the Orator of Paraclete. Okay, anyone with the patience to read an entire Wikipedia page.

"It's a prank," I texted. *"Someone Googled Abelard."*

"One way to find out," Rosalind returned.

Iris turned from her laptop.

"Abelard is looking for you," she said. "And *Christian name* is the name they give you at christening. It means his first name, Peter."

"Yes, Iris, I know."

I sent an email to the address pabelardm@gmail.com: *"Abelard? This is Lily from school."*

"Are you going to talk to Abelard?" Iris said.

"Yes."

"What's he like? Is he taller than you? He doesn't wear skinny jeans, does he? I don't like tall guys in skinny jeans. By the way, who drew that picture? Don't tell me it was you because I know you can't draw that well . . ."

Iris sat on the edge of her bed facing me, her head bobbing happily, her loose brown hair swinging free.

"It's probably not even him," I said.

I heard the ping of an incoming email. The note was short. It gave a phone number and the instruction to text at that number.

I tried to be cool and wait. I made it about a minute

and a half before I entered the number in my phone and texted.

"Abelard? How do I know this is you?"

"You made quite an impression—on my cheek. We were seven. I never told anyone except my mother."

"It's him," I said. No one else knew about the lunchbox.

"What does he say?" Iris asked.

I ignored Iris.

"What did he say?" Iris grabbed for the phone. I tried to evade her grasp, but in the struggle I lost my grip, and Iris dove for it.

"So say something funny and sexy back," Iris said.

I paused momentarily to wonder how Iris had learned the nuances of sexy chat repartee, before deciding this was very good advice. It took me forever to complete my text. I'm a slow writer at best, I misspell words, and autocorrect wreaks havoc on what I'm trying to say.

"I'm sorry for exposing your visible to the trolls. They don't deserve to look upon your face."

"What did you write?" Iris asked.

I showed her the screen before I hit Send.

"Oh, that's good," Iris said. "But visible? What do you mean?"

"I meant to write *visage.*"

"Stupid autocorrect," she said.

Iris backed up the text and rewrote my text three times

faster than I could have done it, because she's not dyslexic. She sees mistakes that I don't.

We waited together for what seemed to be a full minute before a message returned.

"The internet! I hate this deceitful, faithless world. I think no more of it," Abelard texted.

Strange and familiar. While we stared at the message, another one came.

"But your picture and words with it intrigued me. I was always vain and presumptive, and I flattered myself already with the most bewitching hopes."

My breath caught in my throat. Why was this so familiar? Like something Dad read to me a long time ago.

Iris looked at the screen and giggled.

"Does Abelard always talk like this?" she said. "How cool!"

My sluggish end-of-the-day, drug-burnt neurons fired. It was so obvious—and so brilliant. I looked across at the picture of Abelard on the bulletin board and felt a swell of admiration. I'd been thinking of his namesake when I wrote the lines on the top of the picture, but Abelard had gone one step further.

"Iris! It's from *The Letters of Abelard and Heloise!* Quick—go get Dad's copy. It's on the far bookshelf in the living room."

Iris bolted out of the room, the first time in recent memory she'd actually done something I asked her to do.

"Your bewitching hopes? What bewitching hopes?" I texted back.

"Haven't you guessed?" he texted. This was not a quote, this was Abelard, asking me to think. In real time. A peculiar shyness overtook me. I couldn't believe I was having this conversation.

"Tell me."

A minute of dead time. I stared at my last text, wondering if my monosyllabic response had convinced Abelard that I wasn't the clever girl he imagined me to be. Or maybe he thought I wasn't interested. A full minute of torturous self-doubt passed before he answered.

"I have wit enough to write a letter and hope that you would permit my absent self to entertain you," he texted.

"Your absent self has entertained me thus far," I texted back.

Iris came back with the book. I snatched it out of her hands and scanned the first letter from Heloise to Abelard. There was a full half-page of her going on about his picture. My eyes roamed the text, but I couldn't focus on individual lines. Even with all the reading I do, I am a slow reader. Because—dyslexia. Iris is faster.

"Read this page and find me a good quote," I demanded. "Something about writing letters. She has a lot of stuff about writing."

"What's he . . . ?" she began.

"Read!" I yelled.

"Good. Because I don't think I can entertain you in person," Abelard texted.

A modern contraction. These were Abelard's own words, not from the book. Abelard, who couldn't hold a conversation in real time. Abelard, who was twenty seconds behind in actual conversation.

"A letter is enough for me," I texted.

"Is that true?" he replied.

"How about this?" Iris held the book out, her finger on a line.

I studied the quote. Perfect. Iris would make a great reference librarian someday if she wasn't huddled in an underground bunker somewhere, growing hydroponic tomatoes.

"Type it in," I demanded. "Quickly!"

Iris grinned and then handed me the phone.

"If a picture, which is but a mute representation of an object, can give such pleasure, what cannot letters inspire?" I pushed Send.

I waited a full minute before Abelard responded.

"We understand each other," he texted.

"Perfectly," I shot back.

I waited for a minute and then two, knowing that Abelard was searching for a quote. While I waited, Mom appeared in the doorway.

"Iris, what's going on?" Mom said. "You ran through the living room like you were on fire."

"I needed a book for an English project," Iris replied placidly.

Iris could build a pipe bomb, and as long as it was for a homework project, Mom would be okay with it.

"Anyway, it's dinnertime," Mom said.

I ignored her.

"Your wit and beauty would fire the dullest heart and most insensible heart, and your education is equally admirable," Abelard texted.

"Tell Rosalind you'll text her after dinner," Mom said.

"I must go. Fulbert has arrived," I texted, referring to Heloise's infamous guardian.

"Then you don't mind if I text you again?"

"I think I'd mind if you didn't," I replied.

"You look happy," Mom said.

Her face held a familiar note of optimistic wariness. My psychiatrist had told Mom to watch my behavior for euphoria or signs of depression. Basically, any flavor of emotion is a sign that the drugs haven't completely killed all normal human response, and my dosage might need to be upped. But at this particular juncture, not even annoyance with my mother could bring me down.

CHAPTER 8

Because I don't have the most well-developed social life, I spend a lot of Friday nights watching old movies with Rosalind and her parents. According to them, old movies are a fundamental part of Rosalind's theatrical education.

Rosalind's house is a mid-century ranch with a flagstone floor and a sunken living room. It's filled with seventies stuff: Danish furniture and burnt orange pottery. It looks like the kind of place where you'd hold a far-out fondue party—if you ate cheese. Which they don't.

Rosalind greeted me at the door.

"My mother is frying tofu," Rosalind said.

Fried tofu is the most indulgent food Rosalind's parents can imagine. Fried tofu is, surprisingly, pretty damn good, anyway. Most fried things are.

Light bulbs went off. Rosalind's mom didn't fry tofu for just any occasion.

"You told them about detention, didn't you?" I asked.

Rosalind shrugged.

"They found your story touching and surprising. They laughed, they cried." She leaned closer and lowered her voice. "What did Abelard say?"

I couldn't help smiling.

"So very, very much and—"

Rosalind's dad appeared in the living room, and I stopped talking.

"Fauxmosa?" He offered around a tray of orange-colored drinks in champagne flutes.

"Sure," I replied, hoping that the drink wasn't some strange tea or worse yet, kombucha. They drink a lot of kombucha over at Rosalind's house, which is a definite disadvantage to visiting. Kombucha is a fermented yeast tea that tastes a little better than it sounds. But not much.

Here's the great thing about Rosalind's parents: They don't think there's anything wrong with me. They think I'm "delightfully madcap."

I tasted the drink. Fresh orange juice and something fizzy. Not bad.

Rosalind's mom emerged from the kitchen with an artfully stacked pile of tofu chunks. She set the plate on the table. Rosalind's mom is an older version of Rosalind—tiny, artistic, doe-eyed.

"Lily," she said, reaching up to kiss me on the cheek. "So sorry about that spot of bother at school. We're watching *Bringing Up Baby.* Guaranteed to dispel the darkest of moods."

The "spot of bother." I liked that. School was definitely a "spot of bother."

"We should be watching *You Can't Take It with You,* but Rosalind refuses," she said.

"Why *You Can't Take It with You*?" I asked.

Her mother smirked. Dramatically.

"It's the spring play, of course. Rosalind got the lead," Rosalind's dad said from behind his laptop. "Didn't she tell you?"

Rosalind blushed. She gets embarrassed when her parents are proud of her like this. It's a completely alien experience for me. I don't think Rosalind gets how nice her parents are.

"No, she didn't." I poked Rosalind in the arm.

"You've been kind of distracted." She raised an eyebrow to let me know that she expected to hear all about Abelard. Fair enough.

We settled in to eat tofu and watch *Bringing Up Baby.* The sight of Cary Grant in a frilly dressing gown—pretty hilarious. But what really got me was watching Katharine Hepburn, as Susan, destroy cars, lose important relics, rip off the back of her dress, and unleash a dangerous animal on her unsuspecting neighbors—all while talking a mile a minute and being adorable. Maybe I should have lived in the thirties. Because—madcap.

"Well, what did you think, Lily?" Rosalind's mom said as the credits rolled.

"Awesome," I replied.

"Really?" she said. "But did you really enjoy it?"

"Oh my god— You know, whatever I break, at least I will never destroy an entire brontosaurus skeleton. Susan was like ADHD on steroids."

I can say stuff around Rosalind's parents because they've known me since kindergarten.

"ADHD—classic," Rosalind's dad said, looking up from his laptop. "Never thought about that before."

"Well, next we're going to watch *His Girl Friday*," Rosalind's mom said. "It stars the actress we named Rosalind after and—"

"Sorry, Mother," Rosalind interrupted. "Regrettably, we must depart for my room."

Rosalind bolted toward the hall, and I followed.

I sprawled on the queen-size bed next to Rosalind in her room that she does not share with another living being.

"So what did Abelard say? I'm dying to know."

I found the text conversation and handed Rosalind the phone. I felt a little strange sharing my texts from Abelard with another person, but then again, Iris had already seen them, and there wasn't anything deeply personal in our messages.

I watched impatiently as Rosalind scrolled.

"Wow," she said finally. "'Your wit and beauty would fire the dullest and most insensible heart, and your education is equally admirable.' Super old-school romantic! Does Abelard really talk like that?"

"Not really," I replied. "It's a quote from *The Letters of Abelard and Heloise.*"

"How do you know? It doesn't say that anywhere."

"I figured it out."

She handed my phone back.

"You're so smart." Rosalind picked up her phone. She pulled up the picture of Abelard and studied it. "So what do you think about this? You and Abelard?"

I struggled to find the right words. But more than that, I struggled to find the right feeling. I remembered the exhilaration of the moment, but now it was like my whole text exchange with Abelard had been shoved into a book and pressed like a dried flower.

"I'm happy, I guess."

"You guess you're happy?" Rosalind looked up from her phone. "If someone wrote these words to me, I'd be ecstatic. Are you sure you're okay being back on medi—"

"I'm ecstatic," I said quickly.

Rosalind shrugged and went back to staring at her phone. Fine with me. I didn't feel like discussing my drug-induced lack of feels with Rosalind.

"So Iris? Did she give you the picture back?"

"Yes. Can you believe this? She stole it for a homework assignment. So typical."

Rosalind laughed. Rosalind has a greater tolerance

for Iris's academic obsession than I do, because Rosalind and Iris are a lot alike. If not for our school's kick-ass drama department, Rosalind would probably have gone to LAME.

"Can I see the picture of Abelard?"

"Sure," I said. "I don't have it with me, though."

Rosalind leaned back into a pile of red-and-plum-colored velvet throw pillows and sighed. Rosalind had dozens of useless pillows and pointless, diaphanous drapes at the head of her bed. Her room was decorated in a style I liked to think of as theatrical Victorian harem. She had an actual chaise longue. Jealous.

"So, the artist who drew this is Richard Hernandez. You know him, right?"

It was easy to see where this was heading. Rosalind had fallen in love with the picture of Abelard—not the subject, the artist. Rosalind's crushes are like this—talent-based, improbable. Sight unseen. She hasn't had a real boyfriend yet, because it's hard to date an abstraction. Not that I've had a real boyfriend before either.

"Richard? I know him. He's taking Algebra I for the second time. We're in the same class."

Rosalind frowned. I knew what she was thinking. She's kind of an academic snob.

"Hey, I'm in that class," I said. "It's not like I'm stupid."

"I didn't mean to imply anything. So what is Richard like?"

"He's about my height. Broad shoulders. Close-set, intense eyes. Great eyelashes."

"I meant as a person," she said with a deep, theatrical sigh. I could see right through her. Everyone likes long eyelashes. Everyone.

I thought about Richard. I didn't know him that well.

"Dyslexic," I said. "He can't read."

"That's terrible," she said. "No wonder he's failing classes."

She didn't sound any less intrigued with Richard because of his dyslexia. If anything, more so. I'd have to introduce her to Richard, eventually. Not that Rosalind would talk to him. But I had a plan for that.

CHAPTER 9

So—the story of Abelard and Heloise. Heloise d'Argenteuil lived in twelfth-century France. She was super smart and completely bored with the normal women's activities of the day—sewing stuff and hanging around inside doing needlepoint. Her uncle Fulbert took pity on her and decided to hire the most educated man in all of Europe to tutor her in philosophy. The most educated man in all of Europe was, of course, Peter Abelard. He was also one of the hottest men on the continent.

Peter Abelard and Heloise had nothing to do but read, drink wine, and argue philosophy all day. Of course, they fell madly, stupidly in love. Stupid, because Heloise became pregnant. Abelard wanted to get married, but Heloise refused on the grounds that married life would mean returning to sewing stuff and needlepoint. Reasonable, if you ask me.

Then her uncle Fulbert found out. Fulbert may not have even been her real uncle; he may have been her pretend "uncle." Ick. And the story only gets more disturbing from there. Fulbert hired thugs to cut off Abelard's genitals. Abelard fell into a deep depression, and I mean, who wouldn't? Heloise entered a monastery and quickly became the mother superior because she was smarter than everyone else there. Abelard and Heloise continued to write each other, and eventually they lived together.

No one knows what happened to the baby.

Monday morning, I took my dad's copy of *The Letters of Abelard and Heloise* to school. I told myself I'd keep the book in my backpack until detention, but I couldn't help it. During English class, I slid the book under my desk to reread Heloise's first letter. The sweet letter, before everything went wrong between them.

I circled a passage from the letter to use in my exchanges with Abelard. Stuff about Peter Abelard's cleverness and worldly beauty.

That would work. Abelard Mitchell, my Abelard, had worldly beauty to burn. When I thought of the way his hair—

"Lily?"

I looked up. Mrs. Rogers-Peña was peering at me over the top of her reading glasses, one eyebrow crooked at an angle.

"I'm sure whatever you're reading has deep literary merit, but the rest of us are discussing *Macbeth*. Would you care to join us?"

I shoved *The Letters of Abelard and Heloise* in my backpack and picked up *Macbeth*.

After my last class, I ran up the stairs past students fleeing the school, pushing my way through the third-floor mosh pit to Coach Neuwirth's room. I hoped to catch Richard before Coach Neuwirth showed up.

I flew into the room and almost ran into Richard. No one else was there. It occurred to me that Abelard wasn't the only one I owed an apology for the picture. After all, I'd stolen it from Richard. Maybe he didn't want his beautiful artwork displayed before the whole stupid world.

"Oh, hey," I said breathlessly. "Have you seen the thread with your picture of Abelard?"

"Thread?" Richard lowered his backpack into the nearest chair and turned to face me. We were almost the same height, eyes at a level. "My picture?"

"Okay, see, what happened is, I took the picture you drew of Abelard home, and I meant to return it to you, but then my sister found it, and she posted it online for a homework assignment, which shouldn't have even been a thing. But then, for some reason, all the trolls came out from under their bridges to . . ."

Richard frowned, and I remembered that he couldn't read. The whole vicious rugby scrum of the internet was unavailable to him. Sad, but at the same time I had to think how nice it was to meet a guy who'd never dipped his toe into the cesspool of 4chan. All actual human qualities still intact. Perfect for Rosalind.

"Look, let me just show you," I said.

I grabbed my phone and pulled up the picture. When I leaned close to hold the phone between us, Richard stiffened slightly.

"I took your picture home and left it in my room. My sister found it and posted it online. I had no idea she would do that. I'm sorry."

"There's something written on the picture. What does it say?"

"Oh, that was me." I felt myself blushing. It hadn't occurred to me until this moment that I had defaced his work. "It's about Abelard, and well, it's hard to explain, but Abelard was named after a famous philosopher and lover from the Middle Ages—"

"You know a lot about the Middle Ages—da Vinci and all—don't you?"

Richard studied me, his gaze roaming from my eyes to my lips and back again as though trying to decide whether my face was aesthetically pleasing or not. Artists.

"Da Vinci was Italian Renaissance, but yeah, I guess I do. My father is sort of a medieval scholar, or he was until he left us . . ."

Until he left us . . . I'd never actually said those words to another person before. My father left us.

"When did your father leave?" Richard asked.

It was a casual question, and yet there was something about Richard that made me want to confess how I felt like I was the cause of my parents' divorce. Maybe it was knowing that Richard was dyslexic. Maybe he'd screwed up his family too.

"I guess it's been four, five years. But I don't think he left as much as . . ." I stopped, remembering that I was on a mission on Rosalind's behalf. I had limited time before Coach Neuwirth showed up. "So, hey—how much longer do you have detention?" I asked.

"Three more days."

"Me too! What are you doing after that?"

Richard opened his mouth, but I was too nervous to let him form a sentence. Clock. Ticking.

"You should come and work crew at the theater Thursday," I said. "Mr. Turner is always looking for artists to work on the set. You'd probably be great at set design, plus they often have people paint the set so—"

"I don't know. After school I go home to—"

"Oh, come on, say yes!" I grabbed Richard by the arm. I do this sometimes, forget the rules of personal space.

Rogelio arrived, followed by Coach Neuwirth.

"Ms. Michaels-Ryan," Coach Neuwirth boomed, "please stop pestering Mr. Hernandez."

Pestering. There was that word again. I guess pestering

means randomly invading someone's personal space. Guilty as charged.

I didn't know if Richard would show up to the theater on Thursday, but I'd done my best. Now it was up to Rosalind.

CHAPTER 10

Thursday afternoon, and Abelard hadn't texted since the weekend. My dad's copy of the book was already beginning to look dog-eared from my near-constant attention. If Abelard didn't text back soon, the book would burst at the seams, dropping pages like tears.

Iris was in the kitchen making a salad.

"Lily?" Mom's voice echoed from the dining room. I'd done something wrong. Again.

I walked to the dining room table where Mom had her laptop and work spread out, a semipermanent collection of papers and bills. Iris trailed in our wake, a few steps back as though a five-foot distance was enough to provide her ninjalike cover. I knew what Iris was doing—getting up in my business.

"Here's what I wanted to show you." Mom turned the laptop to face me. "I just got an automated message from GradeSpeed. You're failing geography."

The sight of Coach Neuwirth's name alone was enough to make me bristle. I scanned the column of grades: 72,

95, 67, 93, 0, 0, 94, 0. My high numbers were test scores, the low numbers and zeros: homework. Because my brain stores random unimportant bits of information like the stellar news that the capital of Sri Lanka is Colombo, but it doesn't seem to have room for the knowledge of what homework assignment is due. The brain wants what it wants.

Still, my grade should have averaged out to a 70-something because tests had more weight. Instead, my average grade for the six weeks was 47.

A 47. There was no extra credit, no talking my way into a slightly better grade with a number like that. Not with Coach Neuwirth.

"I don't understand," I said. "My test scores are good."

"You're not looking at the right thing, Lily. You have a zero for your six-week project. It's forty percent of your grade." Mom leaned over the laptop and pointed to a line, her face lit in the white glow of the laptop.

I tried to focus on the numbers, but the screen blurred into a halo of white, a fuzzy snowball of doom. It didn't matter if the numbers made sense or not. They never do. All that mattered was that my hope for a golden summer with Dad on the farm was gone. You can't argue with GradeSpeed.

"I did my Populations in Peril project," I said. "I made a diorama and wrote a paper. I turned it in, I swear."

"Lily made a kick-ass diorama, Mom," Iris said. "I watched her."

"Language, Iris," Mom said.

"What?" Iris flopped into one of the dining room chairs and folded her arms across her chest. "*Kick-ass* has entered the standard lexicon. Ms. Arbeth says it all the time."

"Your teacher may feel comfortable with the phrase, but I don't particularly care whether it's common usage or not . . ."

I stopped listening to Mom and Iris argue semantics. I stopped thinking about school and cell phones and dioramas. I wanted to text Dad, but he never liked to text because "conversation is all about context and nuance, and texting destroys that." Besides, his number had changed. We used to message each other on Facebook, but about a year ago, he went off Facebook suddenly. I couldn't reach him.

I thought about Dad's favorite word: *quotidian*. Meaning "daily, routine," and therefore unimportant. As in "don't get mired in quotidian details." Something he used to say. But nothing saved me from the quotidian and the ugly, from the Coach Neuwirths of the world.

"Lily, you're crying," Mom said softly.

"Am I?" I swabbed my eyes with the back of my hand—wet. Sometimes my medication makes me feel so numb, I'm not aware of my emotions as they happen. Other people have to tell me. Iris looked away.

"Maybe it's a mistake," Mom said. "You did ask Coach Neuwirth for your 504 accommodations before the project, right?"

"Coach Neuwirth," I said bitterly.

Like I was going to talk about my 504 accommodations with Coach Neuwirth. Who wants to go to the least sympathetic person on Earth and say, "Excuse me, I'm broken. Can you help me?" Honestly, I'd rather fail. At least my dignity would still be intact.

"Talk to him tomorrow, okay?" Mom said.

I nodded. Anything to get out of the room.

I picked at dinner. Later I went to my room and tried to read, but everything was gray and covered with a film of self-loathing. I'd had no idea how I'd screwed up my stupid diorama, but clearly I had.

"Lily?"

A text from Abelard. He was there. My name whispered soft and low over a great distance. All misery evaporated.

"Abelard. You're here again. It's been a week."

I waited, eyes closed, my head propped against the pillows on my bed. Wondering if that sounded like a complaint.

"I'm glad you're back," I added.

My phone buzzed with the arrival of his next message.

"I was worried. I wondered if you, who had raised this passion, had kindly received the declaration, or if it was an offense." A quote from the letters.

"Kindly received, I assure you."

"I thought you would text me. I didn't want to bother you," he texted.

How many times had I wanted to text Abelard? Middle of school, middle of the night. How many times had I imagined that he didn't really like me that much or he'd gotten cold feet?

"Bother me, please. Better that I don't text you. I have impulse control issues."

"If you weren't impulsive, we wouldn't be talking," he wrote. *"If you weren't impulsive, you wouldn't have kissed me. I like your impulses."*

The mention of kissing sent a shiver through me.

"Not everyone agrees. I'm in trouble at school again."

"Trouble?" he wrote back after a short pause. *"What kind of trouble?"*

"I'm failing geography. Coach Neuwirth gave me a zero on a project."

I waited for a minute, then two and three. I was learning to enjoy the pauses in our dialogues, to use the time to look for quotes, to read back through our texts, to roll the lines around my mouth and taste them melting on my tongue.

I evolved an elaborate fantasy of a passionate kiss with Abelard that would happen so organically that neither of us would have to make the decision to move on the other. During a blackout or tornado warning at school, or some other disaster that would subvert the normal logic and rules of behavior so that in an extraordinary moment, we would drift together in perfect harmony of thought and desire. He'd lean forward in the dark, and his lips would magically find mine. I'd run my fingers through his hair as he pulled me closer . . .

I was about to wipe out the top floor of the school with an F4 tornado when my phone pinged with Abelard's incoming text.

"Coach Neuwirth! His discourse is a fire, which instead of enlightening, obscures everything with its smoke."

I recognized the quote from early in the first letter when Abelard describes his divinity teacher, Anselm. I flipped through the book to find the section and the right quote.

"I was too knowing in the subjects he discoursed upon," I wrote back. Peter Abelard's words. I'd broken my own rule, to speak only Heloise's words, but I didn't think my Abelard would mind.

"He is a tree beautified with variety of leaves and branches, but barren of fruit," Abelard texted back.

I laughed at the thought of Coach Neuwirth as a beautiful, stupid tree.

"I've missed you."

Fifteen seconds. Twenty seconds. Thirty seconds. I worried that I'd gone off script and said something stupid and too personal and maybe needy. Because, yes, me—needy.

"And I you."

"Pleasures tasted sparingly, and with difficulty, have always

a higher relish." A quote I had been saving. I was pleased with myself.

"I am unmoved by your argument. I would prefer to taste pleasures daily and, if possible, in person."

I held the phone to my face and studied the screen. A flush of anticipation and something approaching fear spread through me.

"In person?" My heart beat painfully.

"Absolument," Abelard replied. *Absolutely* in French. I love random French! I failed two years of French in middle school before switching to failing Spanish in high school. French—the language of love and delightful idioms, a certain *je ne sais quoi*. And of course, impossible spelling. *Je regrette* that I can't spell.

I giggled. I couldn't help it. I felt stupidly happy.

Iris turned on the bed to face me. "What did he say?"

"Nothing," I replied. "Okay, he wants to meet."

"Are you sure?" I texted. *"I talk a lot. I can't always help it."*

"I don't talk enough. It should average out."

"Just so you know," I texted.

"Just so I know," he replied.

"Are you going to go?" Iris reached for the phone, and I pulled it away. "What does he want to do? What will Mom say?"

"We don't have to talk at all," Abelard texted. *"We could play a game."*

"A game? What kind of game?"

"Do you play chess?"

Chess. I'd played it with my dad, but it had been years. I wondered if I even remembered the rules.

"Chess. Sure," I texted back.

"Come to my house Saturday at 2:00. We'll play chess."

He sent me the directions.

"I'll be there," I replied. Tornados and failing grades could not have kept me away.

CHAPTER 11

Friday I met Rosalind in the courtyard for lunch.

I opened my lunch bag. Tuna fish sandwich and a green apple, small, no doubt sour, and hard. My mother buys bags of Granny Smith apples because they are cheap and never seem to go bad—real apocalypse food.

Rosalind set her lunch aside. She was blushing—actually blushing.

"Oh my god, I just remembered! You're not going to believe what happened. Richard showed up at the theater yesterday. He wants to work on the set. Richard! Can you imagine?"

"Wow!" I said, trying to sound surprised. I am a terrible actress, but Rosalind was too freaked out to notice. "What did you think of him?"

"You're right, he has amazing eyelashes. And he has the most artistic hands. I mean, have you ever looked at his hands?"

"I can't say that I have."

"He asked Mr. Turner if you were coming." Rosalind frowned as though I'd consciously flirted with her crush of five minutes. Never. "Did you tell Richard you would be there?"

"I did mention I work crew sometimes. So what did Richard say?"

"I didn't talk to him." She raised an eyebrow in horror. "As if I would just walk up to him and start a conversation?"

It baffles me that someone like Rosalind can get up in front of the whole school and remember the script for an entire play, but she can't talk to a guy.

"You're going to have to talk to him," I said. "Richard is quiet and a little self-contained."

"Quiet and self-contained? You might as well be talking about me," Rosalind said. "It's not like I have a million friends outside of theater. I would never have talked to you, except that you demanded to try on my shoes."

"What? I did no such thing." She's told me this story before, but I don't remember it happening. Rosalind's shoes are very small and clever and above all, leather free. Her shoes would never have fit me. "Did I really demand to try on your shoes? I thought we met when I spilled red paint on you."

"That was later. Before that, you came up during recess and said, 'Your shoes have pink flowers and purple flowers, and the purple flowers have pink inside, and the pink flowers have purple inside, and I find them fascinating'—and then you asked to try them on."

Rosalind did a perfect impression of six-year-old me, complete with hand-waving, ninety-mile-an-hour speech pattern, and a good deal of bobbing head motion. I'd like to say that I've changed a lot since kindergarten, but sadly, this isn't true. I still wave my arms and talk way too fast. I would have been offended, except that it was spot-on—and it was Rosalind.

"So I've got to ask, Rosalind. How long have you been crafting this impression of me?"

Rosalind blushed and looked away. "I can't help it. It's what I do. I needed inspiration for my character Alice because she's fearless and impulsive, like you."

"Fearless? Hardly." I took a bite out of the green apple. Sour. "So if Rosalind can't talk to Richard, why doesn't Alice talk to Richard?"

"You mean talk to him in character? I can do that." Rosalind brightened. "Do you think that will work?"

"Why not?"

"What happens when he finds out I'm Rosalind, not Alice? Will he even like me?"

I looked at my friend—my best friend since kindergarten. She hates it when I call her this, but she's adorable. There's really no other word for her.

"I'm sure he will."

* * *

Rosalind texted me at 4:37.

"I talked to him!!!" she wrote. Plus smiley face, confusion, blushing emojis. She was still in rehearsal, so she couldn't send more. But that was enough.

CHAPTER 12

Saturday morning. Mom sucked down coffee, eyes glazed over. I drank my tea and took my pill. Iris hunched over a textbook at the table, working.

"I'm going to a friend's house this afternoon," I said quickly. Sometimes, when Mom is in preverbal coffee mode, she'll simply nod and agree to anything I propose. No such luck today, however.

"Rosalind?"

Okay, I don't have that many people I hang out with. But still, she could pretend I had other options.

"No, Abelard," I said nonchalantly, sipping my tea as though we were just having a random chat.

"Lily has a date." Iris looked up from her algebra textbook.

"It's not a date. I'm just going over to his house."

"Abelard Mitchell?" Mom asked. "I'm not sure that's the best idea, Lily. You did hit him with a lunchbox, remember?"

"When I was seven." Mom always overestimates my

destructive powers. "Anyway, he's over six feet tall now. I don't think I could break him if I tried."

Mom narrowed her eyes. "Will his parents be there?"

"Yes," I said, adding a little note of embarrassed exasperation at the end. I actually had no idea if this was true. His parents could have been in the south of France for all I knew.

"Did you talk to Coach Neuwirth about your Populations in Peril project?" she asked.

"Not yet."

"So, you'll go Monday?"

"Yes."

"I'll drive you to Abelard's house," she said. "I know where it is."

The Mitchells lived in an old brick house off Enfield.

Mrs. Mitchell met me at the door. She had shoulder-length snow-white hair held back with a black headband. She wore a necklace made of gigantic rough turquoise stones, a necklace that would be grotesque on any other person. Somehow it worked on Mrs. Mitchell, because she is super old. She has always been old.

"Lily," she said. "What a pleasure it is to see you again!"

I was surprised that she recognized me. I recognized her because she looked the same as she did in third grade when she brought cupcakes for Abelard's birthday. Schmancy bakery cupcakes, mind you, not the grocery store cupcakes with the frosting that tastes like Crisco and stale powdered sugar. Beautiful decorated cupcakes, although some of them didn't have any icing because Abelard doesn't like icing.

"Nice to see you again," I replied, craning my neck to see around her. "Is Abelard here?"

"He's in here somewhere. Come on in."

The entranceway opened into a huge room. An entire wall of bookshelves at the back of the room stretched to a vaulted ceiling and one of those ladders that runs along a bookshelf track. I was surprised. As long as I'd known Abelard, it had never occurred to me that he was rich, but clearly his family had a lot more money than mine.

"Sorry for the mess," Mrs. Mitchell said. "We don't have many visitors."

She swept into the room and removed a newspaper and several books from a coffee table the size of a life raft, flanked by two massive black leather couches and burgundy leather club chairs. Suddenly, everything was perfect.

"Let me go tell Abelard that you're here," she said. She wandered up the stairs and disappeared.

I noticed a chess set at the corner of the table. The pieces were gray stone and squat. I picked one up.

A man burst in through the front door. He was as tall as Abelard with salt and pepper hair, a bulbous nose, and Abelard's dark blue eyes.

I put the chess piece down, worried that he'd seen me.

"Do you like that?" he said. "It's a fairly good replica of

the Lewis set from twelfth-century Scotland." He dropped a gigantic leather satchel on a half-round high table by the front door, one of those weird pieces of furniture rich people have to put their keys on.

I nodded, and he held out his hand.

"Dr. Mitchell," he said. "And you are?"

"Lily Michaels-Ryan," I replied. I shook his hand. "I'm here to see Abelard," I added, in case he thought I'd just wandered in off the street.

"Ah," he said lifting an eyebrow. "Michaels-Ryan? I had a grad student about fifteen, twenty years ago named Alexander Michaels-Ryan. Very unusual. Alexander was a brilliant student and an engaging writer, but he could never seem to finish his work—"

"Ted, you've returned." Mrs. Mitchell descended the stairs. "This is Lily. She's here to visit Abelard."

"So she told me," Dr. Mitchell said. "Anyway, this Alexander Michaels-Ryan, he had some interesting ideas about—"

"Ted," Mrs. Mitchell said sharply. "We don't want to bore Lily with stories about students from twenty years ago, do we?"

"But I was just wondering if she was in any way related to—"

"That would be my father," I said. "Except he's just Alexander Ryan now." My parents hyphenated their names when they married, and unhyphenated when they divorced.

I'd always known that Abelard's father was a professor, but it never occurred to me that his father had been my father's advisor.

"How is your father?" Dr. Mitchell asked. "Please tell me he's not off brewing Belgian ale or working as a stonemason somewhere. You know, so many of my students see the study of the Middle Ages as the first step to an apprenticeship in a craft. If you want to be a craftsman, go visit the Renaissance Faire—don't bother with a real education, I always say. So how is your father?"

"Good, I guess. He's working at a goat farm in Oregon. But they do have a homeschool there, and I think he teaches English . . ." I trailed off because my father's lifestyle was suddenly sounding quite pathetic to me.

"Well, then," Dr. Mitchell said. "Goat cheese."

The three of us stood awkwardly, in silence, Mrs. Mitchell looking at Dr. Mitchell like she wanted to hit him with a shoe.

My father never finished his work. My father failed out of graduate school. These were things I'd known about him in an abstract way, little pieces of information I'd stored away, like how he'd lived in Paris for a year before he met my mother. But now it struck home. My father failed at stuff. Like I was going to fail at high school.

"Ah, Abelard," Dr. Mitchell exclaimed, "your friend is here."

I turned to see Abelard descending the stairs, and

unpleasant thoughts about failure evaporated from my mind. There is something strangely compelling about seeing someone you only see in school in their home environment, like seeing an animal in the wild. Abelard seemed loose-limbed, his hair slightly damp and a little more tousled than normal, and he was barefoot. He looked like he'd just stepped out of the shower, and as he approached, I caught a waft of a scent, something earthy and clean with hints of sandalwood.

"Hi, Abelard," I said.

I wanted to say about a billion things, to quote pieces of our texts that referenced *The Letters of Abelard and Heloise.* Something sly and sexy and personal—but all I could manage was "hi." This was just as well, since his parents were standing around staring at us with an almost scientific interest, as though we were baby tortoises who had just hatched and were about to undertake the perilous trip to an unknown and yet instinctively familiar ocean.

"Abelard, didn't you invite Lily to play chess?" Mrs. Mitchell said gently.

"Chess," Abelard repeated. "Black or white?"

"White, I guess," I said, although neither side was really white or black; they were simply differing shades of gray.

I sat in one of the club chairs nearest the lighter gray pieces, and Abelard sat on the couch.

"White always moves first," he said.

I moved a pawn in front of one of my bishops out two

spaces. Abelard studied this straightforward move with an intensity that led me to believe I was in trouble. Abelard moved a pawn, but it was just a move. I tried to read some end motivation out of it but couldn't. Suddenly, it was super important to me that I be able to win at chess or at least not make an utter fool of myself in front of Abelard's parents.

"Lily, do you play chess?" Dr. Mitchell asked.

"I used to play with my dad, but . . ." I shut up. I was about to say, *But that was a long time ago, before my father left us for his pastoral idyll in the Pacific Northwest.* I didn't really want to talk to Dr. Mitchell about my dad, the hippie goatherd graduate-school dropout, anymore.

"I've got to warn you, Abelard is pretty good. I used to be able to beat him, but not so much anymore. His mind's ability to exclude other sensory input makes him ruthless—"

"Honey, I'm making some lemonade, but I need you to come squeeze lemons for me." Mrs. Mitchell nodded her head toward the kitchen.

Dr. Mitchell pointed to his chest and mouthed the word *Me?* I had the feeling he'd probably never squeezed a lemon in his life.

"Yes you. Now. In the kitchen," she said.

"Actually I have some work to do. I'm going to just go to my study." He departed for a door in the wall of bookshelves at the back of the room. Mrs. Mitchell retreated to the kitchen.

I moved a pawn.

Abelard deliberated and moved a pawn.

I moved my bishop out. Abelard frowned.

"Interesting," he said. "Not what I thought you had planned."

He draped his hand over his right rook, but didn't move.

His forearms, which I had never noticed before, were long, well-muscled, and slightly tanned. He wore a braided black leather bracelet with a silver tag on his wrist. I vaguely remembered that he'd worn a silver link bracelet all throughout grade school because he was deathly allergic to something—peanuts, wasps, who knew? A fresh wave of tender feeling and concern slapped me across the face. How unfair that a random moment could put him on a count-down toward death. I wanted to snatch all the offending wasps or strawberries from the world, whatever threatened Abelard with destruction.

After all that deliberation, Abelard moved a pawn two spaces. Cautious.

I wanted to put my hands somewhere, to run my fingers along the top of his forearm, to finger the strange, subtle med-alert bracelet. My hands itched for action.

I moved my queen out instead.

"Do you really want to move your queen like that?" Abelard asked.

"Why not?"

"If you move your queen like that, then I will be able

to take it away in four moves. Because then you'll want to move your rook, but you'll waste time moving your pawns."

"Alas," I said. "My queen is an impetuous and headstrong woman, given to charging forth on crusades only partially dressed. She will out—there is nothing for it."

I waited for Abelard to respond to my Eleanor of Aquitaine reference. Eleanor of Aquitaine was my favorite medieval figure, because she decided to gather up all her ladies in waiting and fight the Crusades rather than stay at home doing needlework. Okay—the Crusades were kind of stupid, but who wouldn't rather charge forth with a sword than sit at home doing needlework?

If we were texting each other, we'd probably be reciting whole lines of *A Lion in Winter* by now. But we weren't alone. Mrs. Mitchell emerged from the kitchen with two gigantic glasses of lemonade, one with actual slices of lemons in the glass.

"Here you go, Lily." She handed me the glass with the lemon slices. "Abelard doesn't like lemons in his drink, but I think they're festive."

I took a sip, then was filled with panic at the idea that I would knock over the glass. Everything in the room seemed valuable, perhaps irreplaceable. Even the glass was pretty, hand-blown with specks of orange and blue and yellow.

"Abelard, take it easy on Lily. She probably doesn't play as much chess as you do." Mrs. Mitchell handed Abelard a glass of lemonade.

"Eleanor of Aquitaine," Abelard said.

"Eleanor of Aquitaine?" Mrs. Mitchell smiled apologetically at me and shrugged. "Now, where did that come from?"

"We were just talking about Eleanor of Aquitaine," I replied.

Happiness—Abelard had caught my Eleanor of Aquitaine reference. It was just like texting. Only slower—for both of us.

I moved a knight instead of my queen. Abelard didn't say anything, so I guessed it was a decent move.

Mrs. Mitchell nodded and wandered back through the door of the kitchen. Finally, we were alone.

Abelard studied the chessboard, his head tilted at a beatific angle like a painting of a medieval saint, his eyes the darkest blue through thick lashes. I'd never really looked at him for this long or this close up. It almost surprised me that he was real, that his skin had texture and a paler, softer look where he had shaved. He had perfect straight teeth, expensive teeth, better than mine. He didn't smile much, so I'd never noticed, but I did now.

He moved a chess piece and glanced up. I felt embarrassed to be caught staring at him. I looked away, and when I looked back, he was staring at me with the same intensity. And then he looked away.

"Your move," he said.

"Is it?" I replied. "You've made me nervous. I don't even

know which piece to move, or how to fend you off. I haven't played in a long time."

Abelard beat me at chess. Three times in a row, but quicker the first time than the last. I was beginning to get the hang of the game. If I played chess with him every day for ten years, I would eventually beat him. Probably.

Halfway through the third game of chess, Mrs. Mitchell returned with the pitcher of lemonade. I hadn't touched mine. I was afraid of it, afraid of the destructive power of liquids and breakable glass. Things were going so well—too well. Anytime I got too happy, I could just assume something fragile and lovely was lying in wait, ready to shower my world in glass fragments and sticky lemon slices.

"Abelard, do you think Lily is getting tired of losing?" she said. "You two could watch a movie."

"We're going to my room," Abelard said.

He stood, and I followed him up the stairs. His mom followed us to the bottom of the stairs, hands fluttering.

"Leave the door open," she said.

Abelard had a room to himself at the end of a long hall. A low blond-wood platform bed took up most of the room, and the only other furniture was a desk and chair. The wall over the bed held a built-in headboard and bookshelves filled with graphic novels, vintage sci-fi, backlit cubbies with figurines. A flat-screen TV covered most of one wall. His room looked like it had been set-designed for a TV show about genius nerds who devise superpowers in tricked-out labs while playing MMORPGs in their spare time. Must be nice to be rich.

Abelard sat on the bed while I poked around his stuff.

"Your room is amazing," I said. "Why do you ever leave? I share a room with my younger sister, who is super annoying, and smug too. She goes to LAME, so all she does is lie in bed doing homework and watching K-pop videos."

Babbling. Because—nervous. I willed myself to stop talking.

"I applied to LAME," he said.

"Didn't you get in?"

"I got in," he said. "But I wanted to go to a different school. The Isaac Institute. It's an early college program for students with neurological differences. I'm on the waiting list."

"Are you disappointed you didn't go to LAME?" I sat on the bed beside him. "Now that you're stuck in norm school with us slackers and ne'er-do-wells?"

Abelard stared out the window. Short answers, "yes" and "no," came quickly for him. Other answers took longer. I waited, conscious of my breath and the distance between our hands on the bed.

Abelard glanced at me and then away. I felt the heat in his glance. "If I'd gone to LAME, we never would have broken the wall between rooms. You wouldn't have kissed me."

I leaned closer. Then it just sort of happened. As if

Abelard and I had entered a gravitational field and contact had become inevitable and unstoppable without the exertion of external force. We drifted together, and I lifted my head, thinking that he might kiss me or I might kiss him. Anything seemed possible, but at the last moment, his left cheek drifted past me and grazed my lips. He wrapped his arm around me. He smelled of sandalwood and warmth. It felt right, but I wanted him to kiss me.

There was a small, tentative knock at the open door, and I pulled away from Abelard.

Mrs. Mitchell stuck her head inside the door.

"Lily, your mother is here," she said.

Seven o'clock.

"Lily?"

"Abelard."

"I'm sorry for beating you at chess."

"Well, you should be," I replied. *"Next time I expect you to let me win. My ego demands it."*

"Mom said girls don't like to be beaten at games. She said I was being tedious."

Tedious. I didn't think Abelard could ever be tedious.

"I'm not like other girls. I don't feel that my chess skills afford me the luxury to be easily offended."

Two minutes passed before Abelard texted me.

"Good. I had always an aversion for those light women whom it is a reproach to pursue; I was ambitious in my choice."

"Ambitious in your choice? Hardly."

A long pause.

"Are you disappointed?" he asked.

I thought of the warmth of his chest pressed against mine, the confusing moment when I thought he might kiss me but instead slid his face past mine.

"Because we didn't kiss?"

"Yes."

I considered lying. I didn't want Abelard to feel bad, but I'm a terrible liar. It takes long-term memory and considerable impulse control to lie effectively. I just don't have these things.

"I was a little disappointed. I thought you wanted to kiss me."

"I did. But then I was anxious. Usually I don't like to kiss. It's too much sensation."

Usually. Like kissing was a normal daily activity in his life. I wondered how many girls Abelard had kissed. I'd only kissed three boys—including Abelard.

I didn't know what to say.

"Does it matter to you?" he texted.

Yes—no. Maybe. I wanted something better than a monosyllabic answer. I wanted to kiss Abelard. I thought about kissing him—a lot.

"A little. But I'm okay with it."

"I never want to disappoint you."

I flipped through *The Letters of Abelard and Heloise* and found the quote I was looking for.

"You can't. In spite of all our misfortunes, we may be what we please in our letters. Letters were first invented for comforting solitary wretches such as myself."

"Charming Lily," he texted. *"Your beauty alone hath fired my soul."*

Charming Lily. I'd never expected anyone to call me Charming Lily or to effuse about my beauty. It was almost enough.

CHAPTER 13

"Lily! Come on!" Iris pulled my covers off and shook me.

"Why are you bothering me? It's Sunday."

"No it's not. It's Monday. Mom's already gone—and Maggie is holding the bus for me. You have to get up."

Iris turned and left. I stood and went to the window, watched as Iris bounded out the front door. One of the benefits of attending LAME is curbside service and a bus driver who knows that Iris would crawl across broken glass to get to school in the morning. Iris is an educational flower tended by many patient gardeners who want only the best for her.

My bus driver never holds the bus for anyone. I don't know his name, but he knows mine—Monster. He calls us all little monsters, but sometimes he slips and calls us something worse. So, I barely had time to throw on clothes and grab my backpack before my own bus showed. I couldn't find a clean shirt and had to borrow one from Iris—a pink kitty shirt, a little too tight. I forgot my cup of tea, my toast, and my drugs.

After English class, Mrs. Rogers-Peña called me to her desk. She was typing on her laptop, glasses low on her nose.

"How did your apology to Abelard go?" she asked.

"Good." It seemed like a million years since she had asked me to apologize to Abelard. I wanted to tell her that the world had turned upside down. That Abelard and I had found each other, like two people feeling their way through the darkest dungeon of despair. I couldn't find the words. My brain was sluggish.

"I'm glad," she said. "By the way, Lily, if I ever see you in that shirt again, I'm going to have to send you to the office. Dress code."

I glanced down at Iris's low-cut pink kitty shirt stretched tight across my breasts, and I felt embarrassed. Like I'd lost all my feminist cred because of dirty laundry.

"I don't normally dress like this," I said. "This is my sister's shirt."

"Okay, then." Mrs. Rogers-Peña eyed me sadly. "Just keep it in mind."

I'd promised to see Coach Neuwirth about my Populations in Peril project. I arrived at geography early, hoping I could talk to him about my grade before anyone else showed up. I knew I would have to eat a giant pile of "I suck" and "Yes, you're right, I didn't pay attention" just to get the information about how to improve my grade from him.

I stood by his desk in full awkward display in my tight pink shirt.

"Miss Michaels-Ryan," he said, "that shirt is—"

"I know," I replied quickly. "But I didn't have anything clean, and so I had to borrow a shirt from my sister, and she's smaller than me so . . . you know."

Coach Neuwirth frowned.

"I wanted to talk about my grade," I said.

"Fine." Coach Neuwirth glanced at my chest and looked away. "Let me pull up GradeSpeed."

It didn't take him very long. I sat in a chair next to his desk, trying not to read over his shoulder, trying not to twitch, while people filtered in to the room.

"Here it is," he said. "I've just finished the grades for this six weeks. You received a zero for your Populations in Peril project. It's forty percent of your grade."

A zero. So it wasn't a mistake. The air left my lungs.

Coach Neuwirth is one of those lazy teachers who teach via what I like to call the FCP, or the Fucking Craft Project. I was raised on Elmer's glue, and I can collage with the best of them, but the FCP is a peculiar form of grade torture.

My craft project was one of my best FCPs. I'd made a Bangladeshi village on stilts, midflood. I thought long and hard about how to represent the water, and I came up with a mixture of sand, dirt, glue, and water. I worked hard to get the viscosity of the mixture just right. After I built my village on very short stilts on a found piece of board, I tilted the board slightly and ran the mixture down the side until it looked like fast-moving water, bunching up around the stilts. After my sand and mud mixture dried, I built a half-destroyed hut breaking apart and floating downstream alongside tiny little bloated corpses I made out of modeling clay. As disaster dioramas went, it was "thought-provoking and poignant." No less a critic than Rosalind gave it "two thumbs way up." Coach Neuwirth chose it to put on display in the hall by the office, alongside five other really good examples of Populations in Peril.

If I were being graded for my work alone, I would have nailed the Populations in Peril module. But this isn't the way a Fucking Craft Project works. By definition, an FCP will have some tiny specification that will also disqualify my work from consideration. Perhaps I exceeded the width allowed for this particular FCP. Perhaps I was supposed to turn my paper in online, not in hard copy. There was no way of anticipating the multivariate ways one could possibly screw up a Fucking Craft Project, until it was too late. Still, I had to make my case.

"I did the Populations in Peril project," I said. "You liked my diorama. I thought my paper was good."

"It was. One of the best in the class. But you didn't finish the project. You didn't turn in everything."

Coach Neuwirth stopped, a smug look on his face. This was the pivotal moment in our conversation. He knew it, and I knew it. If I could tell him the one thing I forgot and make it seem like just one of those things that normal people do, he might let me turn it in late for partial credit. If, on the other hand, I continued to act like I had no idea what he was talking about, I was screwed. So of course, I was screwed.

"Think about it," he said. "What did you not turn in?"

If I'd been sitting at home in a cool dark room, working on my breathing, I might have had a chance to remember what the hell he was talking about. If I hadn't forgotten to take my drugs, I might have had a clue.

But now I would never be able to remember, even if I did manage to "monitor my breathing" as my therapist had suggested. My breathing was a runaway freight train, careening down the track alongside my racing heart. I couldn't slow my breathing. If I was lucky, I wouldn't cry. If I was lucky. Dakota Smith hovered nearby, pretending she had a burning question to ask Coach Neuwirth. She was there to rubberneck at the scene of my own personal accident.

"You received a rubric on dark green paper. You were supposed to follow all of the instructions on that paper."

"I did," I bleated out. Trying not to cry had left me with nothing other than short-form answers.

"Not all of them," Mr. Neuwirth said. "Where is your rubric?"

This is like asking, *What did you eat for lunch four weeks ago Thursday? What kind of shoes was the guy who died in the first ten minutes of the movie you watched last night wearing?* It's impossible to say.

Mr. Neuwirth sighed, like I was so much trouble for him. "I happen to have a copy of the rubric here. Will you please read what it says on the top line?"

I picked up the paper. The text was hard to read, because it was on a dark green background and the special instructions on the top were written in italics. Italics. Colored paper. Coach Neuwirth could write a textbook on how to format things so they are difficult, nay, impossible for dyslexics to read.

"'All students must fill out the self-evaluation form on the back of the rubric. Any project turned in without an attached rubric WILL RECEIVE AN AUTOMATIC 0. No exceptions.'"

"It's right there, written on the top of the rubric."

"Well, can I turn a rubric in now?"

"That wouldn't be fair to the other students who read the instructions and followed them," Coach Neuwirth said.

Fair. I hated this word. Fair was what teachers said

when they didn't mean fair, they meant something else entirely.

"So, you're just going to fail me?" I said. "Even though I did one of the best projects?"

Coach Neuwirth put on his pretend-to-care-deeply face. "Lily, everyone has to do paperwork. Everyone has to follow instructions. If I let you slide on this, you'll never learn the things you need to know as an adult—"

I stood up. If Coach Neuwirth wasn't going to let me pass his class, then I wasn't going to listen to his humiliating and discouraging meditation on the total craptacularness of adulthood. Really, this grueling reminder that real adult life is a farce and nothing you do matters as long as you fill out the forms correctly, had all the appeal of an angry suicide note. The world is impossible and untenable, and we all suffer, and therefore we make others suffer to ease our own misery. Like we exist solely to propagate paperwork, because paperwork is infinitely more important than actual human beings. Paperwork demands suffering.

My feet pointed toward the door. Door. Just ten steps away. Cool and dark in the hall, empty. Turn.

Walk.

Breathe.

Count to four on the in breath, hold for two, exhale on the count of four. Hold the positive thought in my mind. I could still pass this idiotic class. Happy thoughts. Something could be done. Happy thoughts.

I turned and walked stiffly to my desk, knowing that every eye in the room was on me. Because if I left class, it really would all be over.

Tears congealed in my eyes. I wrapped my arms tightly around my chest.

People watched me. I wanted them to stop. I didn't want anyone to see me like this. I was an animal thing, all limbic brain, full of rage and the desire to bite anyone who came near me. Frankenstein's monster crawling out from a hiding place and into the light to face ridicule and contempt. I wanted to turn over desks and throw books, to run from the room. Rampage through the village. Share my suffering.

Coach Neuwirth went to his podium in front of the class and began to talk about the Columbian Exchange, and I realized that I couldn't endure an hour of listening to him talk about smallpox and potatoes. It wasn't humanly possible to remain in my seat. I grabbed my books and half walked, half ran for the door. Free.

So that was it. I'd failed geography. And I wouldn't be allowed to go to Portland to visit my father. Nothing mattered.

I walked down the stairs with my geography notebook clutched to my chest, and I didn't stop walking. I threw open the front door of the school and practically ran into Abelard.

CHAPTER 14

Abelard had on Wayfarer sunglasses, a dark blue windbreaker over a blue striped shirt, like he was on his way to a casual day of yachting. He looked cool and collected. The very opposite of me.

The heavy metal door clicked shut behind me. The door buzzed loudly to let Abelard in, but he ignored it. I was in his way.

I stood facing him under the small entrance porch, my breath coming in ragged spurts, anger and frustration still coursing through my veins like some terrible drug. And now here, in the worst possible place and time, was Abelard. All my clever words—gone.

"I have to go." I glanced up at the shiny black dome covering the security cam. Someone in the office was probably watching us. And still, Abelard didn't move.

"I can't be here," I said. "I'm ditching school. If I stay here, someone will come and force me to go back to geography, and I'm not going back to geography."

I wanted Abelard to understand, but he'd probably only

been in trouble once in his life—when we broke the wall. That was mostly my fault, and anyway, he was never going to understand how it felt to be a caged animal. If you managed to escape, you had to run.

And then I did the stupidest thing ever. I put my shoulder into his chest and pushed. Impulse control—offline. The laminar boundary between thought and action—dissolved. I was all monster.

Fortunately Abelard was bigger than me. Not easy to move out of the way.

"Sorry," I said to his chest, feeling tears sting my eyes. Mortified to have become marginally violent with my now soon-to-be ex-boyfriend. "I'm really sorry."

Abelard wrapped an arm around me. I lowered my head to his shoulder and felt my heart rate slow to near normal. All the drugs and breathing techniques, all the adaptive strategies in the world, could never have soothed me half as much as being close to him. I was alone in my misery, and then I wasn't. A miracle.

"I'll go with you," he said.

We walked into sunshine side by side. We didn't talk, which was great. Abelard didn't ask me why I left school. He didn't ask me what happened in geography. He didn't even ask me what I planned to do next. Instead, I asked the questions.

"Why were you out of school?" I asked.

"Doctor's appointment."

"How lucky for me. What kind of doctor? Neurologist? Psychologist?"

"Psychiatrist. To talk about my medications."

"I've had that conversation: How's your appetite? How are you sleeping? Do you have any strange random thoughts about self-harm? Only a few? Good enough!"

Yes," Abelard said. "Just like that."

We walked several blocks away from school toward Dan's Hamburgers. I was suddenly tired and thirsty, experiencing that post-drama letdown when all the rage hormones have run their course, and there's nothing left to do but find a cool dark place to hide. I wondered if Bruce Banner felt this way.

"Do you want a Coke?" I asked. "I have some money. I'll buy you a Coke, because I'm really thirsty, and I'd like to sit down, if that's okay."

I lunged through the door of Dan's and ordered two Cokes. Abelard trailed behind me. It was the middle of the afternoon, and Dan's was mostly empty. I took our Cokes to the back, and we sat next to each other in a red vinyl booth. I sipped my drink, enjoying the cool burn, the black-and-white-checkerboard signs, the strange fifties decor. Two hours later, our classmates would pile in, bringing the endless din of the lunchroom with them. For now, the restaurant was ours.

"So, I failed geography," I said. Thirty minutes earlier,

failing geography had been the end of the world, but now it hardly seemed to matter. "I really do suck at school."

"I'm good at school," Abelard said. "Nothing else."

"You should live with my mother. She says there is nothing else."

I studied his face. I could have stared at him all day. In a windbreaker and dark glasses, he looked less like a medieval saint and more like one of those impossibly gorgeous hoodlums from a fifties movie. The little scar on his cheek only added to the mystique. Here I was, having a Coke at the neighborhood malt shop with my rebel boyfriend. Kind of delicious.

"People are important," he said. "If you can't talk to people, it doesn't matter how good you are in school."

"Now you sound like my therapist."

I used to have a *Star Trek*–obsessed therapist named Humberto. I actually liked talking to Humberto; I liked his collection of vintage robot toys and his sci-fi metaphors and random quotes from different iterations of the TV shows and movies. I often complained about Humberto, but I didn't really mean it.

I relaxed into the red vinyl. Perfect afternoon. Abelard had arrived to soothe the monster, and we were together in the quiet cool of Dan's. And Abelard was different somehow. After a moment's reflection, I figured out it out.

"Abelard, you're talking now. Quicker than usual. Why is that?"

"It's the sunglasses. They diminish sensory input."

"Like being in a dark room." I closed my eyes and lifted my face. Through my eyelids I felt the glow of the sunshine through the windows. Lovely and calm. I kept my eyes shut. "You should wear them all the time. What about earplugs?"

"Same thing," he said.

Sensory input. The phrase Ping-Ponged through my head. Sensory, sensation, sensual, sense, sense, sense. Somehow, we'd drifted closer on the vinyl bench, so close that I was conscious of my breath. I forgot what we were talking about. I was distracted by the weight of his arm against mine, the nearness of Abelard.

"I've heard there are restaurants where they put you in the dark and you aren't allowed to talk. You just have taste and smell, and that's all you have. Disorienting, but it heightens the senses." I kept my eyes closed.

Abelard didn't reply. He was staring at me. Even with my eyes closed, I could tell.

"You're looking at me," I said.

He didn't answer right away. "Yes."

"What are you thinking?" I whispered.

An even longer pause. With my eyes closed, I heard the soft sound of bubbles popping in soda. Felt the crackle of energy between us. The warmth of his arm next to mine.

Abelard bent his head toward me.

"I think I should have kissed you when I had the chance," he said. "But now it's too late."

I lifted my face. I kept my eyes closed. Even through the dark glasses, my eyes searching his face might be too much sensation for him. The white of the afternoon sun through my eyelids. The whole world was a soft, lovely blur.

"It's not too late," I said. "We could go slow. No expectations, right?"

I thought he might kiss me. He was so close that I could have shifted slightly and my lips would have been on his, but I wasn't going to do that. It had to be his choice.

The door opened, and a small child chattered nonsense. And then the moment passed, like a change in air pressure. I opened my eyes.

Abelard tilted his head away from me, and I suppressed the sudden, sharp taste of disappointment. No expectations. We might never kiss.

Abelard walked with me to the bus stop, and then he walked back to school. I didn't know how long we'd been gone, or if he would get in trouble. He had a doctor's note, but it was probably time-stamped. Maybe Mrs. Treviño would ignore the time stamp. I hoped so. She was nice like that.

"So you skipped school again," Mom said. We were standing in the kitchen, Iris hovering nearby. "I'm dying to know what you think is more important than staying at school."

"My boyfriend," I said. "Hello, there are other things in my life besides school."

Too much sarcasm. It earned me the full tirade.

"What do think would happen if I left work every time I didn't feel like being there? You have no idea what the real world is like, and I worry that . . ."

Blah, blah, blah—real world. The real world is a glossy brochure for suicidal ideation. So done with the real world.

"Dad doesn't work chained to a desk," I blurted out loudly.

"Your dad isn't here," she said. "I am."

I didn't stick around for her lecture on how goat farming was not a real job and how Dad skipped out on us. I was there, and I remember. Mom basically threw him out.

I retreated to my room to be alone with my happier thoughts. Nothing could put a dent in my afternoon with Abelard. He texted at seven straight up. This was getting to be our thing—seven o'clock, every night. Turned out he didn't get in trouble for staying out of school an extra hour. I think Abelard is immune to trouble, and he only ended up in detention that one time because I was involved.

We didn't talk about failing geography. Or kissing.

CHAPTER 15

Sometimes when the worst thing happens, it's a relief. Knowing with utter certainty that I had failed geography freed me from thinking about geography ever again. Done with rubrics. Done with chemistry and algebra. Since I'd lost my chance to visit my dad, there was no point in trying to pass anything.

School is not the place for bold action or creative thought—for cheating on the Kobayashi Maru. Humberto, the *Star Trek* therapist, introduced me to winning the no-win scenario of the Kobayashi Maru. *Star Trek* is filled with useful allegories. In school we were taught to think inside the box—the Fucking Craft Project diorama shoebox. Well, no more shoebox for this girl. I was done.

Here was my own personal Kobayashi Maru maneuver: if I couldn't pass all my classes, I would fail them all. Once I failed out of high school, Mom would be forced to pursue "alternative scholastic options." Number one alternative option: send me to live with my father. What else could she do?

I was up early, dressed and ready to go. I had important things to do at school. I had to work on my new Total Failure Plan, or TFP. I padded into the kitchen. Mom and Iris were there eating toast at the kitchen counter.

"Lily, you're awake." She handed me a cup of weak tea with milk.

I sipped.

"Now the pill."

She handed me the pill, and I dutifully stuck it into my mouth. The toaster popped, and Mom turned her back. I fished the pill out from under my tongue and rammed it into the pocket of my jeans. Iris caught me spitting out the pill, and I gave her the look of doom. She got the message. If she told Mom that I wasn't taking my drugs, I'd make the silent treatment an epic, semipermanent fixture in her life.

No more Fucking Craft Projects. No more rubrics. No more drugs. No more worrying about school. Done.

Wednesday I met Rosalind in the courtyard for lunch. Abelard was mysteriously absent from his usual spot under the crepe myrtles.

Rosalind opened her black lacquer bento box filled with homemade vegetarian sushi—brown rice, seaweed, avocados. For some reason it looked really good. First day off the meds, and my appetite was already beginning to return.

"Want one?" she asked.

I reached over and popped a circle into my mouth. A tiny bit of wasabi cut through the creaminess of the avocado. Tasty.

"Where's Abelard?"

"I don't know," I said, swallowing. "He didn't say anything about being gone today when we talked last night."

"You guys text every night?" she asked.

"Pretty much," I replied. "How's it going with Richard?"

"So yesterday, I was in the middle of a scene, and he was in the wings working on a backdrop, and I looked over, and he was staring at me. Do you think it means anything?"

"Weren't you onstage?" I asked. "I mean, wasn't everyone looking at you?"

Rosalind put her bento box down and sighed. "What are you doing tomorrow after school?" she asked.

"Nothing," I said cautiously. Truthfully, since I'd formulated my Total Failure Plan, I had nothing pressing to do for the rest of my life. I wasn't quite ready to admit that to Rosalind, though.

"Can you come to the Blanton with me Thursday after school? Thursday is free day, and I have the day off from rehearsal."

The Blanton is an art museum on the grounds of

the University of Texas. It's a field-trip-in-middle-school kind of place: sprawling, memorable exhibits of giant colorful modern artwork and classical Greek statue replicas. The kind of place where you can really burn off some energy.

"Sure I'll go to the Blanton. But why?"

"I was talking to Richard, and he said he hasn't done his Experiencing Other Cultures assignment yet. I told him that I was going to the Blanton with some people, and I invited him to come along."

Once a semester, our school requires every student to attend an extracurricular cultural event and write a paper about it. The catch is, it can't be in your home culture. Last year I made the case for attending church with a friend—because I'd never been to church in my life, and can I say it? So bored. Last semester I took the lazy route and wandered downtown for the Día de los Muertos parade, alongside all the goths in my school.

"So if you're Hispanic, museums count?" I asked. "What if you only go to the Latin American exhibit? And if you're Hispanic, can you count everything that isn't Hispanic? Could you watch *Pretty Little Liars* or wander around Whole Foods . . . ?"

"You're completely overthinking this," Rosalind said. "And you're missing the point."

"Which is?"

"I said I was going with 'some people.' You are 'some

people.' Anyone else I could ask was already in the theater with me. You have to come with me. Please?"

"I'll have to ask Mom. But sure." Ostensibly I was grounded due to my recent attendance and academic difficulties. My mother grounded me a lot, but my activities with Rosalind were generally exempt. Since I don't hang out with many people besides Rosalind, grounding me is pretty pointless.

"Let me know what she says."

Wednesday was my night to cook dinner. I stood at the stove making an Alfredo sauce for pasta while Iris glued stuff to a posterboard at the dining table. The K-pop top one hundred whined away from her laptop, interrupting my thoughts of Abelard.

"You're burning the flour," Iris said. "I can smell it from here."

"Do you want to cook?" I replied.

"I have homework."

Iris was right. I hadn't added the milk soon enough to my roux, and there was a nasty dark spot on the bottom of my pan. I wheeled toward the sink to wash away the burnt flour. The bottom of the pan skimmed the top of a glass on the counter and sent it crashing to the floor.

Iris looked up from her laptop. "If you keep breaking things, Mom is going to know you aren't taking your medication."

"I'm not breaking things." I dropped the pan in the sink, and it landed with a dull crack. I looked in the sink. Underneath the pan was a dark blue salad plate, split neatly in two. I hadn't noticed the plate there. As Iris pointed out, this happens when I go off my medication. I get too busy inside my own head to notice plates and glasses and doors. They just don't register.

"You just broke a glass," Iris said. "And then you broke something in the sink."

Iris stood up and walked over to the sink.

"People break glasses," I said. "It happens all the time."

Iris found the broom behind the refrigerator and began sweeping up the glass. I dropped the two halves of the plate into the trash and began scrubbing the burnt flour out of the pan.

"You broke a glass yesterday. We don't have that many glasses left. Mom's going to notice."

"Shut up, Iris."

Once Iris emptied the dustpan full of glass into the trash can, I ripped up a paper bag and scrunched up a couple of paper towels and put them in the trash can to hide the broken stuff. Iris rolled her eyes and went back to work. There's something deeply humiliating about having to artfully arrange trash to disguise broken objects. I had no choice. Iris was right—infuriatingly right. If Mom noticed disappearing glasses, she'd figure it out.

I had another pan of flour and butter on the stove when the front door opened. Mom stood in the doorway holding her weird unfortunate briefcase, somewhere between an oversize purse and carry-on luggage. The burgundy leather was scrubbed white from overuse at the edges, and she'd refastened a broken strap with a staple gun. If I ever won the lottery, the first thing I was going to do was buy my mother a new briefcase. Not that I played the lottery.

"Hey, Mom, I haven't done my Experiencing Other Cultures assignment yet, so I'm going to go to the Blanton tomorrow with Rosalind after school, if that's okay."

"Sure." She dropped the briefcase on the dining room table. "So did you talk to Coach Neuwirth today?"

"No." Not technically a lie, since I talked to him on Monday. It wasn't yet time to introduce Mom to my Total Failure Plan.

"Lily," Mom said in a tone so weary it matched her unfortunate briefcase, "you promised you would talk to him."

I added milk to my roux, which meant I didn't have to look my mother in the eye as I lied.

"Yeah, but see, what you don't get is that not everybody's turned in their Populations in Peril project yet."

Apparently Mom was just as tired of talking about geography as I was. She turned to Iris.

"So what are you doing?" Mom asked.

"Fucking Craft Project," Iris said, a tad too gleefully.

"Great! You taught your sister the F-bomb," Mom said, shaking her head. "Are you proud of yourself?"

"Kind of," I admitted. There was a guilty pleasure in taking the shine off of perfection.

We ate dinner and watched an episode of *Castle* while Iris attacked her FCP with a variety of pens and colored pencils. I left before the murder was solved to read in my room and to organize my quotes from *The Letters of Abelard and Heloise*. And then, as if by magic, seven arrived.

"Lily?"

"Abelard. I looked for you at lunch."

"I'm in the robotics lab during lunch and after school."

"Trying to take over the world with your evil robots?"

"No, just All-City Robot Competition. But your absence distracted me. I was so far from making any advances in the sciences that I lost all my taste of them; and when I was obliged to go from the sight of you to my philosophical exercises, it was with the utmost regret and melancholy."

I read the sentence from *The Letters*, and then read it again. *Utmost regret and melancholy*. I had to love that.

"Oh, I hope I haven't monkey-wrenched your robotics competition," I texted.

"Monkey-wrench. Sounds like two people trying to fix a sliding wall."

"You are fortunate that we didn't break that wall sooner,

otherwise I might have 'helped' with your robot. Breaking things is my hobby."

"I would gladly throw my robot into harm's way for more time with you," he texted.

Abelard. I wanted to write his name in big scrolling letters with a feather pen in a lavender-scented notebook somewhere. Unfortunately, my own handwriting leans more closely to serial-killer modern block print. Dysgraphia. The inelegant affliction.

"You could join robotics," he texted.

"I would, but I don't think I'll be in school much longer. I'm going to Portland. My dad lives there."

"Portland? Portland, Oregon?"

I hadn't really thought about how my Total Failure Plan would affect my relationship with Abelard. If I moved to Portland, I'd leave Abelard behind.

"I'm not leaving right away," I texted.

There was a gap of a minute or more. I regretted telling Abelard that I was leaving. It felt like a mistake, one of those moments when you break something fragile and lovely that can't be repaired or replaced. Thoughtless, impulsive brain!

"When are you leaving?"

"I'm not sure. I don't even know if I will go."

"So you might stay?"

"Maybe," I texted.

CHAPTER 16

When I got to the flagpole after school, Rosalind and Richard were already there waiting for me.

"We all get out of school the same time. How come it takes you longer to get here?" she asked, squinting into the afternoon sun.

Richard shifted his weight from one foot to the other, the finger and thumb of his left hand tapping as though ready to grip a phantom pencil. Nervous tic.

"Are they closing the museum?" I asked. "Are we on a tight deadline?" Rosalind knows I can't keep track of time.

Rosalind pursed her lips. She wore cat's-eye eyeliner and a new coat of dark magenta lipstick, the kind of color that only works on girls who are small and whimsical.

We walked across the parking lot to Rosalind's car. Yes, Rosalind had a car. Not a car she shared with her mother, not a maybe-you-can-use-the-car-on-Thursday-if-you're-good car, but an actual car of her own. At some point her parents got tired of waiting in the school parking lot at six thirty while the drama teacher coaxed another version of that scene out of her. And they bought her a car.

Rosalind popped the trunk of her bright blue eco-box, and we dropped our backpacks in.

"This is a nice car," Richard said, his eyes set in a frown. "It's brand new."

Rosalind's parents aren't rich, but still. If your parents get tired of hauling you around and pop down to the dealership for a new car, you are rich to most people.

"It's my mother's car," Rosalind lied, blushing. For someone with such a complex range of emotions in her dramatic repertoire, she was a terrible liar.

"Nice, right?" I said. "My mom drives an eight-year-old car, and not all the doors work. Well, I mean, that's my fault. I broke the door, and then I tried to fix it and made it worse. And then I pulled down the headliner in the back. Also, I peeled up the trim strip on the—"

Rosalind shot me a look that said I was babbling. Richard stood with his arms folded like he was having second thoughts about getting in a car with the rich girl and her crazy friend. I lunged for the back seat so Richard would have to sit up front with Rosalind.

At the inevitable line of cars waiting to exit the parking lot, Rosalind reached for the radio, and then pulled her hand back suddenly. If I strained I could practically hear her tortured inner dialogue—*"What if Richard doesn't like rock? What if he only listens to Tejano music?"* The silence became so thick, like a living breathing thing, that I felt compelled to disrupt it with the first thought that popped into my mind.

"So, Richard, how did you end up in detention?" I asked.

"Lily, that's kind of a personal question," Rosalind said.

"What?" I leaned over and craned my neck. "Everyone knows how I ended up in detention. It's not like it's a big deal."

"Still, Richard might not want to—"

"Fighting in the hall," Richard said. "But I didn't start it."

Rosalind stiffened. This wasn't the answer she'd wanted to hear. Honestly, though, I didn't hold it against Richard. Rosalind is diminutive, feminine, and academically perfect, which means she has always been exempt from the occasional hallway bodychecks. She knows nothing about fighting back, because she's never had to. Admittedly, I haven't been in a hall fight since early middle school. There are some benefits to being a girl.

More awkward silence. Unendurable.

"So what do you think about the theater?" I blurted out.

"I like it. I like places that are both dark and well lit." Richard paused. He didn't talk a lot, but when he did, you had the feeling he had thought it through first. "So when

Rosalind was standing on the stage yesterday, and they turned on a light, and her hair was almost red—"

"Auburn," I said.

"And the colors around you were very . . . strong."

"Trevor was testing the spotlights," Rosalind said. "I think he had a pink gel on number fourteen."

Rosalind knows about blocking and lighting, and all sorts of theatery stuff. She knows that she can't play twelve-year-olds forever, and so she plans to be a director someday. She thinks ahead like that.

"Pink gel?" Richard turned toward Rosalind, his face in perfect profile, wide cheekbones, dark brown eyes with those crazy long eyelashes. He wasn't Abelard, but still.

"Gel. It's colored cellophane you tape to the lights," Rosalind said.

The car inched forward.

"You know so much about theater," he said. "How did you learn all that?"

"Well, I . . ." Rosalind began.

Rosalind must have pulled her foot off the brake pedal because the car crept forward, coming dangerously close to the bumper of the Toyota in front of us.

"Rosalind!" I yelled.

She slammed on the brakes, and we lurched to a stop.

Then for some reason, both she and Richard laughed. It was nice to see my best friend distracted for a change.

* * *

At the museum, Richard and Rosalind walked side by side out of the parking garage, past the forest of yellow rubber hoses by the path. Their hands brushed past each other like meteors exploring the possibility of gravity. I veered off and walked through the installation, eager to feel the slap of rubber against my hands and face.

We stepped into the Grecian cool of the lobby to the echo of voices. The entire two-story entrance hall was covered in watery blue acrylic tiles, like the bottom of a swimming pool.

"Do you have a favorite work of art?" Richard asked.

Rosalind said something I didn't catch. Too much background noise, plus I was busy examining one of the blue vinyl tiles on the wall. Up close each one was swirled like a flattened, oceanic bowling ball, perfectly hard and smooth. My fingernails itched to pry a tile free. I put my hand to the wall and . . .

"Lily, don't touch the art!" Rosalind said.

I turned around. "Should we go upstairs? Hey—we could go to the bones and pennies. Talk about dark and well lit—just like the theater. I know you would—"

"I think Richard and I are going to stay down here and wander through European paintings," Rosalind said quickly. "If you don't mind?"

She wrapped her hand around Richard's arm to guide him in the right direction. A sudden look of surprise passed through Rosalind and ended up on Richard's face, as though neither of them expected physical contact this early in the game. I watched them walk away hand in hand.

And I felt a sudden wave of jealousy or loneliness, because I would probably never walk hand in hand with Abelard through a museum. Too many people, too much noise, too much stimulation. Richard and Rosalind hadn't said more than a few sentences to each other, and yet this part was easy. Holding hands would never be that easy for Abelard and me.

I walked upstairs past a gallery full of installations and paintings I'd return to see after I'd been to my favorite place in the museum. In a small room at the back was a pool of bright copper pennies illuminated by a chandelier made of thighbones. The whole pool was surrounded by black net, and dead center of the pool was a towering stack of communion wafers. The rest of the room was pitch-dark.

Really, if anyone asked me about the quickest way to improve our school, I'd have to say installation art. Just pick this piece up and put it in some fundamentally useless space like the girls' locker room. And then anyone who felt bullied by peers or tormented by rubrics could come bask in the quiet copper glow under the bones and contemplate. Breathe.

After a while, I wandered through the contemporary collection, past violent paintings and crayon-colored sculptures on a polished wood floor, and into the Greek and

Roman statues. And then I went downstairs and looked at impressionists. I didn't see Rosalind and Richard anywhere. I circled the entire museum again, but didn't find them.

I went out to the grounds and found them sitting in the grass behind the yellow tubing sculpture. Richard had gotten his backpack from the car, and he had a pad of sketch paper. He'd traced the outlines of Rosalind's hair, roughed out the delicate shape of her face and her lips. He was working on her eyes, catching a look both expectant and knowing. The rest of the drawing might have been a picture of your standard twelve-year-old, but he'd completely captured the lovestruck glow of her eyes.

She looked up as I approached and mouthed, *Best day ever.*

CHAPTER 17

Third period, Friday. I had the feeling Mrs. Rogers-Peña wanted to talk to me. After class, I kept my head low and made an early dive for the door. Not that it helped.

"Lily, can I talk to you for a second?" Mrs. Rogers-Peña said as I rushed past her desk.

I turned back. Mrs. Rogers-Peña wore a navy blazer and a silky blouse. She didn't usually dress like she was filling in for the vice principal. Her blazer reminded me that she is, in fact, sort of old.

"Hi," I said. "You look different."

She ignored my comment.

"You do know that you were supposed to hand in your *Macbeth* rough draft yesterday?"

"I forgot."

This was a truthful statement. When I decided on my failing course of action, all deadlines left my brain like startled birds. None of my former obligations had since flown back to roost. Normally, I'd have had a better explanation, but her jacket was distracting me. It had sharp, unforgiving shoulders, a merciless perma-press quality.

"That's a lazy excuse," she said.

"You can fail me. It's fine. Mea culpa and all."

Mrs. Rogers-Peña sighed. "I really don't want to fail you, Lily."

Last thing I wanted was for Mrs. Rogers-Peña to share in my failure. Some teachers take this kind of thing personally.

"Don't worry about it." And then—because, *Macbeth*—I added, "Screw your courage to the sticking-place."

Mrs. Rogers-Peña pursed her lips in a tight line and shook her head. "Thank you, Lady Macbeth. Clearly you've read the play, so here's what you're going to do: Monday—rough draft. Or you and I will go down to Dr. Krenwelge's office for a chat about *Macbeth* together."

I nodded. When I'd formulated my Total Failure Plan, it hadn't occurred to me that anyone would actually notice or care. A lot of teachers live by the torturous rubric-fail-trap method of teaching. They smirk and twirl their mustaches like cartoon villains as they hand out F's, all the while explaining how you could have avoided your fate. Like Coach Neuwirth.

But every once in a while, you get a Mrs. Rogers-Peña. This is the problem with school—no real consistency. So I was caught. I had to write a *Macbeth* paper. It was only fair.

* * *

Iris and I were cutting up vegetables when Mom arrived home that evening. Mom deposited her hideous bag on the dining room table. She looked more weary than usual, if that was possible.

"Lily, could I talk to you in my room for a moment?"

Warning bells and klaxons, flashing lights and sirens. I braced myself for the inevitable conflict. Mom must have found out that I failed geography. I wasn't really ready to unveil my Total Failure Plan to the world, so I prepared myself for some awkward lying.

"Sure." I followed Mom into her room, the designated quiet place to talk. I slumped on her bed, waiting.

"I got a call from your guidance counselor today," she began.

Unexpected. Some part of my brain shut down. A call from the guidance counselor is never good. Even worse than failing geography.

"People are worried about you, Lily. She's worried about you."

"Worried"—code for suicide watch.

Okay. I saw this movie once. A woman worked in a nuclear power plant, and she set off the radiation detectors at work, two or three times. And every time she set off the radiation alarms, people in HAZMAT suits whisked her away to a shower room to be stripped naked, hosed down, and scrubbed forcibly with the kind of long-handled brushes they normally use at car washes.

This is what it feels like to be put on suicide watch. I know because someone put me on suicide watch last year, too.

Now that I was back on suicide watch, I had to talk about my feelings about being on suicide watch. Again.

"It's okay, Mom. I'm fine."

Mom frowned like she didn't believe me.

"Really."

"Okay," she said slowly. "So why do you think people are worried about you?"

"I don't know. I've been super happy lately. I have a boyfriend."

"Lily, you can't rely on another person for happiness. What if you and Abelard break up?"

"That's not going to happen," I said, with more confidence than I felt.

Mom is hardly an expert on interpersonal happiness. She has been on approximately zero dates in the last year and a half. After the divorce, she went out a lot more and even had a boyfriend for a year or so, a funny, pudgy guy named Stan. Stan wasn't a reader and therefore—doomed from the start. She shouldn't have left Dad. You probably shouldn't break up with anyone who can discuss nineteenth-century women authors over coffee, even if he can't manage to finish a doctoral dissertation.

Mom sat on the bed beside me.

"What do you think we should do about this?" she asked softly.

"I could go back to Humberto," I said, trying to inject a note of hopefulness into the suicide discussion.

I actually wanted to see Humberto. I wanted to tell him all about Abelard and ask his advice about managing a physical relationship with someone who doesn't like to kiss and who isn't great with communicating in real time. Humberto would have perspective. It's his job description—providing perspective.

"You can't," Mom said. "My insurance only gives you six visits a year, which we've already used. And I'm not sure Humberto helped you all that much."

I didn't agree with her assessment of Humberto. To be fair, school is a pretty hopeless and depressing situation, and there wasn't anything Humberto could do about that. I liked Humberto because he kept the "adaptive strategy" talk to an absolute minimum, and he let me ramble on and on about the inherent contradiction of being forced to spend all my time at tasks I absolutely sucked at. Because—school. Being lousy at your "job" is a recipe for feeling worthless.

I said, "Help me what? Get my homework turned in on time? Be a straight-A student like Iris?"

"That's not what I'm talking about," she said.

"Really? Then what are we talking about?"

I realized that I didn't know. I had something to say

about happiness, but I couldn't find the words. My head hurt. I didn't want to think anymore. And I felt angry. I had to go to school—I got that. But it was unfair to expect me to be happy about it.

"I'll find someone else, Lily. We'll work this out."

I ate dinner with Mom and Iris even though I didn't feel like it, but I realized that if I didn't eat, Mom and Iris would read some deeper meaning into my rejection of stir-fried vegetables. Everything I did for the next couple of weeks, from the TV I watched to the way I brushed my teeth, would be interpreted by the general public as either a troubling sign, or a renewed embrace of continuation on this mortal plane.

Suicide watch. World of suck! I would trade it in a flash for a naked shower scrubbing by HAZMAT-suited individuals. I really would.

I thought seven would never come. But then it did.

"Lily?"

"Abelard."

There was a long pause. I didn't have anything to say. Maybe I'd run out of clever things to say, and all that was left was the real me: unclever, unfunny.

"Are you really moving to Portland?" he asked.

"I don't really know anymore. About anything."

"Okay," he texted.

I leafed through my copy of *Abelard and Heloise.* Heloise

was a font of eloquent statements about loss and human suffering. I had so many quotes to work with.

"I am too much accustomed to misfortune to expect any happy turn," I texted.

"Why?"

Short and to the point. I might as well tell him.

"Someone at school put me on suicide watch."

Another pause, even longer this time.

"Are you all right?"

"I have a broken brain," I texted. *"It's not the same thing as a broken spirit."*

A pause of epic proportions ensued. My heart fell. I thought Abelard understood me, I really did. But perhaps Mom was right: you can't rely on another person for happiness. I was bound to scare Abelard off eventually. In a listicle gallery of the fourteen most unfortunate girlfriend archetypes, the "Suicide? Surprise!" girlfriend is rated number seven, just behind the "She-Hulk." To be fair, I probably also qualify as a She-Hulk because—Hulk smash! If only smashing helped. You can't smash your way through an uncomfortable and extended silence. You can't smash your way off suicide watch. You can't smash your way through love.

"Have to go," I texted. *"Talk to you later."*

I turned my phone off before he could answer.

CHAPTER 18

Abelard didn't text me all weekend. I guessed we were over.

I limped through school Monday. I felt like I had the words *suicide risk* tattooed on my forehead. Accordingly, I minimized my human contact as much as possible.

Rosalind was already waiting under the live oaks when I hit the courtyard for lunch, but Abelard was not at his spot under the crepe myrtles.

Abelard. The thought of him brought a tightness to my chest.

I opened my lunch. Peanut butter and iceberg lettuce on whole wheat. Iris's favorite. Tastes better than it sounds.

Rosalind was glowing. She'd done her hair in an elaborate French twist kind of a thing, and there was something different about her.

"Are you wearing false eyelashes?" I asked.

"Have you looked at Richard's eyelashes? I can't compete with that. So yesterday, we met in Butler Park and . . ."

"Butler Park?" I interrupted. "Where's that?"

"It's the newer park down by the river."

"The one with the Dr. Seuss hill?"

"Yes, but let me finish. He took the bus and met me on the Barton Creek side. He wouldn't let me pick him up from his house. Maybe he doesn't want me to see his house, which I guess I could understand. Oh, Lily, he's so perfect. Anyway . . ."

I hadn't seen Rosalind fall this hard since eighth grade when she lost her mind over the admittedly dreamy theater graduate student who directed the summer youth version of *The Frogs* by Aristophanes. And since the dreamy theater graduate student had been twenty-five when Rosalind was thirteen, that relationship was going nowhere.

I was happy for her, but I couldn't focus. I lost track of what Rosalind was saying.

"Someone put me on suicide watch," I blurted out.

Rosalind looked away and frowned.

My phone buzzed. It was Abelard.

"I need to talk to you. Come to the robotics lab."

I stood, feeling a strange mixture of dread and anticipation.

"Where are you going?" Rosalind asked.

"Abelard wants to see me right now. I'm going to the robotics lab."

Rosalind pulled out her phone.

"Seven minutes, Lily. You'll never get there and back in time for geography."

Time, my mortal enemy. Oh, how it taunted me—ugly, unyielding time! Abelard, waiting for me.

I sat down to text Abelard.

"Not enough time before next period."

"Come to robotics after school," he texted back.

After school, I hid in the second-floor bathroom for a while and brushed my hair and waited for the halls to empty as shouts and laughter faded from the hall. Abelard was in the robotics room. I tried to practice my calm breaths. Good things, bad things, endless possibilities of hope and despair. I had no emotional reference point, no way to scale my feelings. At some point, Abelard had become everything to me. What did my mother say? *You can't rely on another person for happiness.* Well, too late, Mom, on that particular bit of wisdom!

The robotics lab was at the far end of the school, underneath the art wing. Rumor had it that the lights flickered in the art wing because of the power drain from the robotics lab and the shop next door. It could have been the lighting or the maker vibe of that whole side of the building, but it was my favorite part of the school aside from the theater. I passed through the art wing, the glamorous smell of wet paint and solvent, past students' work under glass and a pencil study of a transcendent pair of feet. Richard's work. Only Richard could imbue toes with that level of mystery.

Down the stairs. Blue tiles for luck. I stood outside the open door of the robotics lab, a hive of preregionals activity. Abelard was holding a soldering iron in one hand and a spool of solder in the other. He bent over what looked like a disemboweled vacuum cleaner. Like everyone in the room, he wore clear protective eyeglasses, the strap pushing his already shaggy head of sable hair into a wild tumble of mad scientist curls. He was completely focused on the project, his hands moving deftly from one solder point to the next, his face serenely beautiful, opaque. If I stood in the doorway of the lab and watched him all day, I'd never be able to guess at a tenth of the thoughts that passed through his mind. You could fall for a guy because he could toss a football from one end of the field to the other in a moment of perfect poetry of motion, or because of the way his green eyes sparkled in the sunlight, but soon the moment would be over.

But when this moment ended, there would be another just like it. The gears would continue turning, out of my view, beyond my understanding. Abelard had answers to questions I hadn't thought to ask until I met him.

People began to notice me. Mr. Martini wandered over, protective goggles over chunky black glasses, a white lab coat.

"*Issome* . . . need?" he said in an impatient tone. A busy-with-regionals-don't-bother-us tone.

"I'm here for Abelard," I replied. My voice quivered unexpectedly, and Mr. Martini looked me over as if I might be a contract killer or crazed stalker.

"Wait here at the door," he said finally. "Don't come in—you haven't *inspreefed ayftey procols*."

I had no idea what he was talking about. I waited.

Mr. Martini walked over to Abelard's disemboweled vacuum cleaner and watched his soldering technique for a maddeningly long time. I could see Mr. Martini talking, but at that moment, someone ran a drill, covering the sound of his voice. Abelard showed no sign of hearing either, but after a minute, he set his soldering iron down and turned and walked my way.

I moved out of the doorway, arms folded across my chest.

"Lily," he said.

"Abelard," I replied. "You wanted to see me?"

He pushed his glasses up on his head and stared at a spot on the wall to the left of me. "I have something that I want to say to you, but if you talk, I won't be able to organize my thoughts."

"Okay, I won't talk." I waited. The fluorescent light pulsed oddly in time with a twitch that spread along my skin. I studied his face, three-quarter profile, hair pushed back off his high forehead.

"I've been thinking about what you told me Friday night about having a broken brain, not a broken spirit. And

I've been thinking about what it means to be broken, and how we call things broken that aren't—fractured. It made me think about fractals. Do you know what a Mandelbrot set is?"

I shrugged.

"There's a picture of a Mandelbrot set on the wall."

I craned my head to look around the corner of the door at a poster of something that looked like a regularly shaped psychedelic inkblot. I had questions, but I was not to talk.

"So a Mandelbrot set is one kind of fractal," he continued. "All fractals are self-similar, which means they have a pattern that repeats at different levels of magnification. Fractals are infinitely recursive and orderly, but they appear to be chaotic."

"Why are you even in high school?" I blurted out. I couldn't help it. I was following Abelard's train of thought—but just barely. Why wasn't he already at college or something, turning vacuum cleaners into perpetual motion machines, solving some of the world's major technological issues with robots and math?

"If you talk, I won't be able to finish what I have to say." Abelard ran his hand over the top of his thigh, as though slightly agitated. It was probably hard for him to talk this much.

"Sorry."

"Mathematicians use fractals to model things that appear to be chaotic but are really accumulations of complex patterns. Fractured things, not broken, because broken implies that there is a normal, when mathematically there isn't. Normal would simply mean easily predictable—like a salt crystal. Fractured things like snowflakes and mountain ranges are more geometrically interesting and require more complex modeling."

"Abelard," I said, forgetting that I was not supposed to interrupt, "are you calling me a 'special little snowflake'?"

Abelard closed his eyes. He'd thought about this, arranged what he'd planned to say in great detail, and all I could do was throw him off his game. And yet, I couldn't help it. I wanted to ask him a hundred questions. I wanted to pull the goggles off his head and run my hands through his hair. This was more than I'd heard him talk the entire time I'd known him. He was wearing a heather green ringer T-shirt that looked insanely soft, bunny-marshmallow-cloud soft, and I wanted to run my hand over his chest and find out. Hard to be still and quiet at the same time. I leaned closer.

"Yes," Abelard said finally. "You are a fractured snowflake, a pattern repeated in infinite detail in a world full of salt crystals. You're not broken—you're perfect."

Perfect. Some tight, hard shell around my heart cracked open. I hadn't even known I'd walled my heart away from this terrible world.

This had to be a miraculous mistake, a miscalculation on Abelard's part. He'd done the math wrong. I was so far from perfect that I was afraid he would make a spot reevaluation and realize his mistake.

Big, stupid tears welled up in my eyes. I looked away. Several people in the robotics lab watched us through safety goggles like a colony of super-intelligent insect people, confused by off-task behavior. I don't think anyone had ever cried in robotics lab before.

"You think I'm perfect? I don't think the world at large shares your opinion."

"The world doesn't understand complexity," Abelard said. "Not like I do."

I lunged at Abelard, more violently than I had planned to, and pushed him slightly off balance. His arms flew up and went around me as he staggered back against the wall.

"Sorry," I said.

In response he laughed. It was the smallest laugh, a tiny, delighted sound. I'd never heard Abelard laugh before. His arm slid around my waist, pulling me close.

His shirt was as soft as I'd imagined it would be.

"I love you, Abelard," I murmured, before my brain could stop my rash and completely unwise mouth. Like Heloise, my heart surrendered too willingly to the conqueror. And then—miracle.

"I love you too, Lily." He said it back.

I'd spent my entire life as a teacup with a jagged crack running down the side, an imperfect vessel threatening to spill my contents onto the table at any random moment.

Tolerated but not adored. It didn't seem like it would be even possible to love me. Probabilistically unlikely at best. But for Abelard, the jagged crack was the interesting thing about me.

I closed my eyes, and something went slack inside my brain, as some questioning whirring engine of doubt and impatience shut down. Still. There was only Abelard, the warmth of his neck, the feel of his chest against mine, his arm wrapped around my waist.

This moment alone.

CHAPTER 19

Mom was surprisingly willing to drop me at Abelard's house on Sunday. She didn't even ask if I had outstanding homework assignments. I guess she'd seen me pounding away at my *Macbeth* paper all weekend and assumed I was working just as hard at everything else.

Really, finishing my *Macbeth* paper was as much a matter of boredom as anything else. Rosalind was busy with Richard and the play, Abelard with robotics. The All-City Robotics competition was held Saturday, and Abelard's team advanced to regionals. I wanted to go to the competition, but I was worried that I would be a distraction. So I stayed home and worked on my paper.

Sunday at one o'clock, we all jumped into the car together. Mom and Iris were headed to City Hall after they dropped me off so that Iris could write a report. Her school has given her a taste for urban planning and multiuse facilities. She's always looking for storm-secured bunkers and fair-trade coffee shops. Nice to know she will survive the coming apocalypse and complete cultural collapse while the rest of us wander around looking for Cheetos and Wi-Fi.

"Maybe someday you'll actually teach me to drive," I said. "Then I could take the car."

"Maybe," Mom replied in a far-too-cheerful voice, the kind of voice you use on an eleven-year-old who still believes in Santa. A grow-up-and-get-over-yourself voice.

"Everyone drives, Mom. Texas is the drivingest state in the drivingest country in the world. Unless you want me to move to Amsterdam or New York, I really need—"

"Let's see how things shake out this summer," she said. "We'll both have more time then."

This summer. When I would be in Portland. Research had provided me with ample reason to believe that mass transit in Portland did not suck as badly as it did in Austin.

"Fine," I said. "Don't teach me."

We turned off Enfield, and Mom pulled up in the Mitchells' driveway.

"This is where Abelard lives?" Iris said. "It's so big! Are they rich? What's it like on the inside?"

"Like a Victorian gentlemen's club and a library got married and gave birth to a house," I replied.

Mom snorted with laughter. At that moment, I realized she'd probably been in the house before when Dad was a student. The past and the present colliding—again.

"Is that what it's like, Mom?" Iris said. We weren't used to hearing Mom laugh like that.

"Pretty much," Mom replied. "Lily, Iris and I are going to City Hall and maybe out shopping. Three hours, okay?"

Mrs. Mitchell had on another one of those giant silver and turquoise squash-blossom necklaces that always look like they might weigh upward of fifteen pounds. Hard on your neck.

"Lily," she said. "So nice to see you again."

"Thanks," I replied, hands at my side.

Abelard stood in the middle of the room, barefoot. He was wearing different sunglasses than the pair he wore to Dan's. He probably had sunglasses for indoors and sunglasses for outdoors. The sight of the glasses gave me an odd thrill.

"Abelard," I said rolling his name over my tongue, because now it felt like it belonged to me. The Lewis chessboard was set up on the coffee table.

"Are you planning on trouncing me soundly at chess?" I asked.

"Yes," Abelard replied. Simple statement of fact.

"Abelard, you shouldn't say things like that," Mrs. Mitchell said. "Lily will get the wrong idea."

"Pretty accurate, though," I said. "I can't imagine beating Abelard at chess anytime soon."

"Maybe you two would like to do something other than play chess?" Mrs. Mitchell asked. "We have plenty of board games."

I did have something I wanted to do besides play chess. I wanted to go to Abelard's perfect room and sit on the bed next to him and find out whether he still smelled of warmth and sandalwood. I wanted to feel his arms around me again.

"Board games take three people," Abelard said.

"I could play a game with you," Mrs. Mitchell said unconvincingly. "Or your father could . . ."

"Video games," Abelard said.

Yes! Alone with Abelard in his room.

"Sounds great," I said quickly.

I followed Abelard up the stairs to his room.

"Keep the door open," Mrs. Mitchell called behind us.

I settled on the end of the bed platform. Abelard handed me a controller.

"Monsters or soldiers?" Abelard said.

"Monsters are metaphorically appealing," I replied.

Soon Abelard and I were side by side on the end of his bed, crawling through an abandoned state hospital while mutated half-zombies with strange surgical appliances attempted to kill our avatars. Abelard had a sniper rifle, and I had a machete, which turned out to be perfectly suited to my random-movement berserker style of video fighting. I had to learn not to slash Abelard with an accidental backhand. I think I killed him three times, but he was good-natured about my slower-than-average learning curve. He just kept explaining to me how not to kill him.

Mrs. Mitchell stood outside the open door and pretended to be interested in our progress through the funerary tunnels from the morgue.

"How can you stand so much blood and gore?" she said to me.

"You get used to it," I said. Probably a horrifying answer.

She turned and left, her light tread heading down the stairs. I gave my full attention to the floating disembodied head of a child.

"I don't like to fly," Abelard said.

"I don't blame you," I said. "Who wants to run into a floating toddler head? Toddlers — so creepy!"

"I don't like to fly on airplanes."

"I've only been on an airplane a couple of times," I replied.

"I don't like people I don't know touching me. I don't like going through security. I don't like the noise."

Abelard in an airport. I might feel overwhelmed in airports and shopping malls, places filled with noise and distraction, but I could still function. He couldn't.

"How do you deal at school? Doesn't passing period drive you crazy?"

"I leave class five minutes early. It's part of my accommodations."

"Oh, yeah." I remembered last year when Abelard left English class early. I didn't think much about it at the time, but it triggered another memory. Abelard in seventh grade, standing in the middle of the hallway, shrieking. Teachers came running, helplessly fluttering about Abelard like anxious moths to a brightly lit flame. They couldn't get him to move or stop shrieking. I just stood there and watched until Mr. Acosta yelled at me to get to class. That Abelard seemed like a different person from the calm, collected Abelard beside me.

We outran the floating toddler head by ducking down a side corridor. We ended up in an office strewn with paperwork and old files. For some reason, the abandoned office was way creepier than the electroshock therapy room.

"Are you going to fly to Portland?" he asked.

It was beginning to sink in that my father lived in Portland, and Abelard lived in Austin, and I couldn't be in two places at once. I didn't want to leave Abelard, but I didn't have a future here, and I wanted to see my father again. It was all too much.

"I don't know. My father lives on a cooperative farm, and they have a homeschool collective. I could probably graduate if I homeschooled, which is so not going to happen if I stay here. I'm not sure I want to go, but then again, I don't know how things are going to work out here. I'll end up working at the fry station at McDonald's while my sister skips her senior year to go to some fabulous college. But then of course, there's you and Rosalind . . ."

I stopped. I was rambling. But Abelard didn't appear to be listening anyway. He was completely focused on the game, searching the journal of a long-dead medical examiner for clues to what exactly had gone wrong in the asylum. Since we were not under attack, I let him do the reading while I studied his beautiful profile. I missed seeing his eyes, but the dark glasses were weirdly sexy.

"Maybe you could come visit," I said. "I mean, I know you don't like to fly, but there's always the bus."

Virtual Abelard put down the book after ripping out the applicable pages, a very un-Abelard-like thing to do, IMHO. Just because you're being hunted by the cursed undead is no reason to despoil a book.

Virtual Abelard turned, and I followed him back down the funerary tunnel to the hydrotherapy room, where muscular attendants tried to force our characters into blood-spattered bathtubs.

"I like the train," Abelard said. "You can have your own room on the train."

The only thing I knew about train travel came from a movie Rosalind's parents had us watch—Cary Grant and an elegant blond woman making out in a sleek pale green room the size of a walk-in closet. I imagined Abelard in place of Cary Grant, nuzzling my cheek, talking in a low voice about stars and fractals while the world rushed by. Yes. Magical trains.

Mrs. Mitchell appeared in the doorway, completely disrupting my magical-train-ride-to-Portland fantasy scenario.

"I made cookies." She bustled into the room and

deposited the plate on Abelard's desk. "Maybe you want to come downstairs for a bit?"

"Game," Abelard said.

Mrs. Mitchell watched as we made our way back out through the tunnel. Glowing eyes swam out of the darkness, either rats or monsters. Abelard took careful aim with his sniper rifle and fired. Something at the end of the corridor exploded in a flash of dark red.

She shrugged and left the room.

Abelard put the game on pause. We had maybe ten minutes before she came back, and it made me bold. I moved closer.

I draped my hand across his wrist, fingering that strange but attractive med-alert bracelet. His wrist was surprisingly thick. I ran my fingertips along the inside of his wrist, at the place where his arm joined his hand. At any moment he might shake off my hand and turn away. I'd try not be crushed. I'd read that people with Asperger's don't always like to be touched.

Abelard studied our hands with a slight frown. I slid my hand along his wrist into his palm. He hesitated for a moment and then wrapped his fingers around mine and held my hand. Only for a moment.

Then he slid his hand over my wrist in exactly the same way I'd wrapped my hand around his wrist, as though we were inventing a language of gesture from scratch, slowly, through repetition and imitation. *Iteration*—his word. His fingers went all the way around my wrist, overlapped. It gave me an odd thrill, this difference. His hands were so much bigger than mine. Should have been obvious, but it was new information. It was all new. And nice.

"I want to kiss you," he said.

I looked up, startled. Just as quickly, I remembered that he couldn't tolerate eye contact. "Now? Are you sure?"

I felt myself flush. Nervous. What if he didn't like it?

"I mean, you can kiss me," I said. "But don't feel like you have to if it's something you—"

Abelard kissed me. Midsentence. A soft press of his lips against mine. The warm feel of his shoulder as he leaned into me. I closed my eyes. He lingered for a moment before pulling away. Not the F4-tornado-leveling-the-school embrace of untrammeled passion I'd expected. Gentle. Better.

"How was that?" he asked.

"Good." My voice sounded strange, a little breathless. "Very good. And for you?"

"Different," he said softly.

"Is that bad?"

"No, it's good. Different from my last kiss."

"Last kiss? You mean, when I kissed you in the office?"

Abelard frowned.

"Before that. A different girl."

A different girl. Abelard had kissed another girl before me. Of course he had. It was stupid to be jealous of some girl from his past . . .

While my head was running this hamster wheel, Abelard leaned over and kissed me again. And the hamster wheel stopped turning.

"Lily?"

Seven. Our appointed hour. It had only been a few hours since I'd seen him, but it felt like forever. Iris hovered in our room, pretending to work, busy trying to eavesdrop. Hard to listen in to a text conversation.

"Abelard," I replied, just for the thrill of writing his name. The memory of his kiss lingered almost unendurably. Writing was a pleasure, but I wanted more. I reached under my bed, looking for *The Letters of Abelard and Heloise.* I'd dropped it there earlier.

"What are you looking for?" Iris asked.

"Privacy?" I answered. "My own room?"

Iris shrugged and made a face.

"Do you know what I wish?" he texted.

"What do you wish?"

"I wish you were here right now."

"Why? Would you kiss me again?"

I felt like a bundle of nerve endings. Thinking about his arms around me, wanting more. What if he said no?

"Maybe. I've been thinking about that moment ever since."

"You seem surprised."

I waited for him to reply.

"I don't always like to be touched." It probably was hard for him to say this.

"Well, I've been thinking about this," I texted. *"Since we are both in uncharted territory, we could experiment with touching. See what works and what doesn't."*

"Create a series of successful subroutines?" he asked.

"I love it when you speak computationally," I texted. *"It makes me want to slap on a lab coat and get to work."*

Abelard didn't text me back.

"Abelard?"

"I'm sorry," he texted. *"I was distracted by the thought of you wearing only a white lab coat. I believe it is possible that you are the best girlfriend in the history of girlfriends."*

"I do my best." My best. It's not often that I get to say these words.

CHAPTER 20

Monday night, I got home well before Iris. Only two and a half more hours until seven, and Abelard. I felt happy enough to make dinner, even though it wasn't my night to cook. I'd already made a salad and was busy sautéing asparagus and red peppers for a frittata when Iris arrived.

She had the mail.

"Did you see?" she said. "Report cards are in."

"Terrific," I said with as much sarcasm as I could possibly manage. The arrival of the report cards was just another excuse for Iris to gloat.

I assumed that I'd failed two, maybe three classes. I wasn't looking forward to the inevitable confrontation with Mom, but it was all part of my master plan now. Soon I'd be making my case for living with Dad. Screw your courage to the sticking-place.

Mom arrived just as I turned the oven on and began to beat the eggs.

"Report cards!" Iris said, handing Mom the letters.

Mom ripped open the first one, Iris's no doubt.

"Nicely done," Mom said quietly. She didn't want to make a big deal over Iris's success. She didn't want to make me feel bad, but I was sure at some secret private moment later, she would do cartwheels over Iris's report card.

I didn't feel bad. I felt done with school, which wasn't bad at all. Anxious, but not bad.

Iris retreated to our room.

Mom opened my report card. She stared at the paper for a long moment.

I put the frittata in the oven.

"Well," she said finally. A big, sad, slow sigh, which is the worst thing in the world, worse than screaming or hair-pulling or any imaginable histrionics. The sad slow sigh is a sign of utter defeat.

"I thought you promised to talk to Mr. Neuwirth about your Populations in Peril Project," she said.

I turned and leaned against the sink, arms folded across my chest. "I did. He said tough shit."

"Lily! Language. I'm sure that's not what Coach Neuwirth said."

I took a calming breath. Count to four. Use your words, Lily. "Okay, he said that I didn't follow the instructions. He said if he let me slide on the rubric, I would never learn to function in 'the adult world.' Whatever that is."

I expected an argument from Mom, a defense of all things paperworkish and adultly, but instead: silence. I felt the weight of her sadness settle over my chest. Really, failing things was not so bad, because grades, as Coach Neuwirth had amply proven, were arbitrary. But disappointing people who love you is the worst.

"So what now, Lily? You've failed geography and chemistry, and you barely scraped by in algebra. What should we do about this?"

I took a deep breath. It was time to jump in and make my case.

"What if I went to live with Dad for a while? He could homeschool me, or I could take a GED."

Mom laughed. It was a short, bitter bark of a laugh, but it told me—everything. It was a sound of such force and unintentional honesty, that it brought Iris back to the kitchen. She stood in the door frame of the kitchen looking like a sailor of yore, heading into a heavy blow. Ready to batten the hatches, whatever the hell that means. I felt a momentary stab of loss for the carefree albeit busy girl Iris had been when Dad left. The divorce was the genesis of Iris's career in urban planning and disaster management. She'd been cleaning up in the wake of Hurricane Lily ever since. Couldn't have been easy.

"You told me that if I got good grades, you'd let me see Dad this summer."

"But you didn't get good grades, did you?" Mom spat back.

"Mom!" Iris said. "Tone of voice."

Too late. Mom had promised to let me go to Portland

on the condition that I fulfill the impossible quest—all the while knowing I would never in a million years do well in my classes. She knew she'd never have to make good on sending me to Portland. The monster welled up inside me.

"Fuck this," I said.

I pushed past Iris and charged out the front door.

I walked down the sidewalk of our crappy duplex avenue, past rows of trapezoidal seventies houses. I stepped on a chinaberry and was made suddenly, painfully aware that I didn't have shoes on. I reached into my pocket. At least I had my phone.

"You're not wearing shoes," Rosalind said through the window of her car.

"My departure was hastily planned," I replied.

"Do you want to go home and get shoes?"

I opened the door and got in the passenger's side.

"No. I'm not going back there."

"Ever? That might prove problematic."

Rosalind drove in the direction of her parents' house in Zilker Hills.

"So what happened?" she asked after a pause.

"Report cards came out," I said, arms folded across my chest.

"Ah," Rosalind replied. "Call your mom. Tell her you're with me."

This was not the first time I'd called Rosalind and asked

her to pick me up from—wherever. This was not my first bad report card either. Rosalind knew the drill.

"I'll send her a text."

I had dinner with Rosalind's parents, black quinoa salad in front of the TV, some British comedy on Netflix about a foul-tempered bookstore owner who drinks massive amounts of red wine with two friends who have nothing better to do. Funnier than it sounds.

Rosalind's parents didn't say anything about my bare feet. They're nice like that.

At seven, Abelard texted.

"Lily?"

"Abelard. I'm not at home. Kind of distracted."

"You kids today, and your texting," Rosalind's dad said over the edge of his laptop. Pretty meta, Rosalind's dad. You never know whether he's being ironic or not.

"Where are you?"

"My friend Rosalind's house."

"Who are you texting, Lily?" Rosalind's mother asked.

"Lily has a boyfriend," Rosalind said quickly. "They text every night."

Rosalind was clearly trying to introduce the boyfriend idea by proxy, but her mother wasn't getting it.

"Oh, that's nice, Lily," Rosalind's mom said. "What's he like?"

"Make that a lot distracted," I texted.

Rosalind whipped out her phone and scrolled to Richard's sketch of Abelard. She handed it to her mother. Rosalind's mother pored over the picture with a frown. I hoped she didn't read the comment thread.

"Your boyfriend is quite handsome," Rosalind's mother said.

"Come to the robotics lab at lunch," Abelard texted.

"The artist is amazing, don't you think?" Rosalind leaned over her phone.

I couldn't think. I took my phone and went through the sliding glass door to the flagstone patio.

"I failed a bunch of classes. My mom isn't going to let me go to Portland. I'm thinking of running away."

I inhaled deeply. A gust of wind rustled through the live oaks. The air smelled like impending rain.

"I'll go with you."

I stared at the screen, not quite sure I believed the words.

"Are you sure?"

"I want to be where you are. Nothing else matters."

But other things did matter.

"We'll take the train," he said.

"Sounds expensive."

"I have some money saved. My grandparents send me a thousand dollars every birthday and Christmas. I never spend it."

My grandparents are not thousand-dollar grandparents

by a long shot. I wondered when Abelard's grandparents started sending him a thousand dollars. Can you send a four-year-old that kind of money? A ten-year-old?

"Isn't that your college fund?"

"No."

"Okay. So we will go to Portland together. On the train."

"Yes."

A strange and unfamiliar feeling filled me. I had a plan—and a future. With my boyfriend. Happiness.

Rosalind dropped me back home around ten. Mom was working at the dining room table. I steeled myself for another round of conflict about my wildly unimportant grades.

Mom looked up from her work. "Come talk with me, Lily."

I slumped into the chair across from her, arms folded.

"You know, I don't remember telling you that you could visit your father this summer."

"But you did, Mom! We were in the car driving home after I broke the wall. And then earlier—"

"Okay, if you say I did, I did." Mom rubbed a hand over her eyes and left a little clump of mascara on her cheek. I longed to reach over and wipe it off.

"We can see about a visit, but you can't go live with your dad. I don't think he can take care of you. He can barely take care of himself, and it's just not—"

"I can take care of myself," I said quickly.

"You're sixteen! You can't take care of yourself, honey."

A lump formed in my throat. I understood—finally. She was keeping me from my dad because she didn't want me to end up like him—picking beets and milking goats, poor as dirt. Happy. Mom still held out hope of turning me into Iris, but it was too late for that. I'd never be like Iris.

"Well, that makes me just like Dad, doesn't it?" I stood and pushed away from the table. "I should be living with him."

"Lily, that doesn't even make sense. Someone has to pay the bills and get you to school on time. You don't even do your own laundry. Do you think your dad will—"

"Fuck you," I said. Bitter angry tears rose in my eyes, but I wasn't going to cry in front of her. "You never understood Dad. He's not like you."

"I don't even know how to get in touch with your dad," she said, but I wasn't listening.

I went to my bed and put in earbuds and turned up the music too loud. It was too much. I was done. I'd find my dad if Abelard and I had to go farm to farm in Portland looking for him.

CHAPTER 21

I spent lunch hour in the robotics lab with Abelard. On the way, I passed the art wing. Richard's study of feet was gone from the glass case. In its place was his finished portrait of Rosalind. Nice to know things were progressing.

At first, I thought Mr. Martini was going to say no.

"Preparing for regionals," Mr. Martini said. "You understand, miss."

Miss. He called me "miss," like I'd wandered in off the street to sell something. I guessed this was what happened when you weren't in AP Physics.

Abelard did not, however, understand. He stood at the door frowning.

"I asked my girlfriend to come to robotics," Abelard said.

His girlfriend. I'd always hoped that I would find someone to love before I left high school. I just never expected to find someone who would admit to it in public, and even seem sort of proud of the fact.

Abelard.

"*She'en* been *spreefed* on safety protocols," Mr. Martini said.

Safety protocols. That was what Mr. Martini said the last time I was there. I had no idea. Briefed on safety protocols.

"I asked my girlfriend to come to robotics," Abelard repeated. He shook his head lightly and frowned, a look of absolute stubbornness on his beautiful face. I had the feeling he wasn't going to move until Mr. Martini gave in.

Mr. Martini shrugged and walked to the cabinet and returned with a sheet of paper and a pair of safety goggles.

"Read this carefully and *shine* at the *bobbin*," Mr. Martini said. "And don't touch anything."

I nodded vigorously. I didn't read carefully, because careful reading is not my thing. I just decided I wouldn't touch anything. The last thing I wanted to do was to mess up the communal robot. And so I watched while Abelard, two guys I didn't know, and a nerd girl named Eva adjusted actuators and tried to get the robot to play a better hole of mini golf. I kept my hands to myself. Which was hard.

Mom returned home early from work. It was her night to cook, but she'd brought home a sack of something.

"What's in the bag?" Iris looked up from the dining room table. She was hard at work editing her Cornell Notes for biology. Cornell Notes, the cult of synthesizing information through keywords and questions, written in well-defined margins. Teachers at LAME worship at the altar of Cornell.

"Tacos from Torchy's," Mom replied cheerily. "Fried avocado for you, Iris, and for you, Lily, Baja shrimp. And street corn."

Mom deposited the bag on the dining room table and went for plates. Since Mom only took me for tacos after my appointments with Humberto, I took it as a sign. She'd made an appointment with Humberto.

"Did you talk to Humberto?" I asked.

Mom turned.

"Humberto?" She looked confused. "No, honey, I thought I told you. We maxed out our insurance *splog* yearly *scrits* you can have with Humberto *scrubble*."

"What?" Something about her face filled me with alarm. She had an expression both wary and hopeful. I didn't know what the hell she was talking about, but I didn't have to. I sensed a plan.

"You know, Lily, since I work in medical billing, I run into a lot of people in the profession. And I happened to meet a nice doctor who works in my complex, and—"

"I'm not going to another doctor." I folded my arms across my chest and leaned against the drainboard. "I'm not taking any more drugs."

"Maybe we should talk about this later." Mom tilted her head toward Iris. My alarm grew. Things not to be spoken of in the proximity of Iris are generally messed-up things, like suicide watch and detention specifications.

"Iris isn't even listening," I said.

Of course, this wasn't true. Iris had her head down in her Cornell Notes, pretending to pose thought-provoking questions about the Krebs cycle in the margin, but even I could see that her pen wasn't really moving. Iris was totally listening.

"Okay, Lily. He's not another neurologist. He's a surgeon."

Iris looked up in surprise. I met her eyes, glad to have a witness to this most recent bout of insanity.

"A surgeon?" I laughed. "Like he's going to open up my skull and take parts of my brain out? Are you going to lobotomize me, Mom?"

"It's not a lobotomy, honey," she said, deadly serious. "It's more like an electrode implantation. It's very minor."

"Ah—minor brain surgery." I pushed past Mom and flopped down on the living room couch, which was more of a crap-ass love seat, and covered my eyes with my hands.

Mom followed me.

"You don't have to have the surgery," she said. "We could just go talk to the doctor and see what you think. He's very engaging. I think you'll like him."

Anger welled up, so sharp and bitter I thought I might heave. My hand absently searched the coffee table and found a canister full of Iris's colored pencils. My hand longed to hurl the canister, but some part of my brain said no. No, no, no. It was time to say no to everything. I put the pencils down.

"No," I replied. "Not in a million years."

"Lily, is there anything I can do to convince you to just go talk to the doctor? He's been having a lot of success with ADHD patients. The surgery is safe. He's even doing it on younger kids."

I sat on the couch fuming, sick at heart. My mother didn't like me the way I was. Hardly new information, but somehow it hurt every time she found a new doctor to "cure" me. Every new drug, every new life coach, every neurologist was a reminder that to Mom, I was broken. Broken. A fractal, a complexity.

But Abelard didn't think I was broken.

Abelard.

Bells and whistles.

There was something Mom could do for me. It was so simple. I'd been avoiding the question of how I would tell Mom about my trip to Portland with Abelard. I couldn't just run away. And now, here was my moment.

"You want me to see this doctor?" I pulled my hand away from my eyes to look at her. "Let me go visit my father this summer with Abelard. Then I'll talk to your surgeon."

Mom frowned in slow motion. Her eyes glittered. I

could see she was performing some sort of mental calculus. And then she stood—subject to be tabled for discussion later. Good. At least I'd told her about Abelard and Portland.

We ate tacos in silence.

Seven that night. Abelard wanted to know what I thought of robotics. Which was good. I didn't want to talk about my mother or the surgeon.

"Honestly? Jealous. I want to build robots to do my bidding."

"I wish this one would do my bidding. Our kill ratio is still too low," Abelard replied.

"You shouldn't call it a kill ratio. Your robot will get ideas. Before you know it, you'll have to send your father back in time to save the world."

Abelard didn't respond for a long time, long enough for me to wonder if he'd actually seen any of the *Terminator* oeuvre. It was quite possible that he hadn't wasted as much of his childhood watching old movies in front of the TV. Because—Latin lessons.

"If my father traveled back in time, it wouldn't be to save the world," he replied.

There was something mournful about this. I'd always liked *Terminator.* I liked the idea that if I sent my father back in time, he'd be great at destroying homicidal robots. Thinking on his feet. Dad was strong and quick-witted, and better suited for saving the world than he was for filing his tax returns on time.

"He wouldn't save the world? Not even if he knew he was the future's last hope?"

"He would probably use the time machine to send us all back to different eras. He'd probably send me back to fight in the Crusades or something equally doomed."

"Like the librarian in Star Trek*?"* I asked.

"Exactly," Abelard replied. *"You know* Star Trek*? Truly, you are mistress of the most polite arts."*

I beamed at the quote and the compliment. Of course, I owed this bit of trivia to Humberto, the *Star Trek* therapist. In the librarian episode, the sun is about to supernova, and the librarian sends everyone into the past to survive. But when the away team arrives from the *Enterprise,* all the good time slots are gone; all that's left are the Salem witch trials and the Great Ice Age on some alternate planet. World of suck. Humberto's contention was that I got pushed through the time portal to the worst moment in history to be an ADHD person. Bad luck of the draw. This is how he talks, Humberto. Oddly comforting.

"My dad wants you to come over on Saturday and watch a movie."

"Interesting. Your father wants me to come over?"

"He believes you should watch The Seventh Seal *with us. It's about the Middle Ages."*

This would seem odd, except that I'm used to Rosalind's parents. Film is literature, and everyone has a favorite lesson to teach. Apparently.

"OK, Saturday."

CHAPTER 22

Friday, Rosalind found me in the hall before lunch.

"Can you come work the stage tonight? Next Thursday is opening night, and we're down two stagehands. I'll give you a ride home. Richard has agreed to crew but . . ."

"Of course," I replied. "But you do know that with my GPA . . ."

Rosalind rolled her eyes.

"You know Mr. Turner has a 'don't ask, don't tell' policy about GPA, right? See you at lunch."

Rosalind dropped me off at home after theater, but she didn't come in.

"How was the theater?" Mom asked. She sat in the living room, alone.

"Good, I guess. As good as running back and forth in a squat position can be," I said. "Mostly it was talk tonight. We'll get to staging next week."

"Ah." Clearly her mind was elsewhere. "I've made a

salad if you're hungry. Iris and I have already eaten. Come sit down. I want to talk to you."

I followed her to the dining room. A bowl of Asian chicken salad sat on the table, and a bag of those weird crunchy sticks that exist only for Asian chicken salad. I was suddenly not at all hungry because serious conversation was in the offing. I had to remind myself that she'd already seen my report card for this six weeks. How much worse could it get?

Mom inhaled and sighed deeply. "Lily, I want to talk to you seriously about going to the doctor."

Okay—worse. It could get worse.

"I told you I'd only go if you let me see Dad."

"You know, your dad has his own life. I don't want you to get your hopes up."

"Can't I at least talk to him about it?"

Mom handed me her cell phone.

"Your dad doesn't have a cell phone right now. I tracked him down through one of his friends. This is his girlfriend's number."

Girlfriend's number. My chest tightened, which was stupid. Of course my dad had a girlfriend. It wasn't like he'd been in stasis for five years.

I hit talk. It rang twice, and a woman answered.

"Hi, um, can I talk to Alexander Michaels-Ry—I mean Alexander Ryan?" I asked.

"*Splur,*" the woman said in a voice so percussive, I wasn't sure she hadn't just insulted me. She was gone so long I wondered if she'd forgotten.

"Hello?" My dad's voice. It's not like you ever forget the sound of your dad's voice.

"Hi, Dad. It's me, Lily."

There was a momentary silence on the other end, long enough to hear him breathe. Like he was running through the names in his head trying to remember who Lily was. Which—okay—I'm slow on the phone. Names go with faces, but they don't make any sense without them.

"Lil," Dad said finally. "Hey, kid, how's it going?"

"Um, pretty good, I guess. School not so good, but I have a boyfriend."

Silence on the other end.

"So, yeah, it's good," I said.

"Hey, Lil, that's great!" Dad said.

I heard the woman's voice talking in the background, an impatient sound. Dad put a hand over the phone.

"Just a minute," he said in a muffled voice.

I didn't have much time.

"So, Dad, do you remember when you said that I could come to Portland and milk goats with you and stay on the farm?"

"Farm?"

"Yeah, farm. You know, where you make goat cheese?" I paused. "Home-brewed Belgian ale?" I was trying to be funny, but I realized I was just parroting what Dr. Mitchell told me, and it sounded bitter and mean.

"Belgian ale?" Dad said.

"You told me I could come stay on your farm," I said, impatiently now, because Mom was sitting next to me rubbing her temples nervously, looking like she wanted to rip the phone out of my hands.

The impatient woman said something in the background.

"Ohh . . . !" Dad said, like it just dawned on him what a farm was. "Farm. But, Lil, that was years ago. God, I haven't thought about that place for a while. You know, you'd think it would be great to live on a farm, but really farm life is sooo . . . stultifyingly boring. Lil, you could not imagine how totally mind-numbingly tedious farm work is. It reminded me of *Anna Karenina* and all the scenes where Konstantin deals with the peasants—"

"Dad, I haven't read *Anna Karenina*."

"Well, you should. It's on the shelves, isn't it? I think I left it behind."

Left it behind. I wanted to drop the phone and go look at the shelves. The mention of the bookshelves was the first sign that I was talking to my actual dad, not some frightening alternate-universe version of him where everything went wrong.

"So where are you now? Can I come stay with you?" I asked. "Mom said I could come to Portland if—"

"Did I tell you?" Dad said. "I'm in a band again. We have a really good singer. She's a *scrubby crumb lurker* . . . a New Pornographers sound, or maybe Arcade Fire? *Scooby* like Arcade Fire?"

"Yeah, I guess so," I replied. I'd lost his train of thought, lost the point of our conversation. Scooby-Doo, Arcade Fire, *Anna Karenina*—lost.

"Alex, we're going to be late," the impatient woman said, audibly now. "Do you want to miss Caleb's graduation?"

"Lil, I've got to go," Dad said.

"Who's Caleb?" I asked quickly. "Graduation?"

"Caleb? He's only the sweetest kid ever. You'd like him. He's going into kindergarten . . . his daycare . . . graduation ceremony. It's not a big deal but—"

"Alex!" the woman said.

I heard a small child Muppet voice in the background, undoubtedly Caleb, "the sweetest kid ever." A bunch of run-on sentences strung together with long stuttering pauses and repetition. I only caught one word: *Daddy.* Some kid I didn't know called my father Daddy.

"I've got to go," he said. "I'll talk to you later, okay, Lil?"

He hung up the phone.

I held the phone out and had the dim sensation of it being taken out of my hands.

"What did your dad say?" Mom asked softly.

"He said I should read *Anna Karenina*," I mumbled.

"I mean about you going to Portland."

I closed my eyes, congealed in misery, hoping that if I stayed perfectly still, the world would forget about me. Mom would get up and go to bed, and I would open my eyes and find myself in a quiet room. Alone.

"Yeah, that's not going to work out."

Mom put a hand on my shoulder.

"Lily, I'm sorry," she said.

"For what?" I asked. "For not telling me that Dad had a new family and a new kid?"

"What? He has a child? How old?"

"Five." I stole a glance at Mom. She'd gone to some inward place, mentally calculating the age of Dad's kid against the time he'd last lived with us. It hadn't occurred to me that Dad might have cheated on Mom. From the look on her face, I don't think it had occurred to her either, and I felt sorry that I'd called Dad. I'd always thought she drove him away. It had never occurred to me that he might be to blame.

Mom sat down on the love seat next to me. "Your dad loves you. He was just never good at keeping up with people or finishing—"

"I get it."

I was done hearing about my dad. My dad: funny, smart, literate. Failed history graduate student. Dropout goat cheese maker. Father of "the sweetest kid ever." How long before he left Caleb and the impatient woman in the dust to hunt for gold in the Arctic? Like he'd left everything else.

Like he'd left us.

Guess I was just like him. We were both irrevocably broken.

"Make the appointment with the doctor," I said.

"I already have," she said. "Tuesday at ten thirty."

"Lily?" he'd texted. And then later, *"Where are you?"*

It was 7:13 when I finally ended up in my room.

"Sorry I'm late," I texted back.

We talked about robots and chess and *The Seventh Seal.* I couldn't bring myself to tell Abelard about my father. I couldn't bring myself to tell him there wasn't going to be a trip to Portland.

CHAPTER 23

Every day is new. Every day is a giant reset button. Along with my algebra homework and my favorite T-shirt, I've lost memory of yesterday's conversations and the reason my eyes are puffy this morning. The flood of experience, the unexpected rain last night and the cool and moist air, the bran muffins Mom made and the smell of vanilla and raisins in the house, is the now that matters. I have a today with Abelard.

But I also have a dull spot in the center of my chest that is my father sitting on a couch playing Arcade Fire songs for Caleb, "the sweetest kid ever." Some things are bigger than cool rain, bigger than vanilla and raisins, bigger than the reset button. Some things even I can't forget.

And I'm the queen of losing things.

Saturday afternoon. I lost track of time. And then I was late.

"Lily! I'm so glad you're here." Mrs. Mitchell wore a gigantic amber pendant that had what looked like a prehistoric spider or long-legged bug folded up around some ants.

"Sorry I'm late."

"Oh, honey, you should have called me." She lowered her voice. "It's almost two forty. I think you had our Abelard a bit worried."

I looked past her to Abelard on the couch, sitting with his arms folded. He looked agitated.

"Hey, Abelard," I said.

"Lily."

"I'm making some more lemonade. Would you like some? Abelard, you'd like some lemonade, wouldn't you?"

Mrs. Mitchell fluttered away to the kitchen before Abelard had a chance to answer. I sat on the couch, an arm's distance away from him because I was feeling jumpy from being late.

"I'm sorry," I said. I wanted to say more, but for once, words failed me.

Mrs. Mitchell burst through the door carrying a tray with two glasses of lemonade.

"Are you going to start the movie, Abelard?"

Without waiting for an answer, she picked up the remote. I watched the simple white credits on a black background, as the sound of a gong faded ominously into silence.

"Do you two need anything else?" Mrs. Mitchell asked.

"Popcorn," Abelard said.

"Honey, we don't have any popcorn," Mrs. Mitchell replied.

"Popcorn goes with movies," Abelard said, his voice rising.

Mrs. Mitchell smoothed her perfect white hair with one hand and sighed. "All right, Abelard, I'll go to the store. Feel free to help yourself to more lemonade, Lily. Abelard, you'll be okay while I'm gone, won't you?"

She picked up her purse on the table by the front door and left.

The movie started with a scene of clouds in black and white, and a gorgeous shot of a hawk circling. I reached for my lemonade and drank it quickly because I was thirsty and anxious.

Abelard moved closer to me, and the swirl of frustration and anger at myself for being late subsided. I inched his way, conscious of his hand on the couch.

On the screen, the scene changed to two dead or sleeping guys lying on a rocky beach next to a chessboard. Someone was speaking in Swedish, and words scrolled by the bottom of the screen faster than I could possibly read. I only caught random phrases: "silence in heaven," "half an hour" . . . Nothing made sense.

"*The Seventh Seal.*" Dr. Mitchell emerged from his study. He stood behind the couch, looming over us.

"Hello, Dr. Mitchell." I craned my neck back to look at him.

"Hello, Lily. Have you ever seen this movie before?—oh wait, there's Death."

I turned toward the TV. True enough, a man with a white face, a long black cape, and hood showed up at a rocky ocean beach edge and began talking about chess.

"You know the painter the knight is referring to is Albertus Pictor, but of course he shows up later in the film," Dr. Mitchell said. "You know his last name, Pictor, comes from the same Latin root as our word *picture,* because at this point in history, Sweden had not yet fully begun to use patronymic names and—"

"Dad," Abelard pulled away from me and sat with his hands in his lap. "We're watching a movie."

"What?" Dr. Mitchell replied. "I thought Lily might enjoy a little background about Swedish history and . . ."

Dr. Mitchell resumed talking. In the movie, Death and the knight sat down on the beach and began to play chess. I formulated a new opinion that hell is having someone describe the entire history of medieval Sweden in English while other people converse in Swedish and you try to read subtitles. I didn't want to say anything because I was already feeling stupid, hoping to hide my inability to read the subtitles fast enough to have a clue as to what was going on in the movie. Because—dyslexic.

"Dad!"

Abelard moved to the far end of the couch and ran his left hand over the edge of the coffee table, five inches one way, five inches back, over and over. Smoothing the edge over and over. Agitated. He moved his head side to side.

"Calm down, Abelard," Dr. Mitchell said.

Abelard remained at the end of the couch, relentlessly running his hand over the edge of the table, lost in some deep personal annoyance.

Without thinking, I reached over and put my hand on his shoulder. He flinched and pulled away like I'd burned him.

"Sorry," I said.

Abelard made a strange grunting sound as though I'd hurt him.

Did it hurt to be touched sometimes?

"Oh, dear," Dr. Mitchell said. "Normally Abelard's mother would be here . . ."

I looked at Dr. Mitchell as he trailed off. He had moved away from the couch and was looking longingly toward the front door as though he could will Mrs. Mitchell to come home.

"What should I do?" I asked him. I was talking like Abelard wasn't in the room, and I hated it. I hated feeling this helpless.

"You shouldn't have been late. Abelard is very punctual."

Dr. Mitchell glanced around the room, looking for something. "He has a blanket he likes sometimes at moments like these."

There was a loud *pong*, a reverberation on the glass table. I turned. Abelard had hit his head on the table. His sunglasses were on the floor, his hair about his face. He lifted his head, and I had the feeling he was going to hit his head again. It was too much. I couldn't do anything for him, and I felt like if I didn't get up and move around, I would explode.

"Should he be doing that?" I wanted to stop Abelard from banging his head, but I didn't want to touch him again, if touching him only made it worse. That was all I could do—make it worse.

"Perhaps if you gave us a moment?" Dr. Mitchell said. He grabbed a pillow from the couch and slid it onto the coffee table.

I picked up my mostly empty glass and headed for the kitchen.

I left Abelard alone with his father as a woman in a royal dress holding a baby appeared in the middle of the forest.

The kitchen, hidden behind a swinging door, was cool and crisp, white on white—white subway tiles, white marble counters streaked with gray and white plates stacked neatly in glass cabinets. On the marble center island sat the giant pitcher of blue and orange and yellow speckled glass and lemon slices, glowing in the light from the bay window in the breakfast nook. I heard the sound of the movie in Swedish, the occasional murmur of Dr. Mitchell's voice.

I'd never seen Abelard like this. I wanted to help him, and I couldn't.

I turned my glass over and emptied the ice and lemons into the stainless-steel sink. The bottom of the glass was thick—more than half an inch of heavy, pale-green glass like an old Coke bottle. It calmed me. The thickness of the glass was somehow satisfying. A little offset from the center bottom was a tiny half bubble of glass where the glass blower had finished the work and pulled off the long blowing tube. At least, that's how I thought that the bubble got there. I looked at the giant pitcher half filled with lemonade. Did all blown glass have this imperfection?

I set my glass down on the counter, picked up the pitcher, and lifted it over my head to look for the bubble on its bottom. The pitcher was heavy. It tilted in my hands, and a small stream of lemonade hit the counter and dribbled to the floor. In a rush to stop the flow, I set the pitcher down hard on the marble counter.

The pitcher made a strange, hollow thump.

On the side of the pitcher a crack had formed around the base.

I picked up the pitcher and the bottom fell off. The glass

bottom hit the marble counter and shattered, sending a spray of glass, lemonade, and sliced lemons everywhere. I stood for a moment holding the handle of the pitcher, wondering if anyone had heard.

I had to clean the mess up. My Converses were covered in lemonade, soaked through. A pool of lemonade spread across the polished wooden floor. And I mourned the pitcher, because it was pretty, like so many of the things I end up destroying, and because Mrs. Mitchell had gone to all the trouble to make lemonade, and she'd cut up like a thousand lemons to make lemonade from scratch, which was a thing I hadn't even known you could do because my mother never made lemonade, and the only lemonade we ever had was from P. Terry's, but there had to be paper towels somewhere. Abelard was upset, and I was only making things worse.

I found the paper towels by the sink, hidden behind a polished chrome breadbox like they were ashamed of paper towels because of the environment, or maybe they didn't fit the decor. Weird because the Mitchells were rich and nice and had nothing to be ashamed of, and now I'd gone and destroyed a hand-blown pitcher, and I didn't even know where to look for a replacement or if I could afford it if I found one.

Abelard was in the other room with his father. Had they heard the crash? Things had gone horribly wrong. Breathe. Count to ten.

I unspooled the paper towel roll—great heaping sheets of paper towels—and threw them on top of the lemons and glass on the floor.

"Breathe, Lily. Think," I whispered. "Broken stuff goes in trash cans."

I threw an entire roll's worth of paper towels on top of the spill and opened the under-sink cabinet looking for the trash. Nothing. I opened all the under-cabinet drawers and only found pans and glass baking dishes, neatly stacked cookie sheets. No trash can. I skirted the mess of lemons on the floor and opened the larger cabinet near the breakfast nook, but all I found were Christmas decorations, an ironing board, stuff. They didn't have a trash can. How was I going to clean up this mess without a trash can? Were they so rich they didn't have trash? Did they have some magical way of dealing with trash that I couldn't see?

There was nothing, no broom or mop or trash can, but there was the back door.

And then I had my *Frankenstein monster* moment.

I needed to leave, to walk away from the mess without a word, run down the street to freedom. Before I made things worse. Everything I touched went wrong, starting and ending with Abelard.

I went through the kitchen door into the backyard. There was a stone patio surrounded by a well-tended garden of herbs and flowers, and beyond, a small yard ringed by a tall wooden fence. I lunged toward the fence and circled around the edge until I found the gate. It had a black steel hasp, padlocked. I shook the door by the handle in frustration, and the fence wobbled slightly. Who locks their own yard?

I looked to the wrought-iron deck chair for something to stand on to scale the fence, but then I imagined getting to the top of the fence and pulling the whole thing down. It was pretty wobbly.

I'd have to go out the front door and sneak past Abelard and his father.

I opened the kitchen door. Mrs. Mitchell stood by the pile of lemons on the floor, surveying the wreckage of her once-perfect kitchen.

"Lily, what happened?" Mrs. Mitchell said. She held a net grocery bag with popcorn, French bread, greens.

"I broke your pitcher. I'm so sorry it was an accident," I said breathlessly. I stood like a runner on the blocks, waiting to lunge away from my own disaster.

"Are you all right?" she asked, dropping the grocery bag on the dry counter by the sink.

"I tried to clean it up, but I couldn't find the trash can or a broom or anything. I mean I looked all over, and I just—"

"What were you doing in the backyard?" Mrs. Mitchell leaned against the counter, apparently unconcerned by the sticky mess on her kitchen floor. Focused entirely on me. They probably had a maid or something, someone who came every day to sweep the floor. Maybe Mrs. Mitchell didn't know where the trash can was either.

"I couldn't figure out how to clean the mess up, so I just thought I would . . . leave, I mean . . ."

I looked away as tears began to well up in my eyes, tears of shame and rage.

"Oh, honey, don't worry about the pitcher. It was old. Just go back to the movie, and I'll clean up in here."

"It was so pretty, though." The thought of Mrs. Mitchell down on the floor picking up glass in her tan shirtdress and espadrille flats seemed wrong—like she was dressed to tour the Parthenon, not clean kitchen floors.

"It really doesn't matter, Lily." A strange note of impatience crept into her voice.

"But it was part of a matched set. I should just go before I break something else."

Mrs. Mitchell picked up my empty lemonade glass and hurled it at the wall of subway tiles behind the stove. The glass shattered with a loud crack, leaving a tiny little nick in one of the tiles.

For an old white-haired woman, she had a surprisingly good pitching arm.

"There," she said. "Now it's not part of a matched set."

I stood speechless, tears drying on my face as though the force of her blow had swept a wind through the kitchen. I forgot why I'd been upset as the world turned upside down—nice old ladies smashing glasses, lemonade sinking into a polished wood floor.

Mrs. Mitchell shut her eyes and shook her head.

"Listen, Lily," she said in a low voice. "Abelard doesn't have many friends, and very few that even bother to come over to the house to see him. He may not seem that emotional, but I'm his mother, and I know it hurts him. You're the first girl he's had over. If you run away now—"

"Mom!" Abelard was standing in the doorway, his voice a strangled cry, like the moan of a cat.

Dr. Mitchell appeared behind Abelard.

"I heard a crash," Dr. Mitchell said.

"There was a slight accident," Mrs. Mitchell said with exaggerated cheeriness.

"What happened?" Dr. Mitchell said.

"We're breaking things," Mrs. Mitchell replied. "Would you care to join us?"

Dr. Mitchell appeared to consider this. Seriously.

"No thank you." He turned and retreated to his study.

Abelard left the kitchen. I heard his footsteps on the stairs.

I closed my eyes momentarily. All I wanted was a dark room to think in. I wanted to leave. But if I left now, I knew I'd never come back. I'd be too ashamed. And I'd never see Abelard again.

Mrs. Mitchell opened a smooth stainless-steel drawer

in the central island and began piling lemons and glass into it. Trash compactor. One mystery solved.

I turned and walked upstairs to Abelard's room.

Abelard had left the door to his room open. He sat upright on the edge of his bed with his eyes cast to the side, his left hand rubbing the back of his neck, in a way that seemed either soothing or irritating or probably both. Distant, like he was encased in his own bubble of misery.

I didn't sit on the bed. It seemed like a bad idea. I was afraid to sit next to him, afraid that my presence would send him spinning back into smashing his head against things. Along with robots and fractals and medieval poetry, there was a whole universe of chaos inside his brain that was beyond my reach.

Sometimes I felt like smashing my head against things or running into stuff just to remind me that I was real and human. But only once. Once would have been enough to bring me back to myself. I couldn't imagine what it would be like to do it over and over, and not be able to stop. It scared me.

I pulled out the chair from his desk and sat in it. Like many things in his world, it was covered in a fabric that was both soft and invisible, a neutral brown. Abelard didn't look at me, but his hand moved a tick faster on the back of his neck. I worried that he would rub his skin red—my fault.

"You were leaving," he said quickly. "I heard Mom ask you not to leave, not to run away because I don't have any friends. She begged you not to go. Is this why you're here, because she begged you not to go?"

"No. You don't get it. I destroyed your kitchen. I break things, I run away. This is the kind of monster I am."

Abelard moved his head back and forth across his hand, a slow-motion "no."

"People laugh at me every single day," he said. "They think I don't notice, but I do. People think I'm stupid because I don't read social cues."

"No one thinks you're stupid, Abelard," I said. "They may think many things about you, but stupid . . . no."

Mrs. Mitchell stuck her head around the door.

"Everything okay in here?" she said in a cheery voice. She rubbed a dishtowel between her hands, presumably dabbing off the last of the lemonade, or massaging out broken bits of glass and blood.

"I'm good," I said in my equally fake lady voice.

Mrs. Mitchell regarded Abelard with alarm. Her eyes went to his hand on the back of his neck like she was trying to quantify his agitation for a future conversation with Abelard's doctor. I knew that look.

"We don't have any more lemons, but I've made some iced tea," she said. "Why don't you both come downstairs and play a game of chess? I'm making sugar cookies."

Her words dropped into the room like a stone into a

pond and disappeared, a strange awkward noise and then silence. It wasn't just "people" who thought Abelard was stupid, it was his mother. Not stupid really, but ten years old. Like all his complex relationship issues could be whisked away with a plateful of sugar cookies. No wonder Abelard wanted to leave.

"I've got to go check on the cookies," she said. "I'll be back."

I waited for Abelard to speak.

"You were running away," he said.

And for an instant and only an instant, Abelard looked at me. His eyes were a clear bright blue. Dispassionate and utterly truthful.

He was right. I wanted to run away when he started hitting his head on the table. I wanted to help him, and I couldn't, and when I saw that I couldn't help him, I wanted to be as far away from him as possible. Push the reset button and wait for another day. Wait for the Abelard of fractals and poetry to return.

I still wanted to leave. Run. Find a dark and quiet room to think about things. Run. Like my father. Stupid, free-association brain—filled with dark, unseemly truths! My father? Let me tell you about my father!

I put my hands over my eyes. Maybe I was going to cry. Maybe not. Breathe. Count of four in. Hold for two. Count of four out. Forget that I'd tried to touch him and he'd flinched and howled.

"Okay," I said, exhaling noisily. "This is what I have to say. My life has gone to shit. I could go into all the ways that everything in my life has turned to dust but . . ."

I paused. I hadn't even told Abelard about my father. Our lost trip to Portland. Dreams. Smashed.

"Anyway, I was okay with my terrible life before I met you, because I didn't need anyone. I read books. I knew that I was smarter than half the straight-A students in school, and I was only failing because of a bunch of stupid rules. And I thought that if I ended up working the fry station at McDonald's, at least I'd still have my ironic detachment, and my books. So—fuck the world."

"You're not going to work at McDonald's." Abelard resumed shaking his head from side to side. A tic—or maybe a world of no. I didn't know.

"The point is, I was fine until you called me a woman of 'surpassing beauty and purpose.' I was fine being alone, because I didn't even know I was alone until I met you."

I looked up at Abelard through blurry eyes.

"I don't know how to help you. I don't know how to be the person you need me to be. Which sucks, because I've come to realize that I need you," I said. "And it's absolutely terrifying."

Abelard didn't say anything.

The urge to run was still in me. I went downstairs and sat on the couch. I wrapped my arms around my chest. I didn't trust my hands—not anymore.

Mrs. Mitchell crept quietly out of the kitchen.

"Do you want to watch the movie, Lily?"

I nodded. I didn't trust my voice.

Thirty minutes into the movie, Abelard came downstairs and sat on the opposite end of the couch. We didn't talk. When my mother came, I said goodbye, but Abelard didn't say anything. Mrs. Mitchell walked me to the door and waved to my mother. I was kind of surprised she didn't bring Mom a cookie.

CHAPTER 24

Seven o'clock.

"Lily?"

"Abelard."

"You're here."

"Why wouldn't I be?"

"Because I had a meltdown," he texted. *"You've seen me at my worst. I thought you would decide you wanted a normal boyfriend."*

"Normal boyfriend? Really? I'm not exactly normal. I destroyed your kitchen, remember?"

"You're more normal than I am."

I leaned back on my bed and closed my eyes. More normal. It had never before occurred to me that I might be more normal than anyone in my vicinity. But in Abelard's case, it might just have been true. I had a tight spot in my chest when I thought of the moment when I'd touched him and he'd flinched away. A residual feeling of helplessness.

"You scared me," I said. *"I felt like you were lost to me."*

"I was lost. When you were late, I thought you weren't coming. And then I felt lost."

Time. I'd thought Dr. Mitchell was just being a jerk when he suggested that I'd precipitated Abelard's meltdown by being late. Maybe not.

"I'm bad with time, but I wouldn't just not show up."

"Time is important. Time is discrete, and mathematical. You can't just shear off minutes here and there and expect everything to come out equal."

"Sorry."

I waited. A couple of minutes passed, and Abelard hadn't said anything. I thought he was angry.

"Oh, I understand now," I texted. *"Wibbly-wobbly, timey-wimey bits."*

"Thank you, Doctor Who," he replied.

Relief. If we could joke around, it meant he'd forgive me.

"Sometimes I crawl into my blue box, and I think minutes have elapsed, when really it's been hours. Days even. Decades."

"Time is important. Time is absolute. Even for Time Lords."

"I won't be late again. I promise. I suck at time management. It is literally the thing I'm the absolute worst at. But for you, I will do whatever it takes not to be late again."

"I'll try harder" seemed too small for his level of distress. Being on time really mattered to Abelard. I leafed through *The Letters of Abelard and Heloise*, and found what I was looking for.

"Let us not lose, through negligence, the only happiness which is left us, and the only one, perhaps, which the malice of our enemies can never ravish from us."

I wrote it out slowly, arguing with autocorrect over *neg-ligence* and *ravish.* Stupid autocorrect!

His response came quickly.

"I love you, Lily. More than seems wise."

"I love you too, Abelard. I'll try not to be late again."

"Then we understand each other?"

"Perfectly."

CHAPTER 25

The doctor had an office in Meridian Square where Mom did her medical billing for a group of pediatricians. Dr. Carpenter, one of the people she worked for, was also Iris's and my doctor, so I was intimately familiar with the decor—heavy wood doors and pale green carpet and chairs covered in industrial fabric in the weird color that could only be described as "puce."

Unlike my doctor, whose waiting room was crammed with puzzles and toys and magazines—*Parenting* and *Psychology Today* and *Parents*—Brain Doctor had nothing fun in his waiting room. And I appreciated that. It saved me from having to read another "Ten Tips for Coping with Your ADHD Child" article and comparing it to a "Ten Tips for Dealing with Your Tantruming Toddler." Because, basically the same article. Apparently every problem in the entire world could be fixed by "maintaining a regular schedule, encouraging proper sleep habits, and avoiding processed foods and sugary treats."

Mom and I sat in the waiting room, giving each other forced smiles, being . . . nice. It felt awkward.

"What do you want to do after this?" she said.

"Don't you have to work?" I said. Mom always had to work.

"I took the morning off," she replied. "I don't know how long this is going to take, but we could go—"

"Lily?" a woman in pink scrubs called out.

Mom and I followed her to the hallway where the woman weighed me and checked my height. She escorted us into an office where she took my blood pressure and temperature, then asked me about a billion questions about my history with medication, most of which Mom answered.

Mom and I waited, side by side, facing an empty desk. After ten minutes, a smaller, older man bustled in.

"I'm Dr. *Grill*stein," he said, extending a hand to me across the table. He had brownish skin that looked like he'd undergone some sort of skin process that distributed the wrinkles evenly. The most impressive thing about him was his hair. Mostly black with a bone white streak at a left side part.

"Dr. *Krill*stein, this is Lily," Mom said.

"Dr. Frankenstein?" I said, not out of smart-assery, but because it was as close as I could get to his name. Okay, a little smart-assery. Dr. Brainguy. His new name.

"Lily!" Mom said.

Dr. Brainguy laughed.

"Well, that's the first time I've heard that. You must have read the book, Lily. Most kids think Frankenstein is the name of the monster, not the doctor who created him. Tell me, what was your favorite part of the novel?"

Easy question. I'd thought about this so much, but no one, besides Mrs. Rogers-Peña, had ever asked me. I liked Dr. Brainguy. He was actual human material.

"My favorite part is when the monster is watching the old blind man and his family, helping them, and then he kills a deer for them. And then when he finally comes out of hiding, they run from him. And he realizes that no matter what he does, he'll never be accepted for who he is."

Dr. Brainguy held two fingers to his lips and inhaled. I could swear he was sucking on an imaginary cigarette. He lowered his fingers and exhaled. And he looked at me like he could actually see me, not as some conduct-disordered kid off her meds, but a real thinking person.

"Pretty metaphorical, that," he said.

Mom frowned. I don't think this is what she expected. It wasn't what I expected either.

"I don't know much about this surgery. Could you tell us about it?" Mom asked.

"Yes, of course. Well, it is an experimental surgery, so you do have to understand that there are certain risks. Basically people who have ADHD have regions of the brain that remain chronically understimulated, regions that pertain to impulse control and self-regulation. So what we do is we electrically stimulate the part . . . *urgle* . . . cingulate cortex . . . normalized in . . . *screluar* drug therapy. While this is a new surgery, we use a device. . . . *plababble* responsive simulator . . . on the market . . . used for seizure disorder . . . so what we find with ADHD . . . *slibits* autonomic changes . . . expectation of an imminent challenge . . . determined attitude to overcome it. Stop me if you have questions."

I tried to follow what Dr. Brainguy was saying, I really did. If someone is going to peel your head open like an orange and plant electrodes there, you should do your best to listen. But I couldn't follow. I noticed there was a piece of wood on his desk with three small wooden dowels protruding from it. On one of the dowels was a set of five brass disks, stacked largest to smallest.

"Is the surgery reversible?" Mom asked.

"Yes," Dr. Brainguy responded. "But as with all surgery, there are—"

"What is that thing?" I asked, pointing to the game with the brass disks.

Mom sighed deeply.

"It's a game called Towers of Hanoi." Dr. Brainguy pushed it across the desk toward me. "You have to move all the disks from the first tower to the last, but you can't move more than one disk at a time, and you can only put smaller disks on larger disks. Do you understand the rules?"

I looked up.

"One disk at a time. No larger disks on smaller disks," I said.

I moved the smallest disk to the next pole and then the second smallest disk to the farther pole and then put the small disk on top of that one.

"So because this surgery is experimental, we really look for candidates who have exhausted all other options." Dr. Brainguy said. "Can you give me an outline of the drug therapies you've tried?"

My mother launched into a litany of all the drugs I'd ever been on, but I lost the thread of the conversation. There had been so many drugs.

"First there was the . . . she wasn't sleeping . . . then . . . took that one for two years," Mom said. "And it had side effects, but she didn't mind it."

"Yes I did," I said without looking up. "I was too young and stupid to know I could complain. I thought I had to take it."

"You always have to take drugs. Lily. It's just a given," Mom said. "I'm sorry that you have this condition, but really, we can't do anything about that, can we?"

"Well, except pry my brain open like a can of soup and stick a couple of electrodes in there. Maybe bolts in my neck?"

"Lily!"

I glanced away from the game and up at Mom. Her face was turning red. I realized that this whole visit probably sucked for her almost as much as for me. I wondered aimlessly how much the whole thing would cost.

"And the most recent drug?" Dr. Brainguy said softly. "What are . . . your dosage . . . side effects . . . you feeling about . . ."

I prepared to move a larger disk off, but both poles had smaller disks, so I had to backtrack.

"Lily," Mom said. "The doctor asked you a question."

I looked away from the Towers of Hanoi. Dr. Brainguy smiled.

"What about the drug you're on now? Do you always take it?"

Something about Dr. Brainguy's expression made me think he already knew the answer to this question.

"No." I laughed.

"Why not?"

"Well, for the first four or five months I was on the drug, things were okay, but then everything started to flatten out. After a while, I started to think, what's the point of any of this? Nothing tasted good; nothing made me happy; I didn't like reading or listening to music. The drug made me good at things I hated, and made me hate the things I liked, and I just thought—kill me now."

I pointed my finger at my temple and pulled an imaginary trigger before it came to me that this is the kind of thing you probably shouldn't do in front of a doctor. Or your mother.

"So how would you do it, if you killed yourself?" Dr. Brainguy asked.

"I used to have all my medicine in a jar under my bed—" I blurted it out before I could stop myself. I'd never really admitted to myself that I'd been saving my medicine for this purpose. I'd miss a day, and then I'd put the pill in the pickle jar, and sometimes I'd pull out the jar and hold the pile of pills in the palm of my hand. And it would give me a calm feeling to know that if things got too bad at school, unendurably bad, I could pull the ripcord. Handful of pills, swigs from the bottle of vodka Dad had left in my closet, and it would all be over.

"How do you feel now?" Dr. Brainguy asked.

"Fine," I said. "I stopped taking my drugs, and after a couple of weeks, the feeling went away."

"I didn't know," Mom said. It was a voice I'd never heard before. Regretful. I'd been telling her for months how much I hated the drugs. I'd thought she'd understood.

"Suicidal ideation is a common side effect of this drug," Dr. Brainguy said softly. "Treating ADHD with antidepressants is not without *sprigs,* but the important thing is that Lily is . . ."

Dr. Brainguy continued to say soothing things to Mom. I returned to the game. I'd managed to move most of the disks over to the end dowel using an ever-increasing number of steps, but about five steps from the end, I realized that I was going to end up with all the disks on the middle dowel, not the end one.

"Shit!" I said.

Dr. Brainguy laughed.

"You figured it out?"

"Do I have to retrace my steps, or can I start over?"

"Start over. Do you realize where you went wrong?"

I thought about it.

"It's a recursive pattern, like a fractal. The first move determines everything."

Dr. Brainguy smiled.

"You know about fractals," he said.

"My boyfriend is a math and robotics genius," I said. *Boyfriend.* My new favorite word.

"I imagine you have high theoretical mathematical ability yourself. You're probably hampered by low computational speed. These are the things we will want to test before we even consider the surgical option."

I finished the Tower of Hanoi while Mom and Dr. Brainguy talked about the hospital stay and insurance and testing and MRIs and how his research grant would cover most of the expense, which was nice. When he said that, I felt Mom relax.

And then I finished the puzzle.

"Ms. Michaels, would you mind if I talked to Lily alone for a minute?"

Mom stood reluctantly. I think she was worried that I would say all sorts of random Lily things to Dr. Brainguy and discourage him from doing the surgery.

He waited, puffing on an imaginary cigarette, until he heard the door to the waiting room open and close again.

"So, Lily, what do you think about all this?" he said finally.

"I don't know," I said, looking around at his diplomas, the bookcase behind him. "Does it really matter what I think?"

Dr. Brainguy knit his eyebrows and picked up the Towers of Hanoi.

"Do you know why I have this on my desk?" he said.

I shook my head, suddenly very interested.

"It's an informal test of sorts. I needed to see if you were capable of hyperfocus. Do you know what hyperfocus is?"

Hyperfocus. The ADHD superpower. The ability to work obsessively and without regard to the passage of time on something important, like searching a text for quotes to send my boyfriend. Impossible to use for unimportant tasks like paperwork or organization.

"Yeah, I do. So is that what you are going to zap out of my brain?"

Dr. Brainguy laughed.

"Hopefully not. That's the good part. So are you afraid of losing something if we do this surgery?"

I closed my eyes because I couldn't think. There was

something I needed to grab hold of, some essential part of me I didn't want to lose no matter what. Something the drugs took away.

"Okay, so you know, I have a lot of ideas, and when I'm on the drugs, they just kind of . . . disappear. Do you know what I mean? I get better at absorbing information because there's less going on inside my head, but when there is less going on inside my head . . . I mean, it's kind of like being . . . partially dead. I get that that's really dramatic, but I don't want part of my brain to die."

Dr. Brainguy smiled, but not in a condescending way.

"Okay, part of that is a side effect of some drugs, pure and simple. But you will change." He set the Towers of Hanoi back down on his desk. "This proves that you have high mathematical ability, so let me see if I can explain this like a math problem."

"Suppose you have thirty really original ideas in a week. And of those ideas, maybe five are really good, and perhaps one is superlative. And maybe it takes three weeks to develop that one really good idea, but in the meantime, two other really fantastic ideas have come along. What do you do? So you wanted to be a marine biologist because you had an idea worth exploring, but next week you change your major, and you're pulled in another direction entirely because you don't have the focus to pursue any one idea to its conclusion."

I couldn't help thinking about my father abandoning a brilliant, half-finished doctoral thesis about Hildegard von Bingen to go goat farming, which bored the shit out of him, and probably the other fifteen things he hadn't told me about. New family.

"You're talking about my dad," I said.

"ADHD runs in families," he said. "But you know that. There is this theory that asynchronicity leads to ideaphoria. It's an adaptive response to a deficit.

"So, if you do have this surgery, you may generate fewer ideas, but let's think about that. Let's say instead of thirty original ideas a week, you had ten. That would mean you had a really amazing important idea every third week. In the meantime, you'll be improving your self-regulation and impulse control, so when you have that really important big idea, you could run with it. You could go to college and have the focus to finish your course work. It's possible that with your test scores, you could qualify for early college enrollment."

Go to college? Right now? I hadn't allowed myself to think about college: reading novels with people who actually liked novels, long discussions about music and art and architecture and feminism and . . .

"How will I know which crazy ideas are really great and which crazy ideas are just crazy?" I asked.

Dr. Brainguy laughed. For a doctor, he did that a lot.

"If I could figure that one out, I'd be a billionaire," he said. "So, do you want to pursue this? Your mom isn't here. If you tell me no, that will be the end of it. She won't even know. I'll tell her you weren't a good candidate for the program. It's your brain, Lily. You have to make the decision."

College. I could go to college. I could take robotics or be a marine biologist, and if Dr. Brainguy was right, I would still feel things. Pleasure. Love.

"Yes," I said.

He called my mother back into the room. We talked some more and signed about a hundred papers. Mom and I went to a sushi bar for lunch and splurged. She drank sake, even though she had to go back to work. I think she was happy that I'd decided to have the procedure. And nervous. So was I.

CHAPTER 26

Mom went to school with me the next day. I had several appointments scheduled with Dr. Brainguy next week. I was going to miss a lot of school, and Mom wanted to let the office know the reason. Of course, I was more than happy to have a ready excuse to be out of school.

Mrs. Treviño led us into Vice Principal Krenwelge's office. Vice Principal Krenwelge had one of those curled, short haircuts that look like a wig from 1964. She was encased in a square-shouldered navy blue blazer and shiny, red button earrings.

"Ms. Michaels," she said, extending a hand. "Pleasure to see you again. And Lily."

We sat in two ancient green armchairs identical to the ones in the waiting area. Her desk held a picture of two toddler grandchildren so blond they were practically translucent.

"Thank you for making time for us," Mom said.

Mom had on her lucky jacket, a tan safari kind of thing that nipped in sweetly at the waist, over a white linen blouse. For once, she looked well rested, ready for a day of hunting antelope or taking on difficult meetings.

"What can I do for you?" Dr. Krenwelge asked.

"Well, as you know, Lily was absent yesterday. I'm afraid Lily has a number of medical tests coming up. She's probably going to miss a lot of school."

"Is there a problem?" Dr. Krenwelge asked quietly, her face clouded in genuine concern. I was kind of touched. It was always a shock to realize that people in the office actually cared about students. Aside from Mrs. Treviño, who oozes sympathetic concern from every pore.

"Lily is going in for brain surgery," Mom said solemnly. "It's a minor surgery, but—"

"Of course, anything we can do to make things easier on you both." Dr. Krenwelge looked for a moment like she might start weeping, and I felt bad. She probably thought I had a tumor or something. "We'll make arrangements for homework and makeup tests. Whatever you need."

We all observed a moment of silence in anticipated memory of my soon-to-be-surgically-altered brain. For a second, I wondered if I actually did have a tumor.

"Oh, one more thing," Mom said. "Lily failed geography the last six-week period because she made a zero on her Populations in Peril project. Her project and paper are in the hall. I think Lily did a wonderful job, but she didn't quite follow the directions. The thing is, it states very clearly on her 504 accommodations for dyslexia that she needs oral instructions. I don't think Mr. Neuwirth gave her oral instructions."

"Her 504 accommodations? I don't have any accommodations on record."

"They should be on record," Mom said, her voice rising. "We had an exit meeting when Lily left middle school."

"Excuse me for a moment."

Vice Principal Krenwelge turned toward her laptop and typed furiously. She picked up the phone—an ugly beige landline phone the size of a shoebox, punched in a number, and spoke to someone. I didn't actually pay attention to what she was saying, but she seemed annoyed. I had on a short skirt and my thighs were sticking to the strange green chair. I needed to move, but the phone call dragged on. Dr. Krenwelge shook her head and sighed loudly.

"Mrs. Michaels-Ryan—"

"Just Michaels," Mom said.

"Of course. The district changed software last year, and we've had a few glitches. Lily's middle school swears they sent her 504 over, but we never received anything. They are going to email Lily's exit exam. I'm sorry for the mixup."

"Really? A mixup?" Mom said in a tone of voice that made me actually feel a little sorry for Dr. Krenwelge. I've been on the receiving end of that tone before. Not fun.

"Don't worry, I'll talk to Mr. Neuwirth," Dr. Krenwelge said in a voice that suggested she and Coach Neuwirth would sit down over tea and scones, and agree with all civility and due speed that a grave injustice had been done to my person.

Everyone—Rosalind, Mom, Mrs. Rogers-Peña, even Humberto the *Star Trek* therapist—had suggested that I invoke my 504 accommodations at regular intervals. But I had no idea that the phrase "504 accommodations" was a magical spell I could cast that would cause unicorns and rainbows to issue forth from the sky. No idea at all.

I still didn't want to talk about it with my teachers. I mean, who does? But it could come in handy if I really got into trouble.

"There's also chemistry," Mom said. "Lily failed chemistry because—"

"Please don't worry. I'll be talking to all of her teachers. We'll need to set up a 504 meeting next week. Is it possible for you to come in before school?" Dr. Krenwelge rose from her desk.

"Yes." Mom stood.

Dr. Krenwelge reached for the door.

"I'll be in touch. So nice finally meeting you, Ms. Michaels. And, Lily, a pleasure. I . . ." Dr. Krenwelge stammered, and her voice caught in her throat. "I wish you the best of luck with your procedure. Please keep me informed."

Mom and I walked together out of the office. She stopped at my Populations in Peril project. Most people had already picked up their projects, but I'd forgotten mine. My project was looking much worse for the wear. All but two of the bloated corpses were gone, and someone had pulled out one of the stilts, sending my hut sliding into the fake water and mud. If anything, the repeated vandalism of my project only added to the pathos of the scene.

"You never should have failed this project," she whispered. "Total bullshit."

Mom never swears unless she's really angry. Guess she was that angry.

She picked up my Populations in Peril project and my paper and left. I watched her go, wondering why she wasn't this much of a badass all the time.

Before lunch I stopped by robotics to wave at Abelard from the doorway. He was busy, and he didn't seem to notice me. And so I watched as he lifted a wheel assembly to the work surface in a swift, assured move, like he'd been building robots all his life and didn't even have to think about it. His hair curled around his ears and the straps of his protective glasses. He was wearing a gray T-shirt old enough to be really thin and a little small and that clung to his broad shoulders and chest. I stood in the doorway and watched him, and I realized that I could stand there watching Abelard forever.

He was beautiful, and he belonged to me. My boyfriend.

I met Rosalind at our normal spot for lunch. Middle of May and sweltering hot at noon. Like summer anywhere else but Texas. The courtyard crowd had definitely thinned out.

"Should we go to the cafeteria?" I suggested.

"We could go eat in the theater," Rosalind replied.

"Absolutely not. You'll just go back to working." It was the day before opening night, and Rosalind was spending most of her free time in the theater. It was a wonder she actually made it to classes. "Speaking of work, we should stay out of the theater until dress rehearsal tonight. Do you want to go have an iced mocha after school?"

"I can't. Richard and I are going to walk to the taco truck and hang out with a couple of his friends."

Rosalind didn't look at me. It has always been my job to distract Rosalind before dress rehearsal and opening night.

"Is that all right?" she asked.

"Of course," I replied. Because—love. It's not like I don't know. But it still felt weird.

"I saw your mother leaving school. What was she doing here?"

Brain surgery. I hadn't told Rosalind about the brain surgery. I didn't want to tell her. Not right before a performance, anyway.

"So apparently, the school never got my 504 accommodations from our middle school," I said. "Dr. Krenwelge is ever so sorry."

"She is?" Rosalind raised an eyebrow. Dr. Krenwelge is not sorry for much.

"Yes. She's going to have a 'talk' with Coach Neuwirth."

"Well," Rosalind said. "A talk."

"Well, indeed."

I stayed after school for tech rehearsal. I had a little money, so I walked to a neighborhood coffee shop and had a mocha and a bagel and read in peace before rehearsal. Nice.

Mr. Turner thanked me for showing up to theater and then made me promise to wear all black, no white on my shoes this time. There was very little stage arrangement, mostly just moving a desk and a couch back and forth, so I managed to break away at seven and text Abelard briefly.

"Lily?"

"Abelard. I'm backstage at the theater. I'm working tech. Not sure how long I can talk."

I'd put my phone on silent, so I had to stare at the screen.

"Alors tant pis!"

Tant pis—"too bad" in French.

"Indeed," I sent back. *"Suppose we couldn't take that trip to Portland. What would we do?"*

"It doesn't matter. As long as we are together."

"Really?" I texted.

"We could both go to the Isaac Institute. They have an early college program."

College. With Abelard. It was not something I would've dared to dream about, but Dr. Brainguy had almost convinced me that college was a possibility. Maybe he could even write me a recommendation. A whole world of fantasy scrolled through my brain: the two of us at college, strolling down a tree-lined campus, studying medieval texts in a library, kicking leaves and laughing, images culled from a website somewhere. And then another image, a distinctly unbrochure-like image of us alone in a dorm room. Low lights, soft sheets. Bed.

"OK," I texted.

Mr. Turner signaled me from the curtain.

CHAPTER 27

I didn't text Abelard for the rest of the week. It was torture. After catching me with my phone, Mr. Turner had told me to keep it out of the backstage area. Abelard was busy getting ready for the regional robotics competition. We were both busy.

Rosalind's parents came opening night to see the play. So did Mom and Iris. I met them in the lobby at intermission. We all agreed that Rosalind was a great actress. Iris was deeply impressed with her costume, a little green velvet shrug over a pale green floating floral dress. Glamorous. With her hair in a stylized thirties wave, false eyelashes, and bright lips, Rosalind looked less like a twelve-year-old than I'd ever seen her.

Richard was working the stage, too. Like me, he was dressed all in black. I'd catch him in the wings watching Rosalind twirl across the stage, effusing about being madly in love, which is what her character does. And it was as though it was all for him.

Sunday after the last matinee performance, I stayed to

help break down the set. Rosalind's parents were there. I think they came to every performance. They hung out in the theater near the orchestra pit until Rosalind came out from backstage in her street clothes, still wearing the makeup and eyelashes. Richard and I were pulling apart a riser with a claw hammer and a crowbar when Rosalind approached.

"Come meet my parents," she said, holding out her hand, inflecting her voice in exactly the same way her character in the play had compelled her dreamy boyfriend to meet her eccentric parents. Life echoes art. "Come on, Lily. You too."

We trudged down the steps. Richard extended a hand, looking at once serious and awkward. Introductions all around.

"Richard is a great artist. You should go see his portrait of Rosalind," I said. "It's in a glass case by the office."

Sometimes a work of art is so good, so inspired, that the art teachers don't want to leave it on the walls to face the kind of standard asshat vandalism that my FCP endured. Once in a very rare while, they whisk a meaningful piece of art to the glass-enclosed cases in full view of office security. Richard's portrait of Rosalind was such a work. It would be hanging in a museum someday. Pretty sure.

Rosalind's dad lifted an eyebrow. Apparently my endorsement was worth something.

"Yes, go do that," Rosalind said, drifting closer to Richard. "I'm going to the after party."

She looped a hand around Richard's arm, and he smiled reflexively.

Rosalind's mother looked down at Rosalind's hand, snaking down to hold Richard's hand. Another minute and they'd be making out right here in front of everyone.

"Okay, Lily is staying too, right?" Rosalind's mom said in a high voice. "I'm sure she needs a ride home."

Rosalind looked at me beseechingly. I was her only chance to sneak off into the unknown recesses of the theater with Richard. I hadn't planned to stay for the after party. I'd planned to go home and sit by my cell and wait for Abelard. But I guessed I could text Abelard in the theater as well as I could at home.

"Sure," I said.

Richard had his arm around Rosalind's waist by the time they left. They kissed each other delicately in full view of the stage. I had a moment of jealousy. Negotiating a physical relationship with Abelard would never be that easy. But then, he was Abelard. I would never want anyone else.

At seven, I took a break from tear-down, which was almost done anyway. I dropped into a seat in the middle of the theater and pulled out my cell.

"Are you there, Lily?" he had texted.

"Abelard. I've missed you terribly."

"And I you. It's been too long."

"Eons," I texted back. *"Weeks at least."*

"Months."

"Years. Time has ceased to have meaning."

"Then let this separation of our persons more firmly unite our minds," he texted.

I'd left my copy of *The Letters of Abelard and Heloise* at home, so I didn't have a retort. Note to self: Bring copy of book everywhere.

"How was the robotics competition?" I asked.

"We came in second."

"Congratulations."

"We expected to win," he texted back.

"Condolences. Did the winning robot crush your robot within its steely jaw?"

"No, it did not."

"Push your robot over the edge of the cliffs of despair into a bottomless lake of lava?"

"Not that kind of robot," he texted back.

"Don't leave me in suspense. How did their robot destroy your robot?"

There was a pause before Abelard texted me back. I looked up at the stage. Pretty much bare. A couple of people were pulling the big wallpaper backdrop into the wings.

My phone buzzed.

"I love you, Lily. In spite of your disturbing obsession with robot violence."

"I love you too, Abelard."

"I'm leaving town in a few days," he texted. Suddenly. Abruptly.

The pit of my stomach dropped ominously. Someone laughed backstage. The sound reverberated, ghostly in the empty theater. Most people had congregated in the greenroom. It was a weird time to leave. Finals were next week.

"OK." It was all I could think to write. What did this mean, leaving?

"It won't be long."

"Will you be back next weekend? I want to see you."

Okay, now I just sounded desperate and needy. Don't be desperate. Don't act like this is a big thing, because it isn't.

"I don't know. Maybe," he replied. Less than reassuring.

"We could see a movie next weekend. Or play chess."

"Yes."

"OK," I texted back. The end of our conversation.

CHAPTER 28

Abelard and I talked every night for the next couple of days. But we didn't talk about where he was going or what he was doing.

On Wednesday, he left. Abelard was traveling with his parents. Wherever Abelard was, I hoped he was not being tortured by strange smells and odd food. I hoped he was not on an airplane.

I was out of my normal routine as well. I spent much of the week doing tests in Dr. Brainguy's office. I did the Stroop Effect test, where they give you the word *blue* in red ink and ask you to name the color of the word, because apparently having ADHD is a lot like being on Everest above twenty thousand feet. I talked to a very nice psychologist and told a stone-faced graduate student named Karen what was missing from the picture of the barn, what was missing from the duck, what was missing from the boy. I did puzzles, and, ironically, filled out a million bubble sheet tests. I had an MRI, and I was signed up for a SPECT and a full physical with my pediatrician and an EEG and an EKG. I think Dr. Brainguy invented tests just for me.

Friday. I was sitting in the waiting room between tests, reading *Anna Karenina* with only half my brain. It was the only practical piece of advice my father had given me: Read *Anna Karenina*. But I couldn't stop thinking about Abelard, out in the world, traveling to some distant location with his parents.

I couldn't stop thinking about him.

And while I was thinking, my phone buzzed in the way that could only mean one thing: Abelard.

I shoved *Anna Karenina* into my backpack and dug around for *The Letters of Abelard and Heloise*, and my pen and notebook. I still had a few good quotes I'd recorded but hadn't used, lovely things about his superlative intellect and a few choice bits about his poise and bearing and dress, because apparently the original Peter Abelard was pretty hot as well.

I had something saved for when he finally did text.

"Lily?"

"Abelard," I texted back. *"I have made it an observation, since our absence, that we are much fonder of the pictures of those we love, when they are at a great distance, than when they are near to us."* Heloise's words.

No answer.

"You have given me great opportunity to love that picture." My words. And a playful reminder that he hadn't texted me for a day or two. Honestly, though, I didn't care. I was just glad to hear from him.

I skimmed the book, and my eyes lit on a passage full of longing and despair. There's actually a lot of this in *The Letters of Abelard and Heloise*. It's not really a happy story. I circled the passage aimlessly, drew little stars around the edge because the words were beautiful, if tragic.

"My dad finished grading papers and decided we should go on vacation."

"Really?" That was sudden. *"Two weeks before finals?"*

"I only have one final. It's take-home."

No finals. It figured. Most teachers tell you that you don't have to take the final in AP classes if your grade is high enough.

"Where are you?"

"New Mexico."

My stomach did the late-day flip-flop, even though I wasn't on drugs. New Mexico. But Abelard didn't like to travel. I waited.

"I'm at the Isaac Institute," he texted.

"Wow!" I texted back. A stupid text that meant nothing. Just a chance to make sense of Abelard at a school in New Mexico. Funny. I'd imagined the Isaac Institute was in Austin, just across town. It had never occurred to me that it was someplace else.

"I got accepted," he texted.

"When do you start?"

"In June. But they want me to stay for a two-week orientation session before the start of classes."

"So, now?"

"Yes," he replied.

This couldn't be it. No. He had to come back. Abelard had to come back.

"What about the end of the semester? Don't you have to finish school?"

"Mom arranged it with Dr. Krenwelge. I just have to email my final."

Why did Dr. Krenwelge have to be so understanding? So helpful?

I had a sudden memory of the last moment I saw Abelard. Abelard in the robotics lab the moment before he saw me: the way his shoulders sloped down to his narrow waist, the intense look of focus on his amazing face. And I realized that moment now belonged firmly to the age of dinosaurs and medieval lovers, and soon the memory of his smell would be gone, and all I would have left was the picture that Richard drew of Abelard.

Over.

And it hurt. Not a metaphorical my-heart-pains-me-so-and-I-think-I-have-the-vapors feeling, but a real dizzy, nauseous I-might-throw-up-on-the-pale-green-carpet-or-stop-breathing feeling. Strange.

"I've been on the waiting list for three years," Abelard texted. *"I was up before, but Mom didn't want me to go."*

"But now she does?" I texted back numbly.

"Not really. But she agreed to it."

I put the phone down and frantically searched the book for a passage that would make sense of everything. After all, Abelard and Heloise were separated by a great distance, and they still managed to write. I searched for a passage . . . but nothing came. I kept returning to the same paragraph over and over, the one about loss and pain that I'd circled and starred. Lines that taunted me, because love is about sacrifice and suffering.

I had this picture of Abelard in my mind, a horrible image that I'd pushed out of my brain because it was awkward and uncomfortable. Abelard at twenty-five, still living with his parents, his mother washing his clothes and cooking him breakfast and treating him like he was still ten years old. His mother, arranging his social schedule like playdates in the park. His mother, interrupting every moment alone.

And yet, Mrs. Mitchell had agreed to let him go. Abelard might not have another chance to escape the gravitational pull of his family.

"Awesome!! You should totes go!!" I texted. Plus happy face, surprised emojis. Maybe I was laying it on thick. I didn't think I'd ever said "totes" before to anyone.

"Lily?" he texted. Clearly, Abelard was not convinced.

Hard to see my phone. Big fat sloppy tears clouded my eyes. I put my palms over my face to stop them from coming, because I'd already attracted the notice of the receptionist with my sniffling. I stayed there with my hands over my eyes until I heard my phone purr into life.

"Lily, I won't go. Not without you."

"Yes you will," I texted back.

I couldn't find a Heloise response that made sense. I kept returning to the same passage over and over, like a reproach. His next message came before I could find an answer.

"We commonly die to the affections of those whom we see no more, and they to ours: absence is the tomb of love. But to me, absence is an unquiet remembrance of what I love, which continually torments me."

"Stop it, Abelard," I murmured.

It was killing me to think of him at the perfect school somewhere in the mountains of New Mexico, where he would take college courses and live in a dorm and have teachers who understood him, and he'd be surrounded by smart, like-minded girls who would see only his beauty and natural brilliance. It was killing me to think I would be here alone with a hole in my head, a little piece of my soul gone, love and purpose and meaning all fled. It was killing me to think that there was a right and a wrong thing to do. Right for Abelard was wrong for me, and wrong for Abelard was right for me. And nothing made sense except that love is sacrifice and pain. He needed to go to that school. It was all he'd ever wanted.

Before me.

I had to let him go. Because pain. Our world together was too golden, too perfect to last.

I knew how to make Abelard enroll in the Isaac Institute. Me and Dad, living the dream in Portland. Abelard would believe that.

"I'm moving to Portland," I typed.

I hit Send.

And then, instantly, I wanted to take it back. Why did I tell Abelard I was moving to Portland? Why did I lie to him?

"Portland?" he texted. *"You're moving?"*

It was too late to tell the truth. Some lies are just too big to retract.

"Yes," I replied.

Silence. Minutes passed, and I wept. I couldn't help it. A woman sitting with a twitchy middle grade boy pushed a box of Kleenex toward me and moved away like I was emotionally disturbed.

It took forever for Abelard to text back. I imagined him sitting on a bench under swaying pine trees on a mountain campus, staring at his phone, trying to make sense of me moving to Portland to become an organic farmer.

"When do you leave?" he texted finally.

"Next week," I texted. Random. The time that popped into my mind.

"Lily?" the nurse called.

I had my book clutched in my hand. As I stood my phone buzzed, and I looked down to see his final text.

"I love you."

I didn't have time to text him back before I went back to see Dr. Brainguy. Just as well.

The nurse didn't take me to Dr. Brainguy's office, or the bare room where I did the majority of my tests. She took me to the small room with couches and multiple Kleenex boxes where I'd met with the psychologist.

I sat on the couch, *The Letters of Abelard and Heloise* clasped tightly to my chest. I tried to stop crying. Really.

The doctor entered and sat in the office chair next to the desk.

"Hey, Dr. Ferbenstein," I said, trying to sound cheery. Trying and failing.

"Dr. Ferbenstein? Lily, you might as well call me Dr. Doofenshmirtz," he said. "It's Dr. Brillstein."

I smiled weakly. I had to admire Dr. Brainguy for the *Phineas and Ferb* reference, but really, I wasn't in the mood.

"How about you tell me what's up," he said.

"Oh, nothing. Just chilling out in your waiting room."

Dr. Brainguy leaned across a small glass coffee table

that held a tissue box covered with gentle wave patterns, and he inhaled through two fingers. I guessed he really needed a smoke.

"Lily, this kind of experimental surgery is a partnership between doctor and patient. And because this involves your brain and your emotional responses, I really need to know what you are feeling and thinking. If you have concerns about the surgery, it's important—"

"Oh, it's not that. It's just, well, it's just my boyfriend."

Dr. Brainguy exhaled and leaned back in his chair. I expected him to get on with his busy day because—teenage girl, boy troubles, mystery solved. But he didn't leave. He waited. Clearly, I was going to have to tell Dr. Brainguy a little bit more.

"Okay, so my boyfriend has Asperger's or some sort of processing delay. I don't really know his diagnosis. I guess it's ND. Neurodifferent, right?"

"This is the young man with the interest in fractals? What's his name?"

"Abelard," I replied.

"Quite a name," Dr. Brainguy said.

"Well, his father is a medieval history professor. Which is weird, because my father was one of Abelard's father's graduate students before Dad decided to move to Portland and become a goat farmer, which isn't even a thing he's doing . . ." I shook my head. Best not to talk about my father. "So basically, we've both read *The Letters of Abelard and Heloise,* and we started texting each other quotes from the letters, and then we started seeing each other . . ."

Most people have trouble following a Lily story, the kind of oral narrative that should have footnotes, but Dr. Brainguy appeared to be listening. Really listening.

"Was that difficult?" he asked. "Attempting a physical relationship?"

There was something so straightforward and honest about Dr. Brainguy, I didn't even feel like blushing. Talking about my sex life with my brain surgeon should have been all kinds of awkward, but surprisingly, no.

"We were working on it."

"Were? Did something happen?"

"Abelard is in New Mexico with his parents at this place called the Isaac Institute."

"Oh yes, the Isaac Institute," Dr. Brainguy said. "Quite a waiting list to get in."

"Abelard just got accepted."

"Ahh. So what did you tell him?" Dr. Brainguy ran a hand through his hair, ruffling his white streak.

"Awesome, dude! You should totes go!" I said bitterly, and for some reason, repeating these lines started me crying again.

"'Totes'? That's a far cry from quotes from *The Letters of Abelard and Heloise.* Doesn't sound much like you."

I looked up. "Abelard didn't think so either. He said he

wouldn't go to the school without me. 'Absence is the tomb of love,' he said."

I clutched the book tighter to my chest. Shut my eyes to keep the tears at bay.

"So to get him to go, I told him that I was moving to Portland to live with my dad on his organic farm. My dad doesn't even have a farm. He has a new family, and he doesn't really want me there because . . ."

I couldn't continue because—weeping. Embarrassed that I'd told Dr. Brainguy that my father didn't want me and that he would now go back to his office and write "unloved by father" on my chart. I'm sure he would conclude that all of my problems with boys and half the problems with my brain were due to an uncertain paternal attachment.

Dr. Brainguy watched me weep. Maybe he was trying to decide if all this messy emotion made me a bad test case. Or maybe he was thinking that he might need to shove the electrodes in deeper and up the voltage. I didn't care either way. My brain seemed massively unimportant at this particular moment.

Dr. Brainguy reached over and gently lifted the book from my hand and began reading the passage I'd circled and starred.

> *You cannot but remember (for what do not lovers remember?) with what pleasure I have passed whole days in hearing your discourse. How, when you*

were absent, I shut myself from everyone to write to you; how uneasy I was till my letter had come to your hands; what artful management it required to engage confidence. This detail, perhaps, surprises you, and you are in pain for what will follow. But I am no longer ashamed that my passion has had no bounds for you; for I have done more than all this: I have hated myself that I might love you; I came hither to ruin myself in a perpetual imprisonment, that I might make you live quiet and easy.

"Well," he said.

I heard Dr. Brainguy set the book down on the coffee table. He shifted in his chair and sighed. I didn't care if he was thinking that he might have to throw me out of the program because—emotional basket case. I didn't care about anything. Really.

"Lily," he said softly, "this probably won't help you, but if I had a child on the autistic spectrum, I would move heaven and hell to get them into the Isaac Institute."

He stood to leave the room. At the door, he stopped and turned.

"Your boyfriend is a lucky young man."

CHAPTER 29

Life just goes on, which is kind of stupid. I wished that I could put myself in suspended animation for a couple of weeks, just until I could think about something else besides Abelard. In a way, I was looking forward to the surgery because I had been warned that the anesthesia would leave me feeling groggy and disoriented. It might take several days of fine adjustment of the voltage levels on my responsive neurostimulation device before I felt quite like myself. I looked forward to a few days of feeling not quite like myself, because feeling like me sucked right now.

Things were better in school. I don't throw the term "ironic" around lightly, but sometimes it fits. Now that I was close to being done with school forever, everything was sunshine and roses and rainbow unicorns. Coach Neuwirth called me to his desk before a test and asked me if I needed extra time or a quiet place to work. He was actually kind of nice. It was disconcerting.

On Thursday, Mrs. Rogers-Peña handed back our

Macbeth papers. Mine had a *99* on top, plus a smiley face with stars on it and a Post-it note with the words *come talk to me about this.* I wondered why the Post-it note. I didn't have long to wonder. She called me over after class.

"Great paper, Lily," she said. "You should save this for your portfolio."

Mrs. Rogers-Peña had gotten new glasses. They were extra thick and chunky black, like she was planning on playing a scientist on TV.

"Portfolio?"

"Some colleges ask for writing samples. This one is stellar. You should save it."

"College," I replied. I should have guessed. Mrs. Rogers-Peña was always college this and college that. Frankly, I didn't mind, especially now that Dr. Brainguy had led me to believe that college was in my imminent future.

"Are you all right, Lily? You seem a little—down."

I was tired of concealing the truth from everyone. I was tired of keeping the loneliness and sadness inside my head. I hadn't even told Rosalind about Abelard, because I didn't want to rain on her happy new love parade.

"Abelard moved away," I said. "I guess we broke up."

"You and Abelard? I didn't know you were a couple." Mrs. Rogers-Peña paused. I could tell she was curious but didn't want to say anything indiscreet. Curiosity won out. "How did that happen?"

"Well, after you asked me to apologize to him, we

started texting each other quotes from *The Letters of Abelard and Heloise* because we've both read it. Weird, I know, but his father was my father's graduate advisor. Anyway, he got a chance to go to an early college program for people with Asperger's, and so . . ."

I stopped. Tears welled in my eyes. I struggled to pull them back in. Cardinal rule number one for all circus freaks: Never cry in school. The blowback will be relentless.

"I'm sorry, Lily," she said. "Though I'm glad for Abelard. Have you thought about a long-distance relationship?"

I shrugged. For all our talk, it was the feel of Abelard's arms around me that kept me going. He calmed me. I didn't know if I could stay focused if I knew we could never be together.

"I wanted more," I said.

Abelard and I hadn't talked since I'd told him I was moving to Portland. I was reading the last chapters of *Anna Karenina* when the soft whir of the phone announced Abelard's text. I hesitated. Maybe Abelard had come back from New Mexico. I'd have to tell him that I hadn't moved to Portland after all, which would probably necessitate another awkward lie, but then everything would go back to the way it was meant to be. Abelard would invite me to come over on Saturday, and maybe his mom would be out and we'd be alone for the whole afternoon . . .

"Lily?"

"Abelard."

Iris looked up from her homework. "Is that Abelard?"

"Yes." I stared at my phone, texting slowly as though issuing a magic spell that would reverse everything that had gone before. "Why do you ask?"

"What's up? Are you still in New Mexico?"

"It's just that he hasn't talked to you in a while." She dropped her feet over the edge of the bed and leaned over to watch me text.

My phone buzzed with Abelard's next message.

"Yes. I'm in New Mexico."

Iris read the text upside down before I could pull my phone away.

"Oh my god. Abelard is in New Mexico?" she shrieked. "Lily, what are you going to do?" she asked.

"I was thinking of getting a couple of holes drilled in my head, just for fun."

Iris looked like she was going to cry. I felt bad. Maybe she was worried that something could go wrong with the surgery, worried that she'd find herself alone in this room come summer. My tendency to blurt out alarming stuff was probably reason enough to have a couple of holes drilled in my head.

"Don't worry about it, okay, Iris?" I said. "It's not a big deal. The doctor says so."

She wiped her eyes with the back of her hand. Sometimes Iris seems like she's twenty-two, so I'm always surprised that she believes pretty much everything I say.

"So what are you going to say to Abelard?" she asked. "Do you want me to look through *The Letters of Abelard and Heloise* for a quote that—"

"No," I shot back. Abelard and I were done with lovely prose, done with lavish statements of unending affection. Over, so quickly. I picked up my phone.

"How is school?"

"Excellent. They have an awesome robotics lab here. Better than the one at school. There's a girl on my floor who reminds me of you. She's funny and well-read."

A girl. So soon, another girl. I pressed the phone to my chest. In my mind suddenly this new girl was Emma Stone: funny and gorgeous with glowing green eyes and strawberry blond hair, and madly in love with Abelard because how could you not be?

"Cool," I replied.

"Are you there?"

"Where?" I texted back.

"Portland."

Portland. I was supposed to be in Portland, living a magically special life with my father.

"Yes. It's just like Austin. Only: goats. And rain."

"It's hard for me to text at seven. My schedule is different. I'm still getting used to it," he texted.

Different schedule. Was this Abelard's way of telling me that he would rather be hanging out with the funny girl with the strawberry blond hair in the tricked-out computer lab than texting me? It hurt too much to contemplate.

"Maybe we should call a moratorium on texting for a while," I wrote back.

Abelard didn't answer for a long time. A very long time. And then finally: *"Are you talking about breaking up?"*

"IDK, do you want to break up?" I sent back.

An even longer pause.

"Do you want to break up with me?"

A thousand thoughts careened through my mind about how hard it would be to keep up the façade of Portland, of tending organic goats, or pretending to be happy every time he mentioned another girl, and how I was sort of terrified that I would awaken from surgery another person entirely, and how much I wanted to be with Abelard, to touch him, and that was never going to happen, and it all hurt too much.

"Yes. I want to break up with you."

"What happened?" Iris asked.

"The end."

CHAPTER 30

Saturday. Iris told Mom that Abelard and I broke up. Iris was kind to me. Mom was kind to me. They both spoke in soft voices, stopped talking when I entered the room. It was more than I could take. I fled to Rosalind's house. Mom gave me a ride.

"I broke up with Abelard," I said, standing on her doorstep. Not even waiting for that moment when we were alone, not caring that her mother was hovering nearby, listening.

"I didn't want to break up with him, but he had a chance to go to a really good early college program for people with Asperger's, only he didn't want to leave me, so I told him that I was going to live on a farm with my dad and raise goats, and also, I'm going to have brain surgery two weeks from Monday—"

"Your father lives on a farm now?" Rosalind's mother asked.

"No," I said. "I think he spent a couple of weeks on a farm once."

Rosalind opened the door to let me in. Richard sat on the couch looking uncomfortable. I was screwing up a date. Rosalind had a social life now.

"Hi, Richard," I said, waving awkwardly. I turned back to Rosalind. "You're busy. I should go."

"Nonsense, Lily," Rosalind's mom said. "These two were just going to watch a movie. You're welcome to join."

"Mom," Rosalind said, "maybe you could make us some nice, soothing tea?"

"Tea?" Rosalind's mother said. "I'll make a chai with almond milk. And bring out some cookies."

Rosalind's mother scurried to make tea and find the cookies, although what she considered a cookie was more like some kind of compressed fruit and nut thing rolled in unsweetened cacao nibs. Like all the food in her house, the cookies weren't bad as long as you divorced them from the idea of the real thing.

"I should go," I whispered. "And leave you and Richard alone."

"Too late for that." Rosalind rolled her eyes in the direction of the kitchen. "We were going to go to a movie, but Mom wanted us to stay in. She gave me some stupid excuse about a storm moving this way and driving at night in the rain."

I followed Rosalind into the living room and sat in an armchair. Rosalind sat next to Richard.

"Did you say brain surgery?" Rosalind asked, fire in her voice.

"Should I go?" Richard said. "I could walk around outside for a minute."

"No, it's fine," I replied.

"Once again, brain surgery?" Rosalind repeated, a little louder this time.

"It's just a small device that they're going to implant in my brain."

"Okay, so nothing important, then," Rosalind said. "When is this non-important brain surgery happening?"

"In a couple of weeks."

"In a couple of weeks?" She raised an eyebrow, pausing for dramatic effect. "You're going to have brain surgery in a couple of weeks? So this is why you've been absent so much. When were you planning on telling me this?"

"I don't know." I rolled my head toward Rosalind. Ever since my breakup with Abelard, even small movements, like forcing my neck to hold up my head, seemed to require too much energy.

"So if you don't like having a chip in your brain, can you have it removed?"

"Supposedly," I said. "Look, it's not that big a deal. I didn't come here to—"

"Not that big a deal? I'm your best friend. We're supposed to tell each other everything."

"You've been busy with . . . theater." I glanced at Richard.

"Not that busy," she said.

Richard twitched uncomfortably. Maybe we should have released him from the conversation.

"Look, I just wanted to tell you about Abelard. I shouldn't have come over to bring you down with tales of my unrequited love."

I stood to leave, but at that moment Rosalind's mother returned with the three cups of tea and a plateful of cookies.

Richard accepted a cup of tea but politely passed on the cookies. Apparently, he had been subjected to her "cookies" before.

"Unrequited love?" Rosalind's mom headed for the DVDs. "Do you know what you need, Lily? Bette Davis and a big box of tissues, that's what you need."

Rosalind rolled her eyes, but I was fine with it. I wasn't in the mood for any more madcap comedies, and I certainly wasn't in the mood to talk about my brain anymore. Arguing with Rosalind took too much effort.

Rosalind turned all the lights off so she and Richard could make out discreetly without being observed, which was also fine with me. Rosalind's mom came in every fifteen minutes or so, basically to make sure that Rosalind and Richard hadn't escaped to Rosalind's bedroom. On one of these trips, she left a box of tissues in front of me. I guess she knew what to expect.

We watched *Now, Voyager.* I liked the movie right away. The guy who played the doctor, Claude Rains, reminded me of Dr. Brainguy: small and tidy, a little snarky, his sharp eyes on the world, figuring out the dynamic of everybody and everything.

About the time Paul Henreid's character finds the note pinned to the back of Bette Davis's cape, and she freaks out and tells him that she's fat and old and kind of crazy, and that no one has ever loved her, or ever will, and he just smiles and hands her his handkerchief, I lost it. Maybe because I spent most of grade school with some kind of note pinned to my shirt, and I know that nothing in the world is more humiliating than having a note pinned to your shirt.

But it was more than that. Love is about being broken beyond repair in the eyes of the world and finding someone who thinks you're just fine. More than fine, that you are special and precious because you understand how it feels to be broken and you have a real human heart.

Like Abelard.

I wept. And Rosalind didn't say anything to me because she is my best friend in all the world. Plus, she was busy discreetly making out with Richard.

After the movie, I felt a little better, good enough to face Iris and Mom again. I gave Mom a call. Ten minutes later, she tapped the horn lightly. Rosalind followed me to the door. Mom waited in her car parked by the curb.

"It was good seeing you, Richard," I said.

"You too, Lily," he replied. Richard wandered over to the built-in bookshelves and pretended to be absorbed in studying a particularly ugly piece of burnt orange pottery that Rosalind's mom adored. It matched the room.

Rosalind stood by the open door with arms folded across her chest, a stern look on her face.

"I'm not sure the surgery is such a good idea," she said.

"You don't have to worry," I said. "It'll be fine."

"But I do worry. Someone has to look out for you."

Bells and whistles went off. Rosalind—always looking out for me. I saw the truth that had been before me all the time. The one person who'd always thought I was right in the head didn't think I was so right after all.

"You put me on suicide watch, didn't you?" I asked.

She looked away.

"I'm sorry, Lily."

I shook my head. It didn't make sense. Rosalind, of all people.

My mother honked the horn again, and I bolted for the car.

CHAPTER 31

Two Saturdays before my surgery, Mom gave me money to have fun with my friends. I spent the day with Rosalind and Richard, walking up and down Congress Avenue. Since we were supposed to be having presurgical fun, I'd decided not to mention suicide watch to Rosalind. Talking about suicide and surgery—not fun.

Rosalind hadn't brought up surgery or suicide watch either, but there was an awkwardness that hung between us.

Maybe things were different with Richard around.

We went to St. Vincent de Paul's; to Sfanthor, the sci-fi castle; and over to Lucy in Disguise to try on wigs and military jackets. There was a surf band playing behind one of the vintage stores, and we watched for a while.

"Have you ever been to Hey Cupcake!?" I asked.

Richard shook his head.

"Then I have to buy you both a Whipper Snapper," I replied.

"What's a Whipper Snapper?" he asked.

"A cupcake filled with whipped cream. It's the best."

"Like Pingüinos?" he said.

Pingüinos, the snack cakes they sold at the convenience store down the street from us, like Hostess cupcakes, chocolate with creme—whatever creme was.

"Better," I said.

"You don't have to buy us a cupcake," Rosalind said a little wearily. Both she and Richard looked like they were ready to be done with my adventure.

"Whipper Snappers, and then we'll go," I said. "Come on, cupcakes are essential to my presurgery best-day-ever! montage."

"Will a cupcake really make you that happy?" Rosalind said. "Will it really complete your montage?"

We were at a stoplight, ready to walk across Congress. Rosalind stepped out just as a car turned the corner going too fast, some idiot trying to make a right turn before the crush of pedestrians started walking. Richard grabbed Rosalind's wrist and pulled her back from the street as people around us hurled insults at the driver. Richard wrapped his arms around Rosalind and held her for a moment as though she were the most precious thing in the world. Lucky them.

And I thought of Abelard, and cupcakes, and broken snowflakes. How when Abelard was seven, his mother brought fancy cupcakes to school, but there were some in the box that were plain vanilla, no icing for Abelard, because he doesn't like icing. I wondered if I asked at the Hey Cupcake! window for a vanilla cupcake—no icing—if they'd even have a cupcake with no icing. Maybe all the cupcakes were pre-iced. But it didn't matter, because Abelard wasn't with me. Which made cupcakes, or best-day-ever montages, pointless.

There was no best day ever without Abelard.

Rosalind dropped me off first. She pulled up on the street by my duplex a minute after Mom pulled into the short driveway. There was a man in the car with Mom, and when he opened the door and stood, I realized it was my father.

"Is that your dad?" Rosalind said.

"Yes . . . ?" My dad, here, right now. It didn't make sense. I got out of the car without saying goodbye.

I rushed up to Dad. He looked the same, just tired, like his eyes were permanently worn from lack of sleep. His light brown hair was sprinkled with glints of silver. Otherwise the same. Tall. Iris's close-set, rounded eyes.

"Lil," he said. "Damn, you've grown up."

And we hugged. Mom stood behind us, looking simultaneously nervous and in control, like a wedding planner or funeral director scoping for ways the event might detour from the schedule.

"What are you doing here?" I said. It sounded rude, but really, I was just curious. Okay, a little angry.

"Your mom sent me a ticket," Dad replied.

Mom popped the trunk of the car, and Dad pulled out a small duffel bag, the kind of thing you pack for a weekend visit. So there were parameters to this exchange, an outline to his appearance. It seemed weird and random, but not.

I opened the door to our duplex and rushed in, concerned that I catch Iris before she could be blindsided by this sudden, unexpected reappearance of our father. Iris was in our room, lying on her bed and Skyping with Exene Ybarra.

"Dad's here," I whispered. "He's here—in the house. Right now."

"What?" Exene bellowed on the laptop. "He's been gone like—forever."

Exene seemed to grasp the gravity of the situation, the utter strangeness of the day more quickly than Iris, who sat up on her bed, blinking.

"You mean OUR dad?" Iris said, like she'd forgotten that we actually had a father.

Before I could elaborate, Dad came into our room.

Iris closed the lid of her laptop and stood so suddenly I put a hand out to steady her.

"Iris, so good to see you again," Dad said.

Iris wrapped her arms around her chest and nodded. I put a hand on her shoulder and felt her lean against me, which made me sad. Iris was so young when Mom and Dad split up. He'd really never been a big part of her life like he had been with mine.

"Alex, would you like a cup of coffee?" Mom said. Deus ex machina Mom. Mom—filled with as-yet unplumbed skills. I was overwhelmed by a sudden respect for Mom and her talents.

Miraculously, Dad followed Mom into the kitchen, as though someone had pushed the reset button on their relationship. Off they went on some sort of time-warp coffee date. Mom and Dad used to have late-afternoon cups of coffee on the patio on Saturdays, back when we had a patio and not just a tiny slab of concrete like we do now.

"Dad," Iris whispered like she'd seen a ghost. Maybe she had.

She shook her head, and I realized at that moment that I'd always been Dad's special snark buddy. The one who got all his jokes, the one who listened to *The Prose Edda*, and the one who imagined herself as some psychotic Viking subgoddess, good with an axe and a quip. And Iris, gifted with paperwork, patience, and with playing the long game, could never compete on our imaginary battlefield of now.

Poor Iris. I'd lived in her perfect shadow for so long, it never occurred to me that she'd lived in mine.

Mom made tea. She opened a box of Sweetish Hill gingerbread cookies she'd been hiding from me. Coffee, tea on the back porch. The back slab. A tiny little slab of concrete, opening onto a field of overgrown ivy, overlooking a sometimes stream.

“This is nice,” Dad said. Lying. Maybe not.

We stood on the back porch next to some sad abandoned patio furniture left by the previous occupants, a wrought-iron table and two chairs, staring over a field of ivy under live oaks.

“Do you still go for walks on the greenbelt?” he asked.

“No,” I said, because it was the truth.

“We’ve been in a drought,” Mom said. “But the creek should be full of water now.”

“So, Lil, maybe we should go for a hike?” he said.

Mom handed him the keys to her car. Because, really—and we all knew this—Dad was here to see me.

We drove to the greenbelt entrance on Loop 360 and walked quickly upstream past people with dogs and razor-thin guys on mountain bikes torturing their spines on rock drops. I’d forgotten how fast Dad walked. We hiked the trail as fast as I could go without breaking into a slow jog.

“You know, Portland has miles of hike and bike trails,” Dad said. “You can get just about anywhere in Portland on a bike.”

I didn’t say anything. Even the word *Portland* was an irritant, a cruel joke played on me by the world in general and my dad in particular. Portland was the mythical place where Abelard and I were supposed to live and be happy. I didn’t want to hear about Portland.

We walked on in silence until we reached a widening in the creek at a small swimming hole. But no one was swimming here; they were all at Campbell's Hole or Twin Falls. Dad stopped and sat down on the place where an oversize live oak jutted almost horizontally out over the creek, forming a bench. I sat down next to him.

"Your mom told me about the surgery," he said. "Is this what you want to do?"

I shrugged. "Want" didn't really enter into it.

"I guess."

"You don't seem happy, Lil. I'm just wondering if this is the right thing for you."

"I'm unhappy for other reasons. But I like my surgeon. So, yeah, I'm good with the surgery."

I looked over at Dad. I really didn't want to have the deep serious talk about my life, like he had some kind of answers. Clearly he didn't.

Dad stood and walked to a small pile of stones by the trail, looking for one smooth enough to skip. Not good at sitting still for long, Dad. Unless he was drinking, I guess.

"So why are you unhappy?" he asked.

I sighed and gave up. Conversation was happening, apparently. We were just going to stay here and look for nice rocks until I talked about something.

"If you really want to know, I had a boyfriend, but we broke up. He's wicked smart, and he reads actual books, but now he's gone." I exhaled. "So there's that."

Dad settled on a perfectly smooth disk, rare in the jagged white limestone.

"What's this perfect boyfriend's name?"

"Abelard Mitchell," I replied.

Dad stopped sorting rocks, a momentary twitch. And I was gratified to see it. There was something oddly satisfying about knowing that I'd wormed my way into his past, even while he was off with the new family in Portland.

"Dr. Mitchell's son?" he asked.

"Yup."

Dad pitched a rock out across the water, but the angle was wrong. We were too high above the water here for stone skipping.

"So why did you two break up?"

"Abelard has some sort of autistic spectrum disorder, and he got invited to go to school in New Mexico."

"Ah," Dad said. "So he broke up with you?"

"No, he didn't, because I told him that I was moving to Portland to live with you so he'd go to the school. I broke up with him."

I gave the word *you* an extra note of bitterness, just in case Dad missed the deep irony of the whole situation. Dad threw another rock upstream with such force that he managed to skip it a couple of times.

"So you didn't actually give the kid a choice," Dad said. "You lied to him and then went, 'later, dude.'"

"Said the king of 'later, dude,'" I shot back. "How many lies did you tell us?"

Who was he to accuse me of pulling a cut and run?

"I guess that's fair." Dad sat down on the tree limb next to me.

I waited for him to say something else, to explain what had happened to him. But he didn't say anything. We just sat there in the sticky May heat, waiting for god knew what.

"Can I ask you something?"

Dad nodded.

"Dr. Mitchell told me that your dissertation idea was original and brilliant. He said you were a great student. Why didn't you finish your dissertation?"

Dad rubbed his hands over his face.

"That was such a long time ago, Lily."

I waited. I wanted to know—really wanted to know. It seemed the most important thing in the world. I wanted to go to college, but not if I was doomed to failure.

"When I first started writing my dissertation, I was excited. But then there was so much editing and revising and research, and, in the meantime, there were students I had to teach—Dr. Mitchell's students. And the students were horrible, Lil. Even if they were history majors, they didn't give a shit about women in the Middle Ages, or Hildegard von Bingen, or anything past securing a teacher's certificate. They thought it was boring. And I realized that I was spending years of my life just to get a doctorate so I could teach horrible students in some shitty little college town of fifty thousand in the Midwest—if I was lucky enough to get a teaching position at all. And your mom made it clear she didn't want to leave Austin, but all my friends who stayed in Austin ended up teaching American History 101 at ACC for practically no money. American history to college freshmen—I mean, what the fuck? And I knew your mom wouldn't be happy with that either. I had a band then, a really good band, and all I wanted to do was play the guitar, but I still had a metric shit ton of paperwork to do, and I'd already had all my best ideas, and I couldn't stand to roll the same words around day in and day out. And suddenly, my best ideas began to seem pathetic to me. I had to have something new to think about." Dad stopped. "In the end it was all too much."

All too much. I thought about Dr. Brainguy and the tyranny of new ideas, his belief that if you think too much and too fast, you can never settle into anything long enough to bring anything to actual fruition. Finishing the doctorate. Meeting the criteria of the crappy rubric. High school. Enduring boredom.

I looked out over the blue-green pool of water as a big slow sadness replaced my anger. I'd thought Dad was a superhero of noncompliance, and then I'd thought Dad was a deadbeat, but really he was neither of these things.

"When Dr. Frankenstein is done fixing my brain, maybe he can do yours," I said, only half joking.

Dad laughed.

"I think it's a little too late for that," he replied.

CHAPTER 32

Life is slow. Homework is a Sisyphean boulder of paper to push up a pointless hill. School is a molasses eternity. As bad as high school is, college is supposed to be worse. Slow, slower, slowest. There is only one possible escape from drudgery, one Kobayashi Maru scenario. Run. Make a snap judgment and take off in an entirely new direction. Decide. Break up with your boyfriend so he can attend the kind of school you can only dream about. Agree to have electrodes planted in your brain because you want to go to college and this is your only chance.

Take bold action. Run.

I woke up late the next morning. Dad and Iris were in the kitchen, talking. Iris was telling Dad a story from a Model UN conference about an imaginary, fast-moving zombie plague outbreak in Western Australia, and how quickly the crisis committee resolved to nuke Perth, and even the Australian delegation was for nuking Perth. Dad leaned against the sink, coffee cup in hand, and peppered her with questions about Model UN. Iris loves to talk about Model UN.

Dad looked tired, dark circles under his eyes, a slightly ashy tone to his skin, as though he hadn't slept too well on our crap-ass love seat. His hair was the same rumpled mess but shot through with gray. Maybe this was just how Dad looked now. I didn't like to think of him aging.

Instead of pouring a single cup through a drip filter, Mom had pulled down an old coffeemaker from the top of the pantry and made a full pot of coffee.

"What are you making?" I asked.

"Blueberry pancakes," Iris said. "Because you like blueberry pancakes."

The condemned prisoner ate a hearty meal. I thought about saying it but decided not to. Iris was worried about my surgery, and I didn't want to make it worse for her.

Dad took a chair next to Mom at the dining room table as Iris pulled the last pancake out of the pan. He bowed his head and closed his eyes while Mom sipped her coffee and stared off into the middle distance, like there was nothing at all strange about this. To be fair, Mom usually spent Sunday mornings sucking down coffee with her eyes glazed over.

"Are you praying?" I asked. Disconcerting. It was bad enough that Dad disappeared for five years and reemerged with a new family—but a new religion?

"Just meditating for a moment," Dad replied, his eyes still closed. "Mindful awareness."

"Cool!" Iris said. "I studied mindful meditation in my Religions of the World seminar last year. We had a field trip to a Buddhist temple and . . ."

I zoned out as Iris and Dad began talking about prayer bowls and different states of consciousness. I wanted to be somewhere else. I wanted to be with Abelard, walking one of the many mountain trails that "dot the rustic landscape surrounding the Isaac Institute." I'd been reading the Isaac Institute website just so I'd have visuals when my mind returned to Abelard. Because my mind always returned to Abelard.

". . . I live near a temple. We'll make a visit when you come to Portland."

"Could I go to Portland, Mom?" Iris said, her eyes shining with enthusiasm.

"Yes, let's all go to Portland," I said bitterly. I was done believing anything Mom or Dad told me.

Mom and Dad exchanged a look. For some reason, Mom and Dad had jumped right back into communicating by gesture and eye contact over the rims of coffee cups, and it annoyed me deeply. Everyone perfectly happy but me.

Dad dove for the pancakes.

"These look great, Iris," he said. "So, Lily, this boyfriend of yours—what do you do when you guys are together?"

Present tense, like he'd forgotten that I'd broken up

with Abelard. What was it Dad had said? I didn't even give him a chance.

"He's in New Mexico, so nothing."

Dad helped himself and handed me the pancakes. I took one, tore a bit off the edge, and shoved it into my mouth.

"I think your dad meant when Abelard was living here," Mom interjected.

"We played games." I pushed the pancake around on my plate. "Mostly we played chess."

"Chess?" Dad smiled. "I remember teaching you how to play chess."

"That must be why I suck at chess," I said.

"Language, Lily," Mom said. She threw Dad an apologetic look. I didn't know why they were suddenly best friends. Even Mom had to see that Dad had fallen down on his paternal chess instruction duties. Who knew how many things I would have learned if he had stuck around. I'd probably be driving now.

Because—five years. Five years was a hopeless lifetime of failing algebra and taking stupid drugs, of skipping class and thinking that my dad might show up at any moment and rescue me. I flashed on a memory of Humberto the *Star Trek* therapist gently trying to steer me toward the notion that maybe my mother wasn't the only thing keeping Dad away. I never wanted to hear it, but now I understood. Humberto knew the truth. Dad had moved on and never looked back.

"But I do suck at chess," I said. "It's not like I've played a lot since you left. Now that Abelard's gone, I'll probably never play chess again."

I pushed back from my plate and folded my arms across my chest, feeling the monster rise up. My feet itched for the door. It had been a couple of days since I let my impulses off the leash and followed where they led. I missed the freedom. And soon my impulse to bolt would be gone, excised from my brain forever by the implanted electrical device. Perhaps one last run—for old time's sake.

I stood. And Dad stood. Almost simultaneously, as if he knew what I was thinking.

"I thought we might all go for a walk on the greenbelt after breakfast, burn off some spare energy," he said quickly.

"I can't. I have to work on a project with Exene," Iris said. She looked genuinely regretful, as if she actually wanted to cancel a homework assignment for more time with Dad. I'd never seen this expression on her face before. "Can we go later in the afternoon?"

"Sure," Dad said, still standing. "What should we do until then, Lil?"

I sank back into my chair. My impulse to bolt evaporated. I regretted the loss.

"Still have a chessboard?" he asked.

I would have sworn we didn't have a chessboard, but Mom dug out an old glass set from the back of the hall closet. It was just like the one Magneto and Professor X played with at the end of one of those movies. Appropriate, since I felt like I was playing under duress.

We cleared the breakfast dishes and set up the game at the dining room table. Dad beat me the first game, but I watched him play and realized that he relied heavily on his knights and his rooks. So for the second game, instead of targeting his king, I went for his knights and took them both away pretty quickly. It was gratifying.

"You've been practicing," Dad said. He seemed, if anything, pleased to be on the receiving end of a chess beat down. Weird.

"You haven't."

"I've been kind of busy."

"It must be hard work raising the 'sweetest kid ever,'" I blurted out.

Dad moved a pawn away from his left rook. Rooks, the Hulk-smash pieces of the chessboard. Dad played like me—he moved pieces out quickly and ignored his delicate bishops. If I could slow down, plan, and play cautiously, like Abelard, I could beat him. Big *if.*

I moved a bishop three spaces.

"You're angry with me," Dad said.

"Duh."

I crossed my arms and leaned back in my chair. Dad contemplated his next move, and the way he knit his eyebrows and bit his lower lip reminded me of Iris working on her Math POW. He looked like a bigger, rumpled version of Iris, same straight eyebrows and deep brown eyes. Iris in male form, left out in the sun too long.

"Do you want to talk about it?" Dad moved his rook out.

"No," I shot back.

There was something I'd planned to do with my bishop three moves down the road to take his rook, but now I couldn't remember. Distracted. Annoyed.

"Okay, maybe I do want to talk about it. So little Jacob is what, six years old?"

"Caleb?" Dad replied. "He's five."

"Five years old." My voice trembled. "So were you already with someone else when you were living with us?"

"Lil," Dad said softly, "Caleb is not my biological son. I'm the only father he's ever known, but I didn't meet Mara—his mother—until two years ago when I played a show at his daycare."

I'd held this image in my mind for so long of Dad herding goats, farming organic beets, and teaching English and history to misfit weirdoes. Waiting for me. Now I had to replace that image with Dad playing the lute for toddlers. And Caleb, the "sweetest kid ever." Strange.

"Two years ago. That's when you went off Facebook and you stopped messaging me."

"I'm sorry, Lil," he said. "I meant to get back to you,

but . . ." His voice trailed off. I guess he was not completely unaware of how lame this sounded.

I moved my bishop to place both his rook and a pawn in peril. He moved his rook, and I had to settle for taking the pawn.

"So what did you do for the first three years after you left us?"

"What did I do for three years?" Dad laughed bitterly. "I drank. And then I stopped drinking."

I flashed on the mostly empty plastic quart bottle of cheap vodka that was still in the back of our closet. A middle school friend had wanted to drink the vodka, but I stopped her from having more than a swig, because it was a memento of my dad. Stupidest keepsake ever. I could see that now.

"So you messaged me while you were drinking, but after you stopped drinking, you stopped messaging me? That's messed up, Dad."

"It had more to do with your mother. When I finally sobered up, I realized I needed to leave her alone for a while. And frankly, I thought you guys would be better off without me."

Dad moved his left bishop. Quickly and decisively, like he'd just remembered he had a bishop and it had to be somewhere in a hurry.

He went to the kitchen and poured himself another cup

of coffee while I pondered my next move. It was his third, maybe fourth cup of coffee of the day. Mom had made an entire pot of coffee, while knowing that Dad would drink it all and probably not even wash his cup. He might forget his cup on the bookshelf, or the bedside table, leaving milky rings on the furniture. I remembered how you could always tell that Dad was working because half-drunk cups of coffee littered the house, cold and skinned over, like liquid land mines. I never saw the cups until I sent them flying. Poor Mom. She was always cleaning up after the both of us.

"You were pestering her," I said absently.

"Pestering—Jesus, what a terrible word!"

"Sorry. Coach Neuwirth says it all the time. I guess it stuck in my brain."

"Yes, I was pestering your mother." Dad sighed deeply and sat down across from me. "So, Lil . . . about your mom. Do you think she's happy?"

"No," I shot back. Annoyed. It was like Dad had completely missed the point of this little familial get-together. We weren't happy. None of us. Well, maybe Iris.

"Why not?" Dad seemed genuinely surprised.

"Dad, I make her miserable. Why do you think I wanted to come live with you? If I were gone, she'd be happy again."

A lump rose in my throat. Sometimes you don't see the truth until you say it out loud. The jar of antidepressants under my bed, all my ridiculous fantasies about picking beets and milking goats and homeschool cooperatives was about one thing. Leaving. I was wearing my mother down to a frazzled nub of her former hopeful self. She and Iris would be better off without me.

"That's not true," he said.

"How would you know?" I asked. "It's not like you've been here."

"Happy or not, your mom is never going to give up on you. She'd worry just as much if you came to live with me." Dad moved his rook out. It was a careless, doomed move. If he'd been paying attention, he wouldn't have made it. "Probably more."

"I guess so." I took his remaining rook with a pawn. "Once I have the surgery, Mom won't have to worry about me anymore."

Dad tipped his king over so abruptly I wondered if the gesture was accidental. I'd probably beaten him, but I wasn't sure. I probably could have chased his one sad bishop around on the board for a while. He might have battled back.

"Just make sure it's what you want," he said.

Dad and Iris cooked dinner together, curried cauliflower and brown rice. Now that Dad was a Buddhist, he'd also become a vegetarian. I could tell that the moment Dad left,

Iris would insist on enforcing a vegetarian diet on all of us, and of course Mom would cave. She always does where Iris is concerned.

When Rosalind texted, I went to my room.

"Hey, is your dad still there? How is he?"

"Good. It's like he never left. He and Mom are being super congenial with each other."

"Well that's nice," she texted.

I thought about it. The decision that we would all act like the best of friends was sort of nice, but sort of not.

"Actually, it's kind of creepy. Like someone replaced my normally argumentative family with pleasant robotic duplicates."

"Weird. So why did your dad decide to come visit now?"

The question annoyed me. I had the feeling that she was fishing for dad's opinion about my impending surgery.

"No reason," I texted.

"So does he know about your brain surgery?"

I knew it. She wanted to know if Dad approved of the surgery.

"Yes."

"So what does he think? Does he want you to have the surgery?"

"Not really. But then, he doesn't have to deal with old-brain sad me." I finished the line with a super-tragic emoji. Normally I don't use emojis, but in this case it seemed—applicable.

"You're angry that I put you on suicide watch," she texted.

"No," I shot back. I realized the moment I sent the text that this was not true. I was angry. Angry with her, angry with Dad, angry with everyone. *"Okay, yes. I'm angry."*

"Can we talk in person? You could come over."

I didn't really want to talk to her about suicide watch or my surgery.

"I can't do it now."

"Meet me for lunch tomorrow?" she texted.

I had an appointment with Dr. Brainguy, but I'd probably be done by noon.

"Lunch," I replied.

CHAPTER 33

"Wake up," Dad whispered urgently. "The secret is in the old clock. It's been there all along."

I rolled over.

"Really, Dad?" I mumbled. "Nancy Drew?"

He laughed.

I sat up in my bed. Sun streamed in the window. "Where's Iris? What time is it?"

"It's nine o'clock. Iris has already left," he said. "Your mom sent me in to wake you up. You have an appointment with your doctor in an hour."

Ever since I agreed to brain surgery, Mom had become extremely lackadaisical about my school attendance. It was like I'd had a semipermanent Get Out of Jail Free card.

"I have to go," Dad said. "Your mom is taking me to the airport. I wish I could stay longer, but I have work."

I blinked. My brain refused to process this new information. Dad was leaving just when I was starting to get over being angry with him for leaving the last time. "Bye—I guess."

"Why don't you come to Portland? We have a spare room I use as my office, but you'd be welcome to stay as long as you like. You'd like Mara and Caleb."

Portland. With my dad. This was all I'd wanted for so long, but now everything was different. Now I was heading into surgery, and maybe I had a chance at going to college, without the clever homeschooling I'd imagined. Who knew when I'd see Dad again?

"Could Abelard come with me?" I asked.

Stupid question. Abelard was in New Mexico, and I was here, and we weren't together, but I couldn't let go of the image of Abelard and the train trip, stars rolling by our window.

"I don't know if your mother would be okay with that." Dad glanced toward the door as if Mom was lingering in the hall, eavesdropping.

"Yeah, I don't actually care what Mom thinks about my boyfriend," I said, in case she was.

Boyfriend. A word for what Abelard once was to me.

Dad laughed. The skin around his eyes crinkled and folded in unexpected ways; otherwise, he was the dad I remembered. Making fun of Nancy Drew when I was six. Laughing at random comments. I'd spent so much time imagining our new life on a farm with goats and the children of freaks and nineteenth-century novels that I'd forgotten Dad was a real person. And Dad had forgotten that I'd grown up. Weird.

"I think you have to talk to Abelard first." He leaned over to hug me. "I love you, Lil."

"I love you, too, Dad."

And then he was gone.

An hour later, Mom dropped me off at Dr. Brainguy's office.

The nurse called my name and escorted me into the conference room. Dr. Brainguy was at the head of a long table with his serious-as-a-heart-attack students, two men and two women in scrubs who trailed in his wake, always taking notes, asking questions. It was dawning on me that Dr. Brainguy was kind of a big deal. I didn't get that when I first met him. It wasn't until I cleared his intake round that I began to see Dr. Brainguy as the king of a small, nervous fiefdom, filled with surgical students and psychiatry residents. They tended to talk to me as if I were just a little smarter than the average trained monkey with an active understanding of several hundred words of English.

"Hello, Lily," Dr. Brainguy said. He nodded in the direction of a chair across from one of the doctors. "How are you today?"

"My father made a surprise visit this weekend. He just left," I said. "I guess my mom told him about the surgery."

Two of Dr. Brainguy's students dove for their pens and frantically scribbled notes. It didn't improve my mood.

"How did that go?" Dr. Brainguy said.

I shrugged. If we'd been alone, I probably would have told him all about the visit, playing carnage chess, walking on the greenbelt with Dad and talking about Abelard. But I wasn't going to say anything while his students were recording our conversation for posterity.

Dr. Brainguy glanced around the room and smiled as if he got it. "Today you're going to work with Dr. *Sheerrlll*, and we're going to observe."

I sat across the table from Dr. Golden, feeling surly. Dr. Golden brought it out in me. He was like the straight-A captain of some mythical high school football team in Perfect Everywhereland. Like everything in his experience was completely antithetical to everything in mine. His sandy blond hair and easy smile predisposed me to hating him on sight.

He began reading words from a verbal test that I swear I'd done five times already with Dr. Brainguy. The other students watched.

And suddenly, I needed to leave. Something my father had said about Abelard stuck in my head, but I couldn't focus on it with Dr. Golden looking at me like I'd just crawled out of a petri dish and developed a couple of brain cells. I twitched in my seat and reduced my answers to yes and no.

Dr. Golden turned to Dr. Brainguy.

"Isn't it pointless to try and test for emotional lability in a *splinkal* setting?" he said. "What if the subject doesn't honestly *spork*?"

"You want to see emotional lability?" I said. "Keep talking like I'm not in the room."

I left for the bathroom. Behind me, I could hear Dr. Brainguy's voice, low and measured. Lecturing. Perhaps he was congratulating Dr. Golden for pushing me into demonstrating a lack of impulse control. This was why I was here, after all. Hulk smash!

I pushed through the satisfyingly heavy bathroom door. The bathroom—cool, dark, industrial. An oasis. What the hell was I doing here? It wasn't like I was having a wart removed. I was here to trade in my emotional lability for something else. But what? Would I wake up after surgery as smooth and untroubled by actual human empathy as Dr. Golden?

I could walk away. Dr. Brainguy's office was on the edge of campus. The Blanton wasn't far. I could sit by the pennies and bones. Breathe. I closed my eyes and leaned against the door.

Alone, my brain always circled around to Abelard. What was he doing now? Building robots with the funny girl from his floor? Hanging out at the student union playing pool, laughing? Damn college websites! Heartbreak shouldn't have glossy pictorial spreads.

I couldn't stay in the bathroom forever. I opened the heavy door slowly, unsure of whether my feet would take me out into the bright May sunshine or lead me back to the testing room. I needed to run.

I peeked around the door, hoping to avoid bumping into one of the nurses or his office staff.

Dr. Brainguy stood in the hall, sucking on an e-cigarette. When he saw me, he slipped the cigarette into his pocket.

"You caught me," he said.

I sighed. What Dr. Brainguy meant was that he'd caught me trying to make a run for it. We both knew he wasn't talking about his suppressed smoking habit.

"Aren't all these tests redundant?" I asked. "I'm beginning to think this is some kind of prank. Maybe this is some meta-test of my emotional lability?"

I paused to make air quotes. I was sick of emotional lability. The idea of it, the reality of it, the embarrassment of it.

"No, Lily, we wouldn't do that," he said. "But when it comes to the brain, we like to be redundant."

I leaned against the wall, like we were just hanging out in the hall between classes. I was tired, even though it was morning.

"So how was the visit with your dad?" Dr. Brainguy asked.

"Good," I replied. "He has a new family now. He's going

to try very hard not to run away from them. You wouldn't know this, but apparently relationships are hard work."

Dr. Brainguy laughed. There was a weird, bitter edge to his laugh, and I realized suddenly that I knew absolutely nothing about his personal life. He could be an axe murderer or four times divorced for all I knew. I'd come to trust him because he was the most honest adult I'd ever met, aside from my father. But what did that mean, really?

"I miss Abelard," I blurted out. Random.

"Ah, the young man with the poetry." Dr. Brainguy inhaled between two fingers. "How is he liking the Isaac Institute?"

"He loves it."

"Good," Dr. Brainguy murmured. He pulled his e-cig out of his pocket. "You don't mind, do you?"

"No. What does 'good' mean?"

"Good means good. So, have you been in touch with him?"

"Not recently." I rubbed the toe of my shoe across the carpet, wishing for something to kick. "I broke up with him."

"Really?" Dr. Brainguy seemed genuinely surprised. "Why?"

"I don't know why. I mean, I told him that I was in Portland, and then I wasn't in Portland, and his school has an amazing robotics lab, and Abelard is taking college courses, and what am I doing? I mean, other than having surgery? And who am I going to be after surgery, aside from a girl with a totally attractive one-sided head shave and a weird scar? Not that Abelard cares about that, but will I be the same person? I just feel . . ."

I stopped. I was babbling again.

"Overwhelmed?" Dr. Brainguy said.

"Yes." That was it. Overwhelmed.

"It's natural to feel that way before any surgery, but especially brain surgery. Trust me when I say that you will be the same person."

"Do you think I should tell Abelard about the surgery?"

He tapped the e-cig in the palm of his hand like it was a pipe or something and slipped it into his coat pocket.

"I can't tell you what to do, Lily. You have to decide for yourself."

"I should text him."

"Later," Dr. Brainguy said. "We need to get back to work."

"Do I have to go back in there?" I glanced down the hall toward the room full of doctors, the last place on Earth I wanted to be right now.

"Here's my problem, Lily. Someone has to teach those monsters how to be human."

"Is that my job?"

"No, it's mine. But I could use your help."

I could face Dr. Golden again, if Dr. Brainguy needed me to. Dr. Brainguy—real human material. Soon he'd plant electrodes in my brain, and he'd be off to the next patient. And I'd miss him. Not follow-him-to-his-Swiss-mountain-home-and-threaten-to-destroy-everything-he-ever-loved-unless-he-revealed-to-me-the-deeper-truth-and-meaning-to-life miss him. But still. Very few people are worth hunting down for the general life secrets in their possession.

CHAPTER 34

Dr. Golden's test took a long time, and lunch period was half over by the time I walked out to the courtyard. Montana Jordan or Jordan Montana and her emo boyfriend had taken up residence at Abelard's place under the crepe myrtle.

Rosalind was at our normal spot, hands folded in her lap, a frown of concentration on her face. She moved her lips slightly, as though memorizing dialogue, which was odd because she wasn't in a play at the moment. I remembered that we were supposed to be having a serious talk about suicide watch. I did not want to talk about suicide watch. No, I did not.

I dropped my lunch bag and sat down beside her.

"Well, here I am," I said. "I guess we should talk."

Rosalind didn't look at me. My stomach lurched as she began her prepared speech.

"So I'm used to you being bleak about school, but last semester you changed. You were flat, and you weren't interested in anything. And you started saying some pretty disturbing things, which is why I went to your counselor."

"You could have talked to me," I blurted out. "You didn't have to put me on suicide watch."

"Actually, I did have to put you on suicide watch. I couldn't talk to you. You aren't yourself when you are on drugs."

"Isn't that the point of the drugs?" I replied, a little more bitterly than I should have.

"To be someone else?" Her voice rose. "Even if it makes you unhappy?"

Happy. It's the stupidest word in the English language. It's a sprinkles-on-your-ice-cream, My-Little-Pony kind of a word, and yet we are all expected to be happy about everything, including that which makes us miserable, like school. It's a bully of a word, *happy.* Not only am I required to suck up all the misery and injustice of the scholastic world, I have to pretend to enjoy it. *Mais, je refuse.*

"So now you're going to have the surgery. And you're going to be someone else—permanently. That's just great, Lily."

I shrugged. I wanted to talk about my surgery even less than I wanted to talk about suicide watch. "If you really want to know, I'm going to have the surgery because being me is an unmitigated disaster. Clearly."

"Listen to yourself," Rosalind said. "What if Abelard wanted to have brain surgery? What would you say to him?"

"It's different for Abelard."

A blast of hot air rolled across the teachers' parking lot and sent a dusty breeze over the courtyard. Somewhere, hundreds of miles to the west, a storm descended. Maybe it was raining in the mountains of New Mexico on pine tree forests, the Isaac Institute, and Abelard.

I'd never really thought about the difference between us before. I'm sure it sucked to be Abelard in middle school in ways I couldn't begin to imagine. Of course, it was no picnic for me either. Middle school is where I truly began my career as an academic failure. Up until then, I'd just been dabbling. But Abelard had it worse. He'd been bullied in middle school. Physically, in the hall, in front of everyone. And Abelard had been desperately lonely—his mother had told me as much.

Honestly, though, I was a little jealous of Abelard. I couldn't escape the feeling that high school was easier for him than it was for me. No one expected Abelard to be normal. His issues were accepted by the school because he's a genius, and he rocks all his classes. You can talk all you want about age-appropriate socialization and sensory integration, but if you're good at school, no one cares. Making good grades earns you a pass on everything else.

"So how would it be different if Abelard decided to have brain surgery?" Rosalind demanded.

"It's different because he doesn't need it."

Rosalind shook her head.

"That makes no sense, Lily. Abelard is, well, he's not normal. You can tell just by talking to him. You seem like everyone else."

"That's my problem—I seem just like everyone else. If Abelard leaves class suddenly because he can't stand to be there anymore, everyone worries about him. If I leave, I'm skipping class."

"Maybe you should try not skipping class."

I glared at her.

"Sorry, that was a stupid thing to say," she said. "But you could a better job of asking for help. What about your 504 accommodations and—"

"I don't want to ask for help—ever," I said. Even the idea of asking for help made my skin itch. "Having to ask for help with directions makes me angry. I'd rather have electrodes in my brain than spend the rest of my life asking for help."

"Asking for help makes you angry? I don't understand." Rosalind shook her head. It was too much for her. She'd never understand what it was like to be me because the world loves her. The world loves her quiet thoughtfulness and her insistence on showing up fifteen minutes early to everything. Her stubborn refusal to need further instructions. She's clearly never heard the deep, long-suffering sigh that says, *Everyone else gets this. Why don't you?*

The first bell rang. Rosalind picked up her lunchbox

and hesitated for a moment. She looked like she had more to say. But in the end, the thought of being late to class was just too much for her. She can't stop being on time, any more than I can stop being late.

"That looks good," Mom said, peering into a pot filled with some sort of chickpea, kale, and onion thing Iris was making to go over brown rice. We'd been eating a lot of brown rice since Dad's visit. I was kind of done with brown rice. I couldn't wait until Iris discovered the paleo diet and decided all grains were evil.

"We didn't have a chance to talk earlier," Mom said, dropping her tragic purse on the dining room table next to where I was absently playing a game on my phone. "How was your appointment today?"

"Fine."

Hours at the doctor's office and my lunchtime conversation about suicide with Rosalind had left me feeling spent. I didn't want to talk about my stupid brain.

"What did they have you do today?"

"Tests," I said, not looking up.

"Care to elaborate?" Mom asked.

Fireworks and explosions on my phone signaled that I'd won a level. I slapped my phone face-down on the table. "What else do you want to know?"

Mom slid into the chair across from me. "Who did you work with?"

"I worked with Dr. Golden," I said, feeling the monster rise again. "We did the same tests I've been doing for weeks now."

"Dr. Golden? I don't remember meeting a Dr. Golden."

I leaned back in my chair. "Tall, blond, kind of a douche."

"Lily, language," Mom said.

Iris dumped a pile of sliced carrots into the pot and hovered nearby, attracted by the undeniable lure of conflict and forbidden words.

"I think you mean Dr. Jarrell," Mom said. "Actually, I found him quite charming. And handsome."

"For a douche," I replied.

"Can I go to Lily's next appointment with her?" Iris leaned over the kitchen counter, spoon in hand.

"No," Mom and I answered in unison. At least we agreed on something.

"Even Dr. Brainguy thinks he's a douche."

"I have a hard time believing Dr. Brillstein referred to a colleague in that way," she said. I couldn't tell whether the word bothered Mom or if it was my assessment of Dr. Jarrell.

"Not exactly," I said. "But I knew what he meant."

"I could tell Ms. Arbeth I was researching brain surgery," Iris said. "She'd let me out of class if—"

"Why would you even want to go to my appointment?" I asked. "What do you think we're doing over there, holding

TED Talks about the exciting future of brain research? It's just a lot of blank people with laptops asking me the same stupid questions over and over. It's worse than school, and probably just as futile, and I . . ."

Mom stared at me with a look of concern. Iris caught it too. She turned back to the stove and pretended to be absorbed in stirring her chickpea concoction.

"Are you having second thoughts about the surgery?" Mom leaned across the table and put her hand on my arm.

"No, I'm not having second thoughts," I lied.

Mom did not look convinced. "Do you want to talk about it?"

"I don't really have anything to say."

I had more to say about surgery, a lot more. My best friend thought the surgery was a nightmare mistake that would kill my remaining joy in life. Maybe my problem wasn't my brain, it was school. If we had the money for a place like the Isaac Institute, things would be different. And there was no guarantee the surgery would even work. It was experimental, after all.

There was no point in talking to Mom. She'd made up her mind. So had Rosalind. Neither one of them could understand me. They weren't broken.

There was only one person I wanted to talk to. Abelard.

CHAPTER 35

I am broken because I have a disability. I am broken because I am incapable of sitting still for hours at a time and performing the mind-numbing, repetitive tasks that I am required to do. Abelard is broken because he can't smile and say hello, and he doesn't like crowds, which is basically what high school is—one giant, swirling, chaotic crowd.

Still, if the warp drive on the starship *Enterprise* was set to go critical in thirty-nine minutes, you'd want Abelard in a quiet room working on the problem. And you wouldn't dare call Abelard disabled. For thirty-nine minutes, he'd be your hero. The dividing line between broken and brilliant is the slim margin of context. Perhaps I'm not disabled, I'm just in the wrong place at the wrong time.

I don't know. But maybe Abelard does.

"Abelard."

"Lily," he responded almost instantly.

I clutched the phone, not quite believing it was him. It was as though he'd been waiting by the phone.

"I need to talk to you," I texted.

He didn't answer back right away. I waited impatiently for his next word.

"Why?"

There was an icy eternity in that word, a distance of more than just miles. I'd thought of Abelard as a beautiful shiny object, and I'd thought of Abelard as my secret text admirer, and then as my boyfriend. But he had been so much more than that. Abelard had been my friend. He'd understood me in a way no one else had, except maybe Rosalind. I'd thrown it all away.

"Never mind," I texted back. *"I shouldn't have bothered you. Sorry."*

I dropped the phone in my purse and slumped back on the bed. In my rush to offload geography assignments like spent fuel canisters, I'd mistakenly jettisoned Abelard as well. Stupid, impulsive, rocket brain.

My phone whirred softly. I fished it out of my purse.

"Why?" Abelard texted.

"Everything is wrong," I texted.

"It's statistically improbable that absolutely everything is wrong," Abelard texted. *"Some things, but not everything."*

Funny. Or maybe Abelard wasn't being funny; maybe he was being very, very direct. Strange how often these two things collided.

"My mom wanted me to have this surgery. Mom said I could

go visit my dad if I talked to the surgeon, but now my whole life is upside down."

I stopped. It was too complicated to make sense of in a text.

"Visit your dad? I thought you were living with your dad in Portland."

"No, I'm still in Austin."

His answer came back faster than I expected.

"You said you were moving to Portland. You broke up with me."

"You needed to go to the Isaac Institute," I texted.

"I only agreed to go to the Isaac Institute because you moved to Portland," he said. *"I wouldn't have gone if you'd stayed."*

"Which is why I lied to you," I texted. "I'm in Austin. I never left."

Abelard didn't answer for a very long time. So long I became convinced that he'd turned off his phone. So long I had plenty of time to contemplate the wisdom of telling someone you love over a text that you lied to change the course of their life. I still believed Abelard belonged at the Isaac Institute, but my methods for getting him there were as impulsive and destructive as pulling up hard on a handle just because you see it moving. I hadn't thought it through.

"You could have let me make my own choice," he texted eventually.

"Are you angry?" I said.

"Yes," he replied.

Another long pause, long enough to make me wonder if we were done.

"What kind of surgery?" he asked.

I'd forgotten that I'd even mentioned the surgery.

"Brain surgery. It's not that big a deal. It's an electrode implantation to make me less impulsive."

"When are you having surgery?"

"As soon as finals are over."

Abelard didn't reply for a long time. I couldn't blame him. It was a lot to process—brain surgery, lying. Complexity. A whole pile of crazy-girlfriend drama. I sat staring at my phone.

"I'm coming back," he texted finally.

"You don't have to do that. What about school?"

"The summer semester hasn't started. I'm in orientation right now. I won't miss classes."

Abelard, coming to see me. I worried about him traveling by himself.

"How would you get here?"

"I'll fly. Someone will drive me to Albuquerque. There's a direct flight to Austin."

"You hate airplanes."

"I have to go," he said.

"I want to see you, but don't do anything impulsive." Me, telling Abelard to be sensible. Strange how things work out.

I waited to see if he'd text anything else. He didn't.

CHAPTER 36

Wednesday. I was in English class in the middle of a sleepy conversation about an indifferent short story, holding my phone under my desk on the lowest level of vibrate imaginable.

"Lily?" Abelard texted.

Mrs. Rogers-Peña looked up as though she had X-ray vision and could see my phone through the desk.

I waited until she turned her back, and then texted.

"Yes." It was all I could get out before she turned around again.

"I'm in Austin. Come to my house."

I shoved my phone in my pocket, grabbed my backpack, and stood by Mrs. Rogers-Peña's desk. "I need to go to the bathroom."

I swung my backpack in her direction as though I expected an imminent tampon catastrophe. Mrs. Rogers-Peña eyed me dubiously before handing me one of the giant plastic hall passes our school uses, because apparently carrying a fluorescent green piece of plastic the size of an iPad cuts down on drug use. In two years, I'd never bailed on one of her classes, and I felt bad. She knew something was up, but she was giving me the benefit of the doubt.

Plus, I had her only bathroom pass.

I moved quickly through the hall, worried that I'd be spotted before I could make my escape.

All of my life I've run from things: lengthy homework assignments, arguments with my mother, hours spent in a desk watching pointless PowerPoint presentations. All this disappears in the rush of a run. But I'd never run toward something. I'd never had a destination. And it made all the difference.

I stood outside the Mitchell house and rang the bell. Abelard opened the door—instantly, as though he'd been standing a few feet away. He startled me. Usually his mom answered.

"You came," he said.

"I left school. How long have you been home?"

"Since last night. Mom said it was too late to call you."

Everything about him, from his bare feet and sunglasses to the dark hair curling around his ears, was just as I remembered. Better even. We may grow fonder of the picture of the person we love when they are at a great distance, but it's still just a picture. Abelard was real, and he was here. He shifted in the doorway, and I took it as an invitation to come inside. We stood in the entryway, close enough for me to catch the scent of sandalwood, soap, and warmth.

"How did you get here?" I asked. "You didn't fly, did you? Tell me you didn't fly."

"I didn't fly. I took the bus. My dorm mentor drove me to the bus station."

"And that was okay? No one touched you or anything?" Hard to imagine Abelard on a bus for a whole day.

"Lubbock," he said. "Someone sat next to me at Lubbock, but then they moved. Mom drove out to meet me in San Angelo."

"Where is your mother?" I realized that she wasn't there. She was always there.

"She's at school. When I went to the Isaac Institute, she decided to finish her master's in child development. She's working part-time in a learning center."

I was quite happy that Mrs. Mitchell wasn't in the house, hovering nearby. But I was also pleased to find that she had a life outside of taking care of Abelard. I'd imagined her as the Miss Havisham of cookies, sitting in her kitchen covered with cobwebs, surrounded by uneaten baked goods she couldn't stop making for her absent children. Okay—*Great Expectations*—ninth grade. Visually useful.

"You came to see me," I said. "You got on a bus. I've never been anywhere—on a bus."

"Yes."

Abelard frowned at the half table, or the floor, not at me, but I was used to that. I was suffused with an almost unendurable golden happiness at his proximity, and I wanted to lunge at him. I put my hand on that strange little half table that held a wooden bowl for keys, and another for sunglasses. I wondered if the wall held the table up. If I pulled it away from the wall, maybe it would fall over. I gave the edge a slight tug. Bad idea—to break something—just to keep my hands busy.

"You broke up with me," he said. "I want to kiss you, but I'm still mad."

At the word *kiss,* a thrill passed through me. I'd had the suspicion that Abelard had only come back on a pity mission, because—electrodes in my brain. Not true. He wanted to kiss me.

"I guess you have every right to be angry with me," I said. "I had my reasons for breaking up with you, which in retrospect, were probably bad reasons, but if you could hold two contradictory thoughts in your brain, I'd like it if you kissed me. But only if you felt like—"

Abelard kissed me. Midsentence. This was getting to be a habit. I closed my eyes as words fell out of my brain and the hamster wheel of thoughts stopped turning.

Abelard wrapped his arms around me. We leaned together against the weird little half table with the keys and the sunglasses as though we were both trying to melt into the wall. My face nestled into the side of his neck while his hands searched beneath my shirt and found bare skin at the back of my waist.

"This table thing has only three legs," I whispered. "Are we going to break it?"

I didn't want to break anything else in Abelard's house. I'd pretty much met my household destruction limit with the unfortunate lemonade incident.

"The lower shelf adds structural integrity," he said. "It's stronger than it looks."

I laughed. I couldn't help it. Because—happiness.

"Is that funny?" He tightened his arms around my waist and frowned.

"Yes. You and I are always talking about breaking things. Most people don't think about structural integrity this much."

Abelard turned his head away. Thinking. "Do you want me to stop talking about structural integrity?"

"Please—don't stop. If you stopped talking about structural integrity, then I would have to think about it by myself, and I don't ever want to be that alone in the world of breakable objects again."

"Can I kiss you again?" he asked.

"You don't have to ask every time," I said.

But I knew he would.

He kissed me again, and my thoughts turned to his room, miles of soft bed and warm light. We were alone in the house. Would we ever be this alone again?

"I don't want you to have brain surgery," he said.

"Okay." My too-happy brain, not forming complete thoughts.

"Brain surgery," he repeated.

"What would I do if didn't have the surgery?"

"Come to New Mexico with me."

"Really? How would I do that?"

"I have money," Abelard said. "We'll take the train."

It was all so simple.

I was tired of Dr. Golden and all the tests, the thought of having my head shaved and a scar over my ear. I didn't want to think about how I'd be seeing one of Dr. Brainguy's students every two weeks for the next three years, and probably for a long time after that, maybe forever, because you don't just shove an electrode in someone's brain and then say, "Later, dude!"

I didn't want the surgery. I didn't want to go to school. All I wanted was to be with Abelard.

"Maybe we should go to your room," I said.

There was a sound of a key sliding into the lock. Mrs. Mitchell opened the door and nearly ran into us both.

"Oh!"

She stood with her keys in her hand, frozen in place. She wore an oversize lilac linen shirt, amethyst beads the size of kumquats.

My shirt was up in the back, and my skirt had ridden up high on my thighs. I didn't quite know how it got there.

I pulled my skirt down, and the bowl full of sunglasses clattered to the floor. And still Mrs. Mitchell didn't move. She stared at Abelard as if she'd just discovered bones of all the missing neighborhood dogs in the backyard.

"Abelard, what are you doing?" she asked finally.

"Lily is my girlfriend," he said after a long pause.

I thought about confirming this, but Abelard and his mom were locked in some kind of subterranean battle of will, and anything I said would make it worse. I knew this. Plus, Mrs. Mitchell sometimes threw things. We stood in a hall the size of a walk-in closet. I couldn't stop twitching.

"Abelard says you're going back to graduate school." My voice boomed in the small space of the hall. Abelard flinched.

It was as though my voice broke a spell. Mrs. Mitchell moved into the main room, and we followed her.

"Yes," she said. "I'm not taking classes yet, but I'm working in the learning lab with preschoolers. I'll be a full-time student in the fall for the first time in—"

"Lily is coming to the train station with me," Abelard said.

"Oh, that's nice, Lily." Mrs. Mitchell set her bookbag down on a long table against the wall by the kitchen. "You'll have to be at the station by tomorrow at six, or Abelard will already be on the train. You know where the station is, don't you?"

Clearly, she thought I was going to the station to say

goodbye to Abelard. I glanced at Abelard. I didn't think he understood, but I couldn't tell.

"Um, by Town Lake, right?" I felt like I should say something about the plan, but I didn't quite know what to say.

"That's right, behind the YMCA. You turn on Blagersfield and go under . . . realized that Abelard would be . . . making a visit . . . I called his doctor and . . . ."

Mrs. Mitchell stumbled over the words "making a visit," and I had the feeling she had a less ladylike term for Abelard's cross-country adventure. Traveling was hard. Soon I'd be traveling with Abelard. I'd have to give him a lot of space and not touch him randomly. I could go online and read up about this, but maybe things would be easier for us—because trains. Abelard loved trains. I'd never been on a train, but I was prepared to love trains just as much, if it meant we could be alone together in our own little compartment. Hours and hours in a tiny room with him while the stars rolled by our window and—

"Lily?" Mrs. Mitchell was standing by the open door. "We need to go. When I found out Abelard was coming home, I asked the neurologist to squeeze us in, but he only has a few minutes. We can't miss our appointment. Can I drop you somewhere?"

"Appointment?" I realized Mrs. Mitchell was asking me to leave. "No, I can take the bus."

I walked out the front door and it shut behind me. I was

out blinking in the bright afternoon sunlight. I'd thought Abelard had come home to tell me not to have the surgery. Instead, he'd given me another option, a way forward, like he'd opened the door to my cage. We loved each other, and that was all that mattered. Everything else we could figure out. I had to go home and pack. I did have a future. With Abelard.

CHAPTER 37

Mom owns exactly two pieces of luggage. One is a small black carry-on bag she bought for a medical convention three years ago. The other is a gigantic, ancient brown and yellow suitcase she and Dad bought for a trip they took to France the year before I was born. Mom wanted to go to Paris, and Paris was just as close as Berlin to Bingen am Rhein, the place where Hildegard had her monastery and where Dad did a big chunk of his graduate research. Mom and Dad spent three days wandering around Paris before taking the train to Germany.

I would have liked to take the big suitcase, the one that had been to Paris with my parents, but I wasn't ready to confess to my mom that I was leaving. I took the small bag, hoping I could hide it until tomorrow. I wanted to tell her, but I was afraid she'd try to talk me out of going. All that stuff about not relying on another person for your happiness. I guessed that was fine if you were Iris and you found your happiness in making straight A's and embodying the hope for a bright and shiny future. But that wasn't me. I'd never found true happiness anywhere but with Abelard.

I'd have to tell her at the train station. It would be hard on her. I felt bad, but I couldn't see any way around it. I hoped Mom would come to understand eventually. She'd always been in denial about how miserable I was at school. Like every time I got put on suicide watch, she'd scramble around looking for someone to "fix" my broken brain.

Why couldn't she understand that the obvious cure for misery was happiness?

Abelard texted at three.

"Lily?"

"Abelard."

"Our train leaves at 6:37 tomorrow night. Meet you at the 5th Street station at six."

"I'll be there. Did you tell your mother?"

"Yes."

Mom came home early. I continued peeling carrots for dinner, trying to look like carrots were hard work and at least I was being responsible at home.

"You skipped school today." Mom stood at the door, clutching her sad purse to her chest. Apparently the strap had broken—again. "I got the robocall."

Robocall—like a heavily armed cyborg from a 1980s

sci-fi horror movie. No one can escape Robocall's path of destruction. I briefly contemplated lying. Nothing came to mind.

"Abelard is back in Austin. I went to his house."

She strode to the dining room table and gently laid her purse down. "So I heard."

I looked up, startled.

"You heard?"

"Helen called me."

Helen? Who knew Mrs. Mitchell's name was Helen? Or that Mom was on a first-name basis with Mrs. Mitchell? The whole thing was—odd.

"What did she say?"

A whole host of possibilities crossed my mind. Mrs. Mitchell had caught us in the clinch. Maybe she'd called my mom to tell her that Abelard and I were engaging in dreaded physical contact. I expected to receive another lecture on birth control and "making good choices."

Mom turned to face me. "She was very nice. Apologetic, really. She said that Abelard refuses to get on a train unless you come down to the station to see him off. She's worried about him getting thrown out of his program. She asked if I could bring you to the train station tomorrow."

"Um—okay." Stranger still. I tried to imagine Mom and Mrs. Mitchell talking about Abelard and his school, but I couldn't. "What did you say?"

"I told her I'd bring you down. I imagined you'd want to say goodbye to Abelard in person." Mom had a soft, almost wistful look around the eyes. "I hope that's all right?"

"Of course. Thanks, Mom."

I felt a tightness in my chest. Mom was being so nice. She hadn't even said that much about me skipping school. It was as though she understood how important Abelard was to me, and not only that, she wanted to help me. I had a sudden urge to confess the truth—that I planned to leave with him.

Because I couldn't bring myself to start a ginormous fight, I didn't say anything.

Dinner was miserable. My secret was a giant lump in my throat.

After dinner, I retreated to my room to pack. I filled the black bag with jeans and T-shirts and bras and underwear and my swimsuit, and makeup. I emptied my backpack. I'd taken books from the shelf—*Daniel Deronda*, *Mary Barton*, graphic novels—which I shoved into it. I hid my abandoned textbooks under a pile of dirty clothes before Iris came in to do homework.

I didn't tell her I was leaving, but Iris is no dope. She spotted the black carry-on bag under the desk, from her perch on her bed.

"You're leaving," Iris said.

"Yes." I went back to playing a game on my phone.

"Where?"

"New Mexico, to be with Abelard."

"What?" Iris looked up from her laptop. Closed the lid, even. Exceedingly rare that Iris abandons her homework entirely. "That's crazy!"

"You're right, Iris. I'm crazy and impulsive." Why fight it?

"What will you do for money? How will you live? What does Mom think about this?"

"Abelard has money. But I'm not going to be dependent on him. I'll get a job," I said.

"So that's it?" Iris said. There were tears in her eyes because—thirteen. You weep over everything when you're thirteen. "You're just going to leave, and I'll probably never see you again."

"I'll be back. It's not like I'm going to the end of the world or anything."

"That's what Dad said."

"To be fair, Dad did come back." I couldn't believe I was defending Dad's ridiculously long absence to Iris. Five years was practically never.

"I should tell Mom."

"Go ahead." I yawned and pretended to be absorbed in rereading my text from Abelard. "She's driving me to the train station tomorrow."

Iris frowned, baffled. I hope Iris never plays poker. She's super easy to bluff.

"When I get settled into a place, you can come visit me. New Mexico is not that far away."

"Really?" she said.

"Really."

That was enough, apparently, to get Iris to go back to work. Just the promise that she could come stay with me in New Mexico. Iris had the whole world in front of her. Everyone was always falling over themselves to point out how she would probably rule the world one day, and even her teachers at LAME occasionally looked up from their klezmer orchestras and Burning Man robotics projects to mention that Iris was amazing. And yet Iris just wanted to be with me. I loved my sister even though she annoyed me sometimes. I would miss her.

CHAPTER 38

I went to school. You'd think the day you leave high school forever, the last thing you'd want to do was go to geography. It wasn't that I was looking forward to geography, but I didn't want to sit at home alone all day and wait for six o'clock to come. Waiting is horrible.

Still, school was super awkward. All my books and papers and homework were shoved into a box inside my closet. I'd decided to move it from my desk so Mom wouldn't get too suspicious.

My teachers were surprised. Of course, there are always those guys who arrive at class without so much as a pencil and slouch in their chairs and extend their legs to trip anyone who comes down the aisle without looking, but I'm not passive-aggressive, just honestly forgetful. So it was weird to be in class without anything.

Mrs. Rogers-Peña was wearing a skirt patterned with Eiffel towers, Arcs de Triomphe, and champagne glasses. And pink Converses. She looked festive and happy. Until she saw me. She made eye contact, and I shrugged and nodded apologetically.

After class I dug out the bathroom pass from my purse and marched up to her desk. "Here's your pass. I'm sorry for stealing it."

Mrs. Rogers-Peña peered over the edge of her glasses. "If you're going to leave school, I'd prefer if you didn't do it on my watch."

"Once again, sorry. I plead exigent circumstances."

"Exigent, meaning?"

"Immediate and pressing."

"Lily, you frustrate me to no end. It's hard to remain angry with you when you use SAT words correctly in sentences." Mrs. Rogers-Peña sighed. "Just don't do it again."

She looked down to her desk. Conversation over. I realized that I might not ever see her again, and this was the last chance to say anything.

"You're the best teacher I've ever had. You made this place bearable." I searched for an SAT word to use. "You galvanized me."

Mrs. Rogers-Peña looked up from her desk, startled.

"Why, thank you."

I turned to leave.

"Don't go anywhere yet. Galvanized you to do what?"

And now I was caught. I could hardly tell Mrs. Rogers-Peña that her literary lessons on life, love, and becoming fully human had, at least in part, galvanized me to run away with my boyfriend.

"Well, I'm having surgery, and . . . stuff." This felt like a horrible lie. I hated telling it.

Mrs. Rogers-Peña nodded.

"I get nervous when students use past tense. If you ever need to talk, about anything—"

"I got it," I said.

Suicide watch. It changes how everyone looks at you.

I met Rosalind for lunch. I'd been dying to tell her all about leaving for New Mexico with Abelard, but it just didn't seem like the kind of thing you could announce over a text.

For once, I beat her to our bench. I waited, feeling unaccountably nervous. The sky had grown overcast, and a few fat raindrops fell around me. But then the rain stopped like it couldn't quite make up its mind. I opened my sack and took a few bites out of a peanut butter and iceberg lettuce sandwich. The peanut butter stuck in my throat, and I balled up the sandwich and tossed it in the trash.

Rosalind showed up fifteen minutes later, loose hair fighting a light breeze, her eyes bright with excitement.

"Where have you been?" I asked. Trying not to sound cranky, but my voice came out just like my mother's. Rosalind didn't seem to notice. She sat down next to me, leaving her lunchbox untouched.

"I've been with Mr. Turner," she said. "He thinks I could audition for the Zilker Hillside summer musical. They're doing—"

"I'm leaving tonight," I blurted out.

"Leaving? Wait—what?" Rosalind blinked.

"I'm going to New Mexico with Abelard."

She didn't say anything, so I continued.

"He doesn't want me to have the surgery either. I can't stay in the dorm with Abelard, so I will—"

"When?"

"Today at six thirty-seven."

"Today?"

I'd expected Rosalind to be happy for me. Instead she had the look she gets when she knows I'm about to skip school or blow off an assignment. Dubious, with a faint whiff of disapproval.

The wind picked up. An empty plastic pudding cup rattled across the concrete and came to a stop near my feet. A few noisy raindrops hit the ground.

"You were the one who said I shouldn't have the surgery."

"I don't want you to have the surgery," Rosalind said. "But moving to New Mexico with Abelard seems crazy. What will you do for money?"

"I'll get a job."

"Where? Doing what?" Rosalind pursed her lips. "And what will you do for money before you get paid?"

"Abelard has some money. He said he'd help me . . ."

The sky opened up, pouring down sheets of rain, and we ran for the door alongside everyone else in the courtyard. We piled into the hallway, shaking off water, talking all at once.

"I'll text you when I'm on the train, okay?" I yelled, not caring who overheard my plans to bail on school and everything.

I caught a glimpse of Rosalind being swallowed up in a crowd of tall people. And then the bell rang.

It was the longest day ever, and the shortest. Interminable, and then just when it seemed to have started, it ended. I screamed out of my last class, worried that I'd miss the bus home. I paused briefly in the atrium to give my school a last look. My school, although it never had really felt like my school. I'd never belonged here.

New Mexico would be completely different. I racked my brains for everything I knew about New Mexico—green chiles, mountains. It didn't matter. Abelard and I belonged together.

CHAPTER 39

School ended at 4:17, and my bus usually made it home by five. Iris came home and made a big show of ignoring me. She went to our room without saying anything, but I could hear her talking about me in a loud voice to Exene. Annoying.

Five thirty came and went. By 5:40, when Mom got home, I was frantic.

"Where have you been? The train leaves soon."

"We'll get there, don't worry. I'm going to run to the bathroom," she said. "Go put your things in the car."

I piled my backpack and my suitcase in the trunk while she was in the bathroom. Mom didn't see, and I was glad, because I didn't want to tell her I was leaving until I got to the train station. But it was strange that Mom had told me to get my things. Something was off about that. You don't need anything to say goodbye.

Iris stood on the stoop, watching me, her arms folded across her chest.

I closed the trunk and leaned against the car.

"Did you tell Mom that I'm leaving with Abelard?" I asked.

"You said she already knew." Iris spit out her words in an angry, gleeful rush of accusation—like she'd just found out I was planning on skipping school and couldn't wait to tell Mom. "I knew it! Mom would never let you—"

Mom burst through the door and nearly knocked into Iris. I expected Iris to tell her about my plans, but she didn't. Her silence made it all the worse. She stood barefoot in the driveway watching us go, an oddly forlorn figure in jeans and an unfortunate electric green Model UN spring conference T-shirt. At my school, you'd be crucified for mistaking a school event shirt as a badge of cool—and a Model UN T-shirt at that. I'd told Iris not to wear the shirt at school, but she didn't care, which was sort of the best thing about her. I didn't get a chance to say goodbye, and who knew when I would see Iris again.

Mom sped away, but we had to stop on Lamar for construction by the Alamo Drafthouse South. I couldn't stop twitching. Five forty-nine. I'd never watched a clock like this before.

"This sucks, Mom. Abelard hates it when I'm late."

"Doesn't Abelard know you struggle with time management?" she asked softly.

"Yes," I spat back. I hated her gentle tone of voice, her

infinite maternal patience. "You don't understand. Abelard has issues with time too. He has anxiety attacks when people are late."

"You don't choose to be late. Abelard will have to learn that."

We reached the lane closure and had to merge into the other lane. Five fifty-five. I imagined Abelard on a train platform in an ornate cavernous building, nervously pacing back and forth in the billowing steam. Anxious Abelard like a character from one of Rosalind's old movies, scanning a black-and-white crowd for me.

"I won't be late anymore."

"You can't change who you are," Mom said. "Not to make someone else happy."

I laughed bitterly. Everyone wanted me to change, to be someone else, to make a different decision. And Mom was the one who wanted me to change the most. I thought of Dad saying that she would never give up on me, no matter how miserable I made her.

"All I ever do is try to make other people happy," I said.

"Maybe it's time to stop worrying about what other people want," Mom said. "What do you want, Lily?"

We crossed the bridge and got stuck in late-day traffic. Up ahead, under the trestle, was the memorial for Ivan Garth Johnson, a red heart crawling with vines. Ivan Garth Johnson was a teenager killed by a drunk driver. His mother put up the graffiti. The image had been periodically painted over or defaced and had reappeared for as long as I could remember. If Ivan Garth Johnson had lived, he'd have been over forty years old. His mother had committed to repainting the pillar every year until other people started doing it for her. Someone's mother who never gave up, no matter what.

Dad was right—Mom would never give up on me. Whatever I did, whatever happened with me, she would always feel like it was her fault. I couldn't leave my mother here mourning the lost possibility of surgery and a bright future.

But it was more than that. I thought of Dr. Brainguy and his plan to release me from the tyranny of too many new ideas. Abelard would be in school building robots and taking calculus and reading books, and I'd be working? Unless I got tired of one job and went to the next. And then something else. Love doesn't make the endless hamster wheel of new ideas stop spinning. What if I spun away from Abelard?

What did I want? I wasn't sure. When what you want is always wrong, you train yourself not to want anything. I'd spent so much time thinking about what everyone else wanted that I'd forgotten the excitement I'd felt when Dr. Brainguy suggested I could go to college. Rosalind's room was scattered with brochures from small tree-lined liberal arts colleges everywhere. Since I'd agreed to the surgery, I'd pored over all of her letters and invitations and allowed myself to imagine going to college. It wouldn't happen if I went to New Mexico.

It wouldn't happen without the surgery.

Traffic began moving. We circled under Lamar to the Amtrak station.

The train was already at the station, only a few railroad cars, long, sleek, and silver, steps away from the parking lot. Abelard stood by the train, and I felt a sick thrill of fear and love and relief at the sight of him. I couldn't help it.

I jumped out of the car as soon as Mom pulled into a parking spot and ran to Abelard. I stood before him, breathing hard, and almost lost my nerve. He was wearing all black, a tall silhouette against the skyline full of cranes and silver buildings, black sunglasses glinting in the afternoon sun. I wanted to be alone with him in our own private room with strange, key-operated beds and everything sleek except the Texas scrub rolling by outside our window.

What did I want?

I wanted everything. It was impossible.

"I can't go with you," I said.

Abelard shook his head in slow motion. I was beginning to read everything in his tiniest gesture. Slow-moving pain.

"Are you breaking up with me again?"

"No," I said. "No, no, no. More than anything in the world, I want to go with you to New Mexico. But I also want to stay here and have the surgery and maybe go to college and actually take actual math, which I can't right now because—homework. And I didn't even think I was any good at math, but Dr. Brainguy says I have high conceptual mathematical ability. I can't access it, now, but the surgery will change all that. Does this make any sense to you?"

Babbling. I was babbling at the worst possible moment.

Abelard didn't say anything. Mrs. Mitchell emerged from the station house, her hair glowing white-hot in the sun. She wore a necklace of inch-long shards of silver that threw off blinding stabs of light.

"Honey, say goodbye to Lily," Mrs. Mitchell said. "You need to get on the train now."

Mom tapped Mrs. Mitchell on the shoulder.

"Helen, we need to give them a minute."

Mrs. Mitchell turned, a confused look on her face. Mom led her away to the awning by the station.

She knew. Mom had known that I was planning on leaving with Abelard, and still she drove me to the station.

The train hissed impatiently. No time left.

I turned back to Abelard.

"So, I want to go more than anything in the world, I want to stay more than anything in the world, but these two things are antithetical," I said. "What I need is a Kobayashi Maru."

"Kobayashi Maru," Abelard repeated.

"Like on *Star Trek*, when Captain Kirk has to take the

unwinnable challenge because both answers are wrong, so he cheats and combines the answers to win the Kobayashi Maru. I want to cheat. I want surgery, I want to go to college, and I want to be with you. Is that even possible?"

A conductor stepped off the train and yelled, "All aboard!" Just like in the movies. It's surprising how many things are just like in the movies.

"Abelard, you have to get on that train," Mrs. Mitchell called from under the awning.

"Can I kiss you goodbye?" I said.

Abelard nodded his head ever so slightly. Maybe I imagined it.

I reached up and pressed my lips against his. We stood there for a moment, enclosed in a perfect bubble of warmth in the late-afternoon sunlight, while the train behind us huffed delicately. His arms slipped around me if only for a brief moment before they went slack at his sides.

"Kobayashi Maru," he said finally.

And then he turned and was gone.

The train pulled away. I probably would have run down the track waving frantically, but his compartment was on the other side of the train. I couldn't see Abelard.

The train crossed the trestle over Lamar. It made the right-angle turn toward the bridge over the river, glinting in the sunlight. And I wept. Behind me, Mom and Mrs.

Mitchell murmured a discreet conversation. Eventually Mrs. Mitchell left.

When I finally turned around, ours was the only car in the parking lot. Mom stood in the shade of the train station awning, waiting.

We were almost home before either of us spoke.

At a stoplight, Mom took her hands off the wheel and slumped forward a little. "That was rough," she said.

I didn't know whether she was referring to my letting Abelard go, or her awkward half an hour making pleasantries with Mrs. Mitchell while I wept, or the crazy last day and a half when I decided to leave and she knew about it but kept it to herself. Probably a little bit of everything.

"You knew. You knew I was planning on leaving with Abelard, and you drove me to the station anyway." I leaned my head against the window. "Why?"

"Something your dad said to me."

I looked at Mom. "Are you planning to share?"

"It might make you mad."

I shrugged. I didn't think I could find anger underneath everything else I was feeling.

"Fine. He said that if I didn't trust you to make a couple of bad decisions, you wouldn't know a good decision when it hit you in the face."

"Sounds like Dad." I laughed mirthlessly.

I closed my eyes, and the enormity of what I'd done hit

me. I was the queen of yes—no—yes—no. I'd promised to leave with Abelard, and I'd changed my mind—again.

"Letting go of Abelard doesn't feel like a good decision."

"I know," Mom said.

I expected her to say more, to talk of Tennyson and relationships. But she didn't. Thank god.

When we returned from the train station, Iris was slumped, red-eyed, on the couch. She leapt up when she saw me, and I braced myself for a barrage of questions. Instead, she hugged me.

CHAPTER 40

I went back to school the next day, which was really strange. I felt like I'd said goodbye to everyone and everything, but of course, from the perspective of the rest of the world, nothing had changed. I went to English expecting Mrs. Rogers-Peña to treat me as though I'd returned from the dead. I thought she'd be at least moderately surprised to see me, considering that I'd given her such a stirring goodbye she'd expressed concern for my state of mind.

But she hardly noticed me. With thirty students, why would she? She hadn't known I'd planned to leave.

I checked my phone every five minutes looking for a text message from Abelard. Nothing.

At lunchtime I went to look for Rosalind at our usual spot under the live oaks. I didn't really expect her to be there. Since I told her I'd be gone, I'd imagined she'd be eating lunch in the art room or the theater with Richard. The two of them in the near gloom of the empty theater, Rosalind expressing a mixture of frustration and concern, Richard listening.

"Lily has done some crazy things before but nothing as crazy as this . . ."

I didn't expect to find her on the deck. But there Rosalind sat, with her feet together in red velvet ballet slippers, her hair in a matching velvet headband. I remembered what she'd said about me demanding to try on her shoes in kindergarten. I still wanted to wear her shoes.

"Hey," I said.

Rosalind looked up, a flicker of surprise in her eyes. "You're here."

"I decided not to go," I replied.

I settled on the bench beside her and opened my lunch. Iris had carefully packed a veggie sandwich on toasted whole wheat with avocado, shredded carrots, tomatoes, and cucumbers. Mayonnaise. Someday I would break down and tell Iris that mayonnaise wasn't vegan. Not any time soon, though.

"That looks delicious," she said. "You and Iris must be on good terms."

"Pretty much. Iris is happy that I'm still here. Do you want half?"

Rosalind shook her head.

"So why didn't you go?" she asked. "Did you break up with Abelard again?"

"No. It wasn't about Abelard, it was about me."

Rosalind frowned. A group of senior girls arrived back from the nearby Starbucks, laughing loudly, talking about how great it was to be almost done with school. We watched as they sauntered toward the parking lot, and I felt a sudden wave of annoyance. They were done with school; they had plans for the future. Life was golden—for them. The weight of my choice hit me. There were people in the world who went to class, and went to have a vanilla Frappuccino with friends, and never spent any part of the day thinking about what it means to be human. I'd have liked to drink a Frappuccino in the parking lot, blissfully unaware of the inner workings of my brain.

"So what does that mean?" Rosalind asked. "Are you going to have the surgery?"

"Yes." There wasn't anything else for me to say.

"I think it's a mistake, Lily."

"I know you do," I replied. "But I don't want to go back on drugs, and I don't see any other options."

"And you really trust this doctor that much?"

"I do. He doesn't want to change me. He just wants to make me a better version of the person I already am."

Rosalind looked down at her feet. I wasn't going to convince her. In her own way, Rosalind was as stubborn and intractable as I was. Maybe more.

"But brain surgery, Lily? There's got to be another choice. Can't you just go to a different school, like Abelard?"

"It wouldn't matter. Even if I went to the perfect school,

I'd still end up skipping class. I broke up with Abelard, and I didn't want to do that. I don't even know why I did it. It's like my brain wants to be free, and so I run. I run from everything eventually."

"You've never run from me," Rosalind said.

"No, I never have." I hadn't thought about it before, but it was true.

Usually, when I was on the run, I'd wait until my head stopped spinning in hamster wheel circles and then head for Rosalind's house. Maybe a best friend is someone you run toward when you are running away from everything else.

Suddenly I felt afraid. A friendship is a strange and delicate ecosystem. What if my surgery disrupted the balance? I couldn't stand the thought that an electrode in my brain might be the butterfly wing that caused a gale to rip our friendship apart. If I didn't run, would she be as important to me?

Rosalind studied me. I wondered if she knew what I was thinking. Or maybe we were both worried about the same thing.

"So you really think your surgeon doesn't want to change you?" she asked.

I nodded.

"Okay. But I'm going to come visit you in the hospital after your surgery. I'm going to come visit you, and if you aren't the Lily I remember, I'm going to tell them to yank that thing out of your head."

"Mostly the same Lily," I said. "I can't promise to be exactly the same person."

"Fair enough," she replied.

By the time I got home on the bus, I was exhausted and discouraged. Iris wasn't home yet. I flopped on the couch and checked my text messages for about the thousandth time, looking in vain for something from Abelard. And then I noticed that I had a couple of emails. One was from school, but one was from Abelard.

Lily,

I was disappointed that you didn't come with me. I'd spent an hour at the train station, imagining what it would be like to finally be alone with you. But it didn't happen.

When you first told me about the surgery, I didn't want you to do it, but I think I understand. We both have secrets locked deep within our brains. If I could have surgery to unlock the hidden part of my brain, I would. I can't deny you what I'd want for myself.

You asked for a solution to your own Kobayashi Maru — the no-win scenario. You wanted to go with me, but you wanted to stay and have the surgery.

You seemed to think that whatever course you

chose, we'd be blown to bits at the edge of the neutral zone. While I admire your fearless rush toward mutual destruction, there is a simpler solution to our problem.

We continue just as we are.

Was texting hard? I never thought so. I've spent what seems like months looking forward to texting you at night, only to remember that we'd broken up. Broken up. I don't even like to think those words. I wanted to tell someone how I felt, but I didn't know who to talk to. Who could understand, except you?

I won't lie; I want to be with you. But even if we could never be alone together again, it would be enough. Enough is the wrong word, because if we weren't ever together again, I would still think every day of the way you felt pressed against me and the weight of your head against my shoulder. I want more. Until then, this is my answer to your Kobayashi Maru scenario. And I will be back for the semester break in August.

Love, Abelard.

I'd just started on a reply email to Abelard when Iris arrived home. She dropped her backpack on her bed and began unloading her assignments.

"Aren't you supposed to cook tonight?" she asked.

"Can you cook for me? I'll cook tomorrow," I said without looking up.

"Just because you almost ran away from home doesn't

mean that suddenly all the rules have changed to accommodate you." She nudged her backpack and laptop aside, and sat on the bed. "What are you doing, anyway?"

"Abelard sent me an email. I'm writing him back."

Iris sat on the edge of her bed for a moment longer. Then she got up and went to the kitchen. I heard the fridge door open, the click of a knife against a cutting board. By the time she came back twenty minutes later with a glass of sweet tea with lemon, I'd finished my letter.

Dear Abelard,

I know that in an alternate universe somewhere, there is a less destructive version of me who doesn't break things and, consequently, never ends up in detention with that universe's Abelard. In a less chaotic universe, we never would've happened.

Shudder. What if I'd never loved you? What if you'd never loved me?

But in this chaotic universe, I broke a wall, and I got — you. Oh, lucky destruction!

That day in the office when you said you felt rust on the gears in the wall, I was fascinated. I'd never met anyone who felt the same compulsion to fix things that I had for breaking them. And then when we talked, you made me realize that breaking is just inept fixing, inspired by the same curiosity about how things work in the world. And I want to fix things instead of breaking them. It's one of the reasons why I want to have the surgery. I want to be more like you.

I admired your intense look of focus when you worked on your robots. Also, your broad shoulders, your sable dark hair, your wrists. Your bare feet when I came to your house. The little scar on your cheek that I gave you. The way you only wore the softest shirts and how, when you held me, my brain stopped whirling around in tight circles, and I felt calm.

I think about you all the time.

But when you break things like I do, you have to live with the consequences. When you break things, you have to assume that everything in the world is fragile and impermanent — like the blown glass pitcher I shattered on your kitchen counter.

I knew that we would end eventually. It was only a matter of time.

So when you finally got the invitation to go to the Isaac Institute, I was sure our moment of destruction had arrived. I thought it was over between us, and nothing could convince me otherwise.

I didn't consider the possibility of a long-distance relationship. I loved you, but I thought love was a perfect snowflake you held in your hand until it melted against the heat of your skin and vanished. I loved you so much that I thought I would destroy you. Turns out, you are not so easy to break.

I love you, Abelard. And I need you. I need to you to remind me on a regular basis that the world is not simply entropy, chaos, and loss. I need you because you are miraculous and unbreakable. I think we could remake the world together, with love and novels and robots.

"Do we understand each other?"

I sent the email and waited for his response. It didn't take long.

"Perfectly," he texted.

POSTSCRIPT

The night before my surgery, Abelard texts me at five o'clock, our new time. Time is important, so I make sure I am there by five. His dinner call is at six thirty, and he was having a hard time making it back to his room by seven to text me.

I don't know where I got the idea that he had a new girl who looked like Emma Stone and adored him. I'm learning that my brain will invent catastrophic scenarios that bear absolutely no relationship to reality because, like Heloise, I am too much accustomed to misfortune to expect any happy turn.

I have to change that.

Dr. Brainguy tells me that there will be rough days ahead, but after that, sunshine and unicorns. Freedom from the tyranny of too many new ideas. I must learn to expect—nay, demand—a happy turn.

And so, I tell Abelard everything. All my fears and hopes for the surgery.

"Can I text you tomorrow night after surgery?" he asks.

I feel the overwhelming urge to say no. To pull back. Because—fear.

"I may be strange and groggy."

"I don't mind," he texts. *"I like that you're strange."*

I close my eyes and try to formulate what to say next. It's important.

"Abelard. What if the surgery trims the odd angles off my brain? What if suddenly I am more of a salt crystal than a broken snowflake?"

I wait for his answer. It takes a long time.

"I will love you whatever happens. You will still be Lily."

In *Frankenstein*, the monster follows Victor Frankenstein to his Swiss mountain home in a quest for a mate because he mistakenly believes that it is love that makes you human. But love doesn't make you human. Being able to feel pain deeply, or even being able to feel the pain of others, doesn't make you human.

What makes you human is the ability to tolerate paperwork. To fill out the right form because that's what everyone else has to do in the craptacular adult world of Coach Neuwirth. To read every bit of the rubric.

It wouldn't have mattered if Frankenstein created a bride for the monster who shared in his triumph and his sorrows, who felt the pain of isolation and brokenness as deeply as he did. One bad trip to the DMV and a license renewal gone wrong, and the monster would have been ripping the arms off random strangers. All it takes is one petty bureaucrat or stupid form to send the monster rampaging again. I know. The monster is always there, just below the surface.

The monster will out. And so—surgery. It's the right thing to do. I know that now.

Abelard says he will love whoever I become, and I trust him. In spite of our misfortunes, we have always been what we pleased in our letters. When we are together, we become even more than what we please. We become ourselves.

But I worry. Because it is the monster who makes us love. It is the monster who stares through the chinks in the wall at a blind man with a starving family and feels real pain. It is the monster who kills a deer in the forest to feed them.

It was the monster in me who broke the sliding door to see who was on the other side. It was the monster in me who looked at Abelard and saw the delicate and complex gears turning, and thirsted to know more. The monster demands the greater truths of life. I told Dr. Brainguy, my own personal Dr. Frankenstein, that the thing I feared most about the surgery was the loss of ideas, but that wasn't true.

I fear the loss of the monster.

It was the monster in me who cried out in despair to a dead, uncaring universe, looking for someone to love. Someone special and broken and perfect. And the universe answered with Abelard. More than I'd asked for, and certainly more than I deserved. Lucky me.

So what happens if Dr. Brainguy kills the monster? If suddenly paperwork and schedules and rubrics make sense to me? If I become—fully human?

Will I still love Abelard? Will Abelard still love me?

I hope so.

I guess I'll find out tomorrow.

The END

ACKNOWLEDGMENTS

I'd like to thank my editor, Margaret Raymo, for believing in my story. Thanks to my agent, Jim McCarthy, for seeing the subtleties in family life I missed. Best revision notes—ever. Thanks to Ana Deboo for a great copyedit.

I owe so much to my mentor Marty Mayberry, who plucked me out of the Pitchwars slush pile and taught me how to write romance. Thanks to Brenda Drake for Pitchwars.

Brenda Marie Smith has been my writing partner and line editor extraordinaire from the beginning. Thanks to her and the other members of my home group, George Leake and Aden Polydoros.

Thanks to Alex Cabal for Scribophile.

I wouldn't have been able to finish this novel without Jerry Quinn, head of the Ubergroup on Scribophile. Jerry gave me the harshest critique I've ever received—and one I desperately needed. Thanks for his leadership and his unflinching honesty.

I wish I had the space to individually thank all the Ubergroup members who read and critiqued my novel, many of them multiple times. I've learned so much about neurodifference, education, and writing from all of them. Thanks to Dannie Morin, Lucy Ledger, Allison Castle, Erin Merrill, Sydney Oliver, Gabrielle Reid, Jennifer Todhunter, Susan Boesger, Sera Flynn, Sarah Overland, Maria Dascalu, Maggie Giles, Lisa Price, Dustin Fife, Ashley Dunnett Grace, C. C. O'Hugh, Marisa Urgo, Brenda Baker, Maggie Stough, Sam Emerson, Derek Cummings, Valerie Godown, Jefferson Hunt, Eleanor Konik, and Lindsay Diamond.

Thanks to Russell Rowland, kick-ass writing teacher and author.

Thanks to Carol Freeman Athey for telling me that there is more than one way to be a hero in your own life.

Thanks to Morgan McLauren Guidry, Pat Littledog, and Denise Dee for starting me on the writing path.

Thanks to Bob Bechtol. He knows why.

My sister-in-law, Kristen Clifford Creedle, has given me great advice and encouragement. My siblings, George Creedle, Will Creedle, and Dory Grandia, are always willing to discuss writing and neurodifference—and to listen to me moan when things are hard. I rely on them all so much.

Thanks to Isabel Grandia for her thoughts on love and romance.

And thanks to Ethan Brem for his thoughts on love and letter writing.

Thanks to Courtney Cater for the inspiration and encouragement.

Thanks to James Fason, Blair Creedle Reynolds, and Callier Creedle Reynolds for their warmth and humor, and for allowing me to steal bits of their childhoods for my writing. Special thanks to Blair for committing to read this almost as many times as I have.

And finally, thanks to my husband, Henry D. Reynolds. He is the most faithful and fundamentally generous person I've ever known, and he's never wavered in his belief that I would get this done. I am so lucky.